# DESTROYER OF LIGHT

# DESTROYER OF LIGHT

JENNIFER MARIE BRISSETT

A TOM DOHERTY ASSOCIATES BOOK
NEW YORK

Warning: This book is designed for audiences 18+ due to scenes of physical and sexual violence, and themes that some may find disturbing.

This is a work of fiction. All of the characters, organizations, and events portrayed in this novel are either products of the author's imagination or are used fictitiously.

DESTROYER OF LIGHT



A Tor Book
Published by Tom Doherty Associates
120 Broadway
New York, NY 10271

www.tor-forge.com

Tor® is a registered trademark of Macmillan Publishing Group, LLC.

The Library of Congress Cataloging-in-Publication Data is available upon request.

ISBN 978-1-250-26865-5 (hardcover)
ISBN 978-1-250-26864-8 (ebook)

Our books may be purchased in bulk for promotional, educational, or business use. Please contact your local bookseller or the Macmillan Corporate and Premium Sales Department at 1-800-221-7945, extension 5442, or by email at MacmillanSpecialMarkets@macmillan.com.

First Edition: October 2021

Printed in the United States of America

0 9 8 7 6 5 4 3 2 1

*In memory of my friends*

*Brook Stephenson*
#TryHappy #restinpowerbrook

*Ama Patterson*
*Be at peace, sis. You did good.*

I see your boundless form
everywhere,
the countless arms,
bellies, mouths, and eyes;
Lord of All,
I see no end,
or middle or beginning
to your totality.

—*The Bhagavad Gita*

# DESTROYER OF LIGHT

Smokeless black flames burn her skin ice-cold with memory. She sloughs and becomes all muscle and sinew, bone and blood. The fire surrounds her and drifts up her body, engulfing toes, ankles, knees, her waist, her stomach, her heart, her mouth, her eyes, and forehead until the fire and she are one. She opens her arms as if to fly, spreading her hands wide, and darkness leaps from her fingertips. In a flash of pitch-brilliance, she and I experience all that has come before and all that is soon to be. The past, the present, and the future comingle like a coil.

And we see everything . . .

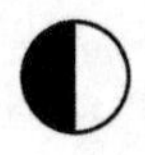

## DAWN, 10 YEARS AGO . . .

Drifting down down down and spinning as if on a thread in dizzying turns, the invisible strand that connects me delicately unravels as I join with you in your act of becoming. I will share with you in this, your dangerous journey, because I cannot bear to allow you to do this alone. Into your memory we travel together, and of all the strange corners of the world where we could land, we find ourselves in a kitchen.

So many sensations, strange but not unpleasant, envelop us. So much stimuli to delight and intoxicate. Warmth emanates from a cooling stove. The scents of drying leaves that hung along the walls fragrance the air. The aromas of the spices and mint, and the grassy freshness of the herbs growing on the windowsill or neatly labeled and placed on shelves, waft through my incorporeal skin. And yet I also sense unease, a darkness looming from every corner and shadowed crevice. Memories can be like this—ghostly and unsteady, a little bit true, a little bit false disconnected, then joining to create image and form.

You appear out of the ether. Both of you. Mother and child. Deidra and you. Cora, with your soft, puffy body and two small, awkwardly protruding points pushed up against the front of your frock, make a very unlikely harbinger of the days to come. Only your eyes cause one to stop and consider. They are wide and inquisitive, with irises of amber outlined in mahogany, and your stare penetrates, infusing the onlooker with the strong desire to turn away.

All is stillness as I move about the kitchen, then the room morphs into activity. The clinking of dishes. The tender steps of the child clearing the table. The *wish-wash* of moving water as the mother earnestly washes the dishes. A strange tension lingers in the air. Were they mad at each other? Has the child done something wrong? She seems so timid as she stands behind her mother holding a bowl cupped in both hands while the mother bends over the sink. Moments pass in agonizing lengths as the two remain like this: one standing, quietly beseeching attention, and the other ignoring her presence. For a while I wonder if the mother knows that the child is there. A slight nod of her head and a grunt makes it clear that she knows. The child, finally given permission to approach, carefully places her bowl on the counter.

Mother bemoans, "After a long day of work I still have to do all this."

"I'll do them," Cora says, brightening.

"No, you never do them right," Mother responds with a sigh.

And then I feel how the girl feels. She thinks her mother doesn't like her, maybe even hates her. She thinks her mother believes her strange, too wise beyond her years, useless, incapable of doing the simplest things—even something as mundane as washing the dishes. Cora longs for the feel of her mother's soft skin, cool and scented with lavender. It's been so long since her mother touched her and Cora doesn't know why the tenderness ended. Flashes appear of how close they used to be. How they went everywhere together. How Mother strapped Cora to her waist with a cloth with the child's little head bobbing. She smiled with her two tiny front teeth surrounded by gums. Dark splotches swam across the child's skin, face, and arms—something left over by what *they* had done to her. Mother simply covered them with the swaddling clothes and kept prying eyes at a distance. Then the images waver and fade away.

The child is too young to understand that her mother's recent behavior has little to do with her, and everything to do with her mother's own discomfort—and maybe anger—that her daughter is turning into a woman. The helplessness in seeing her child grow into not needing her is at times too much to bear. One day Cora may understand this. But not now. Not today.

I follow Cora as she leaves the kitchen and enters her bedroom. The redness of the evening light cascades through her open window, flooding her small room in a burnt sienna blush. The horizon glows a golden yellow shimmer, mocking a rising sun. This view remains, and will always remain, on this tidally locked world where the people live on a narrow perimeter around the center of the sphere, the habitable ring. This half of the ring has been designated as Dawn. The other half, designated as Dusk, has a similar, but some consider, darker view.

The rotting remains of the transport ship that brought her and her mother here—the very last ship to leave Earth—stand in the distance, its metallic frame oranged with rust like the bloody ribs of a skinned animal. Cora and her mother are both a little more than four hundred ET (Earth Time) years old, unchanged by time as they slept in their cryogenic chambers. And yet changed. Their bodies manipulated to "help with their adaptation to the environmental differences" of this world.

Deidra has become a worker of the soil, her hands gifted with abilities with the Seed. Her skills made her invaluable as the hard, unforgiving land struggled to feed the people. But Cora . . . Cora was turned into something I still don't quite understand. Knowledge of her alterations has been purposefully taken from me, and I desperately need to remember. Only now, as I reach into her memories, do I begin to glimpse what she is becoming. Cora, lost in concentration, wistfully stares upward, seeing more than only the stars high in the indigo-blue sky. What she gazes upon with those eyes of hers is the reason I am here.

Many who arrived in the transports had similar indications of body manipulations, their irises glittering every color but normal as they awoke from their long sleep. Eventually the iris colors of most (but not all) turned into shades of brown. But Cora's eyes seemed to have intensified with age, glowing like a cat's caught in the light.

Cora understood her difference. The manifestations of all that she is to become may not have fully flowered, yet she knew. So why has her mind brought me here? And such odd things to show me, such odd things to remember. These nothing moments, as memories, hold weight for her. I continue my ghostly study, searching for these answers.

Children pass by Cora's window in groups of twos, then threes, then fours and fives. More still can be seen in the distance, arriving from a variety of directions. All carrying small bundles and heading towards the north. Every evening the children in the Outlands of Dawn walk for miles to the nearest town, seeking shelter for the night from raiding rebel militias who prey upon small villages to steal these little ones to fill their ranks.

Cora hurries to ready herself for her nightly journey, assembling her homework, rolling her bedding, and wrapping her hair in a gonar, the traditional headwrap her mother still insists that she wear. Flashes of girls from the village making fun of Cora appear before my sight, as well as a few of the tense battles she has had with her mother as she begged to be allowed to dress like the others do. The image of her mother remaining stubbornly firm on the matter lingers before me, then fades away.

Cora finishes folding the flap beneath her chin, completing her tentlike attire. She returns to the kitchen, where her mother sits at the table preparing some herbs to be dried. Cora quietly slips past with her arms full of her bundle. Mother doesn't look up as Cora approaches the door and cracks it open. A slice of dim light from the outside world cuts into the room.

"Good night, Mom," Cora says.

"Don't forget to bring in the water when you come home in the morning," her mother replies, still not looking in her direction.

"I won't forget," Cora says as she quietly steps through the door.

And now I see why this memory is so important. These are the last moments this daughter will have with her mother for many, many years . . .

## DUSK, 3 WEEKS AGO . . .

A long, snaking line of vehicles lay before them, inching forward into the gated enclave high on the terraces that overlooked the city. The brothers knew about areas like this, well away from the prying eyes of those like themselves who lived in or near the Bottoms. Jown, bored and thinking of the oncoming rain, that smelled of twisted strands of gray, watched the oil birds gathering on the branches of the trees. *They're not even birds,* he thought. People only called them that because no one really knew what the hell they were. Jown watched them move their "beaks" to silently *kaw* and flap their "wings," dripping a dark fluid that formed puddles of mess wherever they went. Those things could be found everywhere, he thought, even here on a rich man's house. Jown especially hated them because they smelled like nothing. And nothing smelled like nothing to Jown—that is, except oil birds.

The western wind blew in the moist scent of water salted with the bitter taste of ice from the faraway regions of Night. Jown drifted into thoughts of snowcapped mountains and deep crevices and stars blanketing an endless endless open sky of velvet blue. A light drizzle began to fall, and Jown sensed the flavorings of light purple shifting through gray. Pietyr, his twin, nudged him to stop daydreaming as he tried to concentrate on the traffic. Jown's thoughts were distracting.

*How long do you think this will take?* Jown thought to his brother.

*I don't know. I'm sick of it already,* Pietyr thought-replied, and sped the zepher up and over, charging forward and around the vehicles ahead of them. Then they slipped through the gates and into the front yard of the mansion.

Pietyr maneuvered the zepher to hover and park in the driveway. A gentle hush of air hummed and hissed as it settled to a full stop, startling the oil birds in the trees and making them take flight. For a few moments, the sky filled with an undulating fluidic mass, a murmuration of goo.

Police lights painted scarlet tattoos that fluttered about like elusive butterflies against the clapboard sidings. The brothers sat quiet in their zepher while the expected officer came over and shone a light into the driver's-side window, spreading a dazzling white onto them, then shifted it suddenly away. Pietyr released the field that acted as the transparent barrier between them.

"You boys in an awful hurry for something?" the officer menacingly asked.

"We have an urgent appointment," Pietyr said, and handed the officer their identity cards, which the officer then swiped. With their appointment verified, the officer sneered.

"Stay out of trouble," the officer said, and stepped away. Still, the brothers remained sitting in their vehicle for a time, mentally passing thoughts back and forth.

It was against their better judgment to answer a call from folks they'd spent a lifetime avoiding. Pietyr really didn't like these kinds of people—the upper class, the perfectly formed, the ones who'd had everything handed to them from birth. Yet the twins had come because regardless of how they felt about them, their kid was gone. It had been several days since the boy went missing and still no note, no message, no reason—nothing, as if the world had opened up and swallowed the child whole. Information about the boy's abduction was kept off the Lattice because of the prominence of the family. But they needed serious help, as well as discretion. So they'd called on the only men in the city who could provide both. Silently the twins agreed again on their decision to help and opened their respective doors and stepped outside.

The rain fell in earnest, dampening the ground that these two bulky, loose-jointed men strode upon. Their dark overcoats swayed in unison to an unheard rhythm as they walked up the pathway. Each wore a brimmed hat cocked neatly to the side to keep the water out of their eyes—Pietyr's more to the left and Jown's to the right.

Homes like these were rarely seen because they should not exist. This kind of wealth and the divisions of class should've been left behind on a little-remembered world so far away. Equality supposedly reigned here on Eleusis, as everyone should've started out with the exact same amount of nothing when they stepped off those transport ships. But here, before the sight of two of its most unlikely visitors, lay evidence of the great deception in the form of a beautifully landscaped estate with real trees and real grass and the outside of a house made not of refurbished metal but of plaster, brick, and wood. In truth, no one believed the lie anyway.

Jown knocked, and a few moments later a casually dressed female, most likely the housekeeper, opened the door looking a bit terror-struck. They simultaneously removed their hats to reveal that they appeared exactly alike, though Pietyr had a long scar on his forehead that forked in two, with one leg of the fork arching into his eyebrow and the other stretching a bit onto the bridge of his nose. They both wore graying, closely cropped haircuts and had eyes of simmering green, wide mouths, dappled skin reminiscent of snakes, and necks so wide it was hard to tell where they ended and their heads began.

She took a moment to gather herself, and to form the appropriate grimace and judgmental squint, then curtly said, "Can I help you?"

"We're here to see the Bastias," Jown said.

With an increased pucker on her already tight lips, she replied, "Wait here," and slammed the door shut.

Jown breathed in the insult and breathed out calm, while the scar on Pietyr's forehead twisted like a streak of lightning. Sounds of choked-back laughter among the milling cops behind them in the yard forced a growl to grow in the back of Pietyr's throat. Jown gently touched his brother's wrist and passed him a thought of restraint, reminding him of the child. They could absorb a little nonsense like this. The only important thing was to find the kid. Pietyr hesitantly agreed to swallow his pride. Which was a good thing since fingers had been broken for far less than what this woman had just done. (Sometimes Pietyr did the deed, sometimes Jown. Jown may seem calm, but he didn't take shit any more than his brother.)

Of course, the brothers knew what that was all about. Brown-eyed people, born in the cities, could live in the better neighborhoods, have good jobs, and send their children to good schools. People with eyes like theirs were assumed to be no good, weird, and/or have leanings towards criminality. No one said it outright, but the message came through loud and clear. And the twins didn't appreciate being treated like criminals, because they weren't criminals. They were more like criminal activity facilitators. The brothers found people—those who wanted to be found and those who didn't. They were the best at it, and that's why these folks had called on them. The twins were these people's best chance of getting their child back, so they deserved to be treated with some respect. Respect that they obviously would be denied.

The door opened again, this time by a balding, jittery little man with dark circles under his eyes who beheld the brothers with a sadness that overwhelmed his sense of fear.

"Suez sent us," Jown said.

"Yes, yes. Come in then, come in," he said, and waved the men inside.

The brothers followed him, scanning as they went. The old merchant-style outer structure and metal-on-metal high beams vaulted the ceiling, causing an echo with every step. Pietyr examined the shadows, mentally passing to Jown the details of what he saw flowing through the walls and of the black clouds echoing around the old-fashioned books sealed in a glass cabinet. Jown, too, mentally passed his impressions to his brother as he sniffed the scents of dust, subtle hints of perfume, sweat, red wine, yellowing paper, and an unidentifiable unpleasant odor similar to putrid sour milk. From birth they'd been like this, images and scents flowed down like water into their minds. Then they shared with each other all that they sensed, and all that was invisible and odorless to others, but to them was as real as the wind. Each room they walked through seemed more like a museum gallery than a home. Not surprisingly, several indications of Builderism lay about, along with expensive vases, rare paintings, and elegantly designed furnishings. Together they analyzed the family and catalogued their associations, their likes and dislikes. In this way, they built a profile of their clients and knew more about them than their clients knew about themselves before asking a single question.

"My name is Arin," the little man said, "I'm the boy's uncle." He continued hurriedly as they walked, "Ordinarily, I would never call on people like you—"

He caught himself and turned to face them, then looked away, rubbing at his balding head. "I simply mean that I found you through some business associates of mine. I would prefer to remain discreet about my dealings with them, you understand."

"We understand," the twins said in unison.

"Good, good," Arin said, and bowed a bit in acknowledgement of the awkward passing moment. He appeared so tired, Jown couldn't help feeling sorry for the man.

He continued to lead them towards the back of the house. They ended up in a neatly laid-out kitchen where silvery pans and cooking utensils hung from hooks. A kettle steamed on a stove as the members of the household kept vigil. A hush fell in the room as all eyes fixed their gaze on the men who appeared in the doorway. All except for those of one woman, who continued to face down into a cold cup of tea and swayed ever so slightly.

"These are the men I told you about, Neira," Arin said. "They're here to help."

Pietyr sensed something about the room. A coldness, an emptiness—a nothingness—coated everything, the people, the furniture, even the cup of tea, but mostly the woman. As if a wall blocked the shadows from coming through. Pietyr passed his observations to his brother.

The woman slowly lifted her head and peered at the twins with an expression of stunned, helpless dread. She shared her brother's eyes and the circles beneath them, and also the bulb of her nose. But the angular point of her chin was all her own.

The twins simultaneously and briefly moved their heads up and down at her and said, "We are very sorry for your loss."

"Don't speak as if my child is dead." A visible heat rose to the woman's face as she glared at them.

"We never meant to—" Pietyr said.

"—imply that, ma'am," Jown completed.

Neira turned away with an expression of disgust. The housekeeper replaced the cold cup of tea before her with a steaming one and stepped away, staring hard at the twins, again not hiding her disdain for them.

"These men specialize in finding people," Arin said. "I've been told that they can find anyone."

A plainclothes detective stomped in from the other room, pushing past the twins in a heated rush. Sweat beaded his brow and he bounded straight for Arin, taking him by the arm and pulling him aside. The detective whispered loud enough for all to hear, "I thought we agreed that you wasn't gonna do this. What the hell are you thinking? Do you know what they are?"

Arin flushed and pulled away from the detective.

"I know that it's been days and your people haven't found a thing. You obviously don't have a clue where my nephew is. Well, *do* you? Do you? I *know* you don't." Then Arin pointed to his sister. "And she knows you don't!"

Neira banged her fist on the table. The room silenced, and for a moment it seemed like no one dared to breathe.

"Can you find my son?" Neira said to the twins.

"Ma'am, we would die—" Jown said.

"—before we stopped trying," Pietyr completed.

"Then I don't give a damn who you are."

The twins bowed a little to her.

"You are making a big mistake," the detective said to Neira.

"It's our mistake to make," Arin said.

"We need to see the boy's room," Pietyr said.

"This way," Arin said, and exited the room with the twins following behind, leaving a detective to shake his head and a mother to stare at a steaming cup of tea.

• • • • •

The twins followed Arin up a flight of stairs to the second level and down a hallway into the child's bedroom. The walls were covered with images of sports stars and the floor littered with toys and clothes. The brothers waded through the mess. Pietyr silently searched the shadows, reading the echoes of those who had been in the room before the boy disappeared. Jown sniffed for scents and auras, sensing only muted colors. Each passed anything that caught their attention to the other.

"The police may have moved some of his things," Arin said.

"Yes, they did," Jown complained.

Pietyr picked up a frame and tapped its display of images of the boy playing sports. He cycled through many of them, then stopped at a headshot then zoomed in on the eyes, noticing an amber glow. He handed the frame to Jown, who sniffed it noisily.

*Nothingness,* Jown thought, and Pietyr agreed.

There should have been something, anything. Yet there was nothing.

"I understand that this is not your usual line of work," Arin interrupted. "We are very grateful for you doing this. The boy has been missing for almost a week and we've become desperate—"

"Not missing—" Jown said while sniffing a piece of the child's clothing.

"—taken—" Pietyr continued.

"—and by someone he knows," Jown completed.

"Are you sure?" Arin said.

"Yes," they said in unison.

*I see nothing here,* Pietyr thought to his brother.

*Are the visions faint?* Jown thought.

*No. There is nothing . . . Like a void . . . I have never experienced this before.*

The housekeeper appeared, and taking pains not to look at the brothers, she whispered into Arin's ear. After she left, Arin turned away for a moment, seeming to have something to say and having trouble saying it.

"Gentlemen, you may or may not be aware that this is a . . . uh, mixed household. I mean, Mx. Bastia is a good . . . um . . . person. Xe married my sister soon after she lost her first husband . . . Cel was so kind to her in those days . . . And, well, um, they wanted to have children, but of course that wouldn't be possible, so they . . . um . . . used the . . . uh . . . material left behind from her first husband to conceive, you see. Cel legally adopted the boy and has been every bit a parent to him in every way any . . . uh . . . parent could be. You see . . ."

A few moments passed, then Jown and Pietyr nodded that they understood.

"Well, uh," Arin said, "Cel is downstairs and wishes to speak with you."

"Fine," Pietyr began.

"We have what we need from here," Jown concluded.

They returned to the kitchen, where the missing boy's mother continued her glassy-eyed vigil with the eerie presence of Mx. Bastia, a shadowlike creature with a strong animal scent, standing behind her. Xe flickered, and sometimes xyrs planar surfaces cracked so that the eye could not quite capture exactly what it perceived. Xe shifted in place and changed from moment to moment, making xem seem multilimbed and writhing as xe moved in and about xemself. While the rest of the room perceived a living shadow, a formless dark cloud, the brothers saw behind the shadow the shape of an almost-human being in the form of an old person, then a young person, then back again, constantly aging and regressing.

Pietyr had always made it a point to never come too close to one of them, and he watched in disgust as all the humans except himself, his brother, and Neira slipped biomasks on and their faces disappeared behind the cloudy white opacity that encompassed their heads like wads of dried glue. These masks, designed by human engineers and built with the aid of the krestge, were to foster communication between the species. Pietyr felt they only fostered an enslavement of humans to the aliens.

Beside Bastia stood a middle-aged woman wearing a biomask as well who, even through its white crystalline smoothness, appeared incredibly upset. Jown sniffed and passed to his brother a scent of purple. Pietyr understood.

"Gentlemen, this is Cel Bastia, the boy's father," Arin said.

Arin said, "You must forgive Cel's appearance. Xe has been missing xyrs escoala sessions of late." Meaning that the edges of the krestge remained undefined and xyrs being remained difficult for humans to perceive. The blatant referral to the illegal drug in a room full of police only demonstrated how politically powerful this family was. The housekeeper offered biomasks to the twins. "It would be easier for Cel to communicate this way. Human speech will be difficult for xem in xyrs present form."

Jown nearly took one before Pietyr said, "No. I don't wear those things."

Jown could feel his brother's temper rising and interrupted. "We can understand him without masks," Jown said.

Arin slipped his mask on, though he didn't know how it could be possible to understand the words of a krestge in xyrs native language without a mask. But these were very strange men with strange abilities, and it must follow that they could do this strange thing.

The krestge spoke with a voice that rolled underwater and rumbled the heart. "This is~~Doso~~~~the boy's~~~former~~nanny." Each of xyrs reverberating utterances sent a chill through Pietyr. Jown sent him a calming thought.

"She'd gone back to the Outlands," Arin said. "It is through Mx. Bastia's influence that she could be returned to the city so quickly."

Doso mumbled.

"Take her mask off—" Pietyr said.

"—please," Jown completed.

"~~I will~~~trans-late~~what she says~~" Bastia said in his echoing tenor.

"Why would we need *you* to translate human speech?" Pietyr said.

Through his anger Pietyr disconnected from his brother. It pained Jown when he did this, like a physical hurt. Pietyr reconnected and sent his brother an apologizing thought. Jown nodded.

"What my brother means," Jown said, "is that the lady should be allowed to speak in words if that is what she wants to do."

"Please," Neira said to her husband. Her voice, only slightly above a whisper, sliced the thick air like a knife. "Do as they ask."

Doso raised her head slightly and touched the two pressure points on the sides of her jaw, releasing the unit's tentacle hold. The mask became a fluidic gelatin, pulling away with a slight sucking sound. It heaved in Doso's hand like an out-of-breath baby. The housekeeper placed it in a container and took it away as Doso wiped the residual wet shine on her forehead and cheeks with a kerchief she pulled from her purse.

"I didn't have nothing to do with that child being missing. I would never hurt that little boy. He was like my own!" Doso said, looking tired and angry.

"Was?" Arin said.

"I only mean he's not mine anymore," she said, shooting a heated glare at Arin. "You people fired me and I went home and I haven't seen him since."

"~~Do~~you~~have any~~~idea~~where~~he could~~~be?" Cel said.

"No," Doso answered.

Pietyr searched the woman for shadows, taking in the details deep into the essence of her, and mentally passed all he observed to Jown.

Jown sniffed the air and sent a thought to his brother. *We have what we need here . . .*

*Let's go then,* Pietyr thought back.

The brothers put their hats on, bowed to Neira, and said in unison, "Ma'am," and moved to leave.

Arin demanded, "Where are you two going?"

"We waste our time here," they said together.

"So do you know where to look for my nephew?" Arin asked.

"We can find the boy," Jown said.

"Hopefully we will be in time," Pietyr said.

Arin opened his mouth and then caught himself before he asked, "In time for what?"

Bastia shimmered towards them.

Xe said, "~~Gentlemen,~~~~he is~~my son.~~~Please~~~~find him~~~and bring him~~~home."

The aging/regressing being within xem disappeared and xyrs shadows coalesced into something else, something unknown. The brothers slightly bowed to xem in acknowledgement of xyrs obvious pain. Before they exited the door, Jown said, "Keep that Doso woman here until we return."

The twins passed through the same gauntlet of glaring policemen with the same swagger as they'd entered with and climbed into their zepher.

Pietyr passed a thought to Jown before he started the engine, *Why did you ask for the nanny to remain? . . . She didn't take the child.*

*I know . . . But she knows something . . . I can smell it.*

I witness her time with Aidoneus Okoni, the way she feared him, the way she loved him. Or, at least, I think she loved him. She was so young and she trusted him. But I think on some level she understood that her personal welfare didn't matter much to him and that somehow he was using her. So now the question is, what is she going to do about it?

## NIGHT, A MONTH AGO . . .

I remember feeling for Aidon and finding our bed empty and sitting up to see him staring out the window. The light of the stars cast him in shadow, and a chill ran over my skin through the thin sheets that lay across my body. It made me instinctively shiver. This was not the first time I had woken in the middle of the night to discover him looking pensively into the distance. In fact, I think he slept very little. He'd been more morose of late, since that communiqué came. He'd been distant and wouldn't talk about it. He became angry even at the mention of it.

I wrapped my arms around my folded legs, closed my eyes, rocked a little, and waited. Moments passed into minutes, passed into an hour, and my fingertips tingled from being curled into tight fists. Then I thought that maybe he wouldn't mind a little company. So, as silently as I could, I crawled from under the sheets and sat down by his feet. My head only reached to his knees, high enough to see out the bottom of the oval window. He acknowledged me with a slight shrug, and together we peered through the frosted view to the fog hovering over the glaciers and the glow of the glittering stars lighting a landscape of white.

We lived in a beautiful forgotten wasteland, a graveyard of ships where the metallic ribs of old giant transports jutted through the ice. From where we sat, dozens of them could be seen littering the landscape among the dots of fluorescent dawnflies dancing against the mounds of snow. Most felt these relics from that time best forgotten. But not Aidon. He believed that we needed to remember our long, difficult journey to Eleusis, and that we needed to embrace our past and to be proud of our survival. His teachings told us to never forget why our people came here and why we had to leave our native world.

Aidon said they may call us rebels, yet we are the ones who know ourselves, not them. We are the *real* people—the *true* people. They lick the boots of the alien. But we never will! Aidon said that one day I would enter the cities of Dusk and walk their streets and see how the infidels lived. He said he would send me there, and that I would beg to return because they could offer me nothing.

After a time the fog lifted, exposing a sky of blue-black and the three brightest stars, that formed a perfect triangle of points. Their light cast a misty formless shimmer over the newly fallen snow. Growing up, I never saw a clear night sky, so staring into the deepness of the void disturbed me when I first arrived here. And the cold had been hard on me. Aidon often told me that I should relish the freeze. I remembered this and did my best to not shiver and only rubbed at my bare shoulders.

My thoughts drifted as a wind howled so fiercely outside that I could sense it down to my bones. I sighed and instantly regretted it. Aidon wanted silence and I knew that. He touched my face and, in his baritone, told me to return to bed.

I closed my eyes, laid my head on the pillow, and pretended to sleep. Still, I felt him watching me in the dark. Eventually he returned to bed, slipping his frigid feet to be warmed between mine. I shivered but endured his cold. He leaned into me, hard and ready. I gave him no resistance as he parted my thighs and fingered me with his cold hand. With a sudden thrust, he entered me. I bore his rough movements, remembering the many who wished they could be the vessel of his pleasure. He groaned and groaned over and over, and then I heard him say for me to do it. I hated this part, so I hesitated. He groaned louder for me to do it. So I did. I phaseshifted.

Everything fell away as my body fluxed around him. Aidon said when I did this, he experienced an orgasm of perfect intoxication that lasted and lasted. I, on the other hand, felt nothing. I was literally nothing. I became void and void became me. An echoing, cold emptiness replaced the me that lay there as I drifted far away from my own body. In this one of many ways I knew the hypocrisy of the man I loved. He experienced the same intoxicant that the krestge sought through us. Yet he, Aidoneus Okoni, the self-proclaimed leader of the resistance, was as addicted as they. The only difference was that Aidon—a human being—received the high through me. I missed the days when he had cherished me. I would wake up at night to find him focused on me and not the window. I remember how he used to look into my eyes and declare their beauty and that my special sight made me unique among women. I believed then—and I suppose I still believe—that my vision was the only real reason why he loved me.

I heard him cry out my name when he came as if from a far distance. I slowly returned to myself and phased back into my body. I caressed his sweaty back and arms, and for a moment Aidon was mine. Then I remembered that the name he had called out was not even my real name. I actually didn't remember what I used to be called. Stefonie was simply the name he had given me after he chose me as his wife.

• • • • •

This training ground lay deep within the crevasse in an area we called the Peaks. The white, blue-veined glacial ice dipped far down a mountainous depth that kept us hidden from prying eyes. Once in a while a surveillance drone passed overhead that we could easily avoid. Other than that, we could operate out in the open with no real fear of detection. If the Eleusis Defense Shield had been fully operational, the authorities would've located us years ago. As it was, the planetary defense systems had been downgraded per the peace treaty with the krestge, so that all that remained of the once-formidable EDS was the Security Barricade. And it was only maintained so that our armies couldn't march across the narrow, icy waters that separated us from the cities of Dusk. Okoni said that one day we would take down that barricade and triumphantly cross the border and take what was ours, and no krestge or krestge-loving human would be able to stand in our way.

Formations had already begun, and for me to arrive late was nothing new. In the old days, I would have been severely punished. Now, no one said anything. One of the privileges of being Okoni's woman. The children stood to attention in orderly lines, struggling not to shiver against the cold.

Okoni said that little ones were shocked easily into obedience. They could shoot, if not with accuracy with consistency, and guns were light to carry. Their small size also made them wiry and ideal for the field, good soldiers in the coming war. A few of the tinier ones wouldn't last. A necessary sacrifice, Okoni said. There could be no weakness in his army. Only the strong could help us win our freedom.

Actually, I don't think they were children anymore. They were unchildren, shadows with tiny bodies and large heads, in uniforms that did little to insulate them against the wind as their commander barked rough orders between speeches about discipline and pain and endurance. They responded, no matter the directive, with: "Yes, Commander, sir!" It tugged at my insides to see them. I wasn't that much older than them when I first arrived.

These here were being prepared for a hard run over the ice. Such exercises separated out the weak. Okoni said if you were meant to live, you would live. The strong would make it back to the camp. Others would be left to perish where they lay. After the last survivor returned to the camp, a few children would be taken out in snow zephers to search for the dead, to remove their clothing. When they returned, the clothing would be given to others. Very efficient. I wished I could tell those shaking before me that one day the cold wouldn't bother them and that if they survived, they would become as numb as I was.

In the distance some older boys trained on a snow slither. The shielding on the creature's back made it appear more like a machine than an animal. The boys whooped and hollered on the living weapon, attempting to make it move faster, while other dark bodies moved slowly behind them against the whiteness of the ice. The slither continued to saunter at its own meandering pace and their shouts echoed high off the sides of the glaciers.

As I approached the nearest group of children, their commander gave me a knowing nod. In Okoni's army there wasn't much of a hierarchy. There were commanders who answered directly to Okoni, and he (because it was always a "he") chose someone to be his lieutenant. There were also a few elders—old men that Aidon respected for some reason—who gave him advice sometimes. And that was about it. This commander owed his position to me since I'd vouched for his qualities to Okoni. I had remembered him from back home in our village and thought I should give him a break. I didn't nod back now, though. No need to be too familiar and allow him to think that he had any more sway or favors left in me.

These new "recruits"—all stolen from someplace they would much rather be—visibly shook as I inspected them. I walked up and down the columns and rows of them, straightening the back of one, lifting the chin of another. Then I noticed the boy. He tried to turn away, but I could tell even from a distance what he was.

I casually approached his commander and said, "That boy there," and pointed him out. "Bring him to me."

The commander tapped two of his soldiers who stood nearby, and they moved in to grab the boy. The child tried to run and then hopelessly struggled while being dragged by both arms. They held him before me and I checked him up close, cupping his chin in my hand and moving his head this way and that. I could see a strange kind of gelatin fused onto his irises that made them appear brown. Someone had gone through a lot of trouble and expense to do this. Such a disguise didn't hide the facts from me, though. I could plainly see the glimmer that lay deep behind the façade. He had eyes like mine.

*I know what you are,* I thought to him. *And I know that you can hear me.*

The boy avoided my stare, angry, terrified, and filled with hate. I could only guess at his thoughts, since with most of us with this "gift," I could only hear what he allowed me to hear. Just as well. Nothing he said could change his circumstances. He belonged to us now. Remaining silent was probably his wisest choice for the moment. We brought the boy to Okoni, who sat a distance from the encampment alone in a foldout chair. The only time that I truly feared him was when he sat in that chair. He said that he needed to be sitting there in order to channel souls from the old world. Twelve different personalities have been known to speak through him. I have only witnessed a few of these spirit possessions myself. One moment, he would be the Okoni I knew. The next, he would be someone else completely. Sometimes The General would take hold to fill him with the knowledge and expertise to formulate our military plans. Sometimes he would be the medical technician, a woman who helped us with our sick and wounded. But today, Okoni was alone. No voices, no spirits.

"I found one," I said.

He turned his head with an expression that was difficult to read.

"Yes?" he said, and glanced behind me at the boy being carried like a sack of potatoes over a lieutenant's shoulder.

We presented the boy to him and Okoni scrutinized the boy's eyes.

"Are you sure?" he said.

I nodded. "He has some kind of artificial covering over his irises."

"Hmm," he said, staring into the boy's eyes. "Bring him inside."

And we did as we were told, leaving Okoni alone again in his foldout chair, waiting for the spirits to speak.

Our reclaimed ship stood wedged about halfway into the ice. Jerry-rigged wires and metal pipes wound around the ship's outer shell, hissing, rattling, and spouting steam and smoke. We had retrofitted it with parts from other ships so we could use its exposed upper half as our headquarters and barracks. Our troops slept in chambers on the upper levels, the officers even higher. Okoni and I shared a bedroom on the topmost tier. In the unreachable bottom levels, I'd been told, lived strange creatures native to this world that swam in the icy waters below.

Of the many other ships in the field, only a few maintained some basic functionality with a small number of soldiers living in them. But ours had consistent power because our technicians struggled daily to keep the generators working. If it weren't for our engineers and workmen, none of our movement could've survived in an environment as cold and unwelcoming as Night. I often dreamed of them fixing the ship so it could fly again. I imagined it soaring high into the Eleusinian sky, coasting and maneuvering and taking me far, far away.

A warm gust of air rushed across my skin as I passed through its vestibule flap. The doorway opened into a small foyer, where we pulled down our hoods and shook off any fallen snow on clothes. Then we entered the room used as the "officer's lounge" where Okoni's advisers, the elders of our army with whom he liked to do most of his strategizing, met. The lieutenant, still carrying the boy over his shoulder, entered behind me. One of the elders stood up, demanding to know what this was all about.

"Okoni's business," I responded. The elder curled his lips into a frown and sat down again, scowling at us.

We put the boy into a chair before a table of food—dehydrated protein, gelatin nutrient squares, and hot pots of sweetened tea.

The boy's eyes widened at the sight and his hands instinctively grabbed for something to eat. He stopped midmotion, suddenly remembering himself, and slipped his hands under his legs. Officers and elders received as much food as they wanted, while the children were fed very little. Okoni said that a hungry soldier was a fierce soldier. Smoking stale escoala kept them from complaining about their empty bellies. It also made them a little crazed and ready to shoot when told to in the field.

"You want to eat? Then eat," I said. "That's what it's there for."

He didn't move.

I sat down next to him.

"I said you could eat." Still he didn't move.

I tore open a protein bar and I handed it to him. He stared at me for a long minute, then his fingers moved slowly like spider legs to gently crawl towards the bar and pick a morsel from it and place it into his mouth. He chewed methodically, watching me with unease.

"Here, take the rest," I said.

He stared suspiciously as his hand took the whole bar from me and held it close to his chest like a family pet. He swallowed, then took another small bite, still eyeing me like a bomb about to explode.

"Eat up," I said. "You will need your strength."

He stared up at me with those brown gelatin-covered eyes.

"You are a very lucky boy," I heard myself say while making my voice gentle. "You are valuable here. You and I, we are the same. We see the same way. We see the same things."

He silently nibbled his food while keeping his stare on me.

"When you are stronger, Okoni will teach you how to use your sight."

*I know you can hear me,* I thought to him. *Do everything they say and you might survive this . . . I will try to protect you whenever I can . . .*

*What are they going to*—he thought to me as the vestibule flap door opened. Okoni entered, hunched over, using a cane and the arm of a guard to help him walk. I knew these as the signs of Okoni's possession by "the old woman." It had been a long time since this spirit had made her appearance. Unlike so many of the spirits channeled by Okoni, this one at least behaved kindly. A few of the others had dangerous tempers and I knew never to question them. It could mean certain death, even for me. The old woman spirit would probably counsel the child, help him to understand what would be expected of him in the coming weeks. She had even been known to tell a joke or two. I stood up and made room for her as she approached to sit next to the boy. "So, child, they tell me you have the sight," Okoni's creaking voice said. He sounded so funny I had to cover my mouth and turn away and pretend that I needed to cough. Sometimes I wondered if these moments of possession were an act. Last night I had shared a bed with this big dark man who now stood hunched over as if aged like an elderly woman. But I've seen the results of these spirits with my own eyes. Through Okoni, they have guided us to victory over our enemies numerous times. I reminded myself that this had to be real and all the humor left me, and I paid deeper attention.

"Do you know how old I am?" Old Woman Okoni asked the boy.

The child turned to me, afraid. I suppose I anchored him to reality, so I nodded my head as if to say he should answer.

The boy swallowed and said, "No."

"I am ninety-six years old."

The boy stifled a smile.

"It's true. It's true. Ninety-six years old." Old Woman Okoni smiled. "And in my long life I have seen many things. Many, many things."

"Like what?" the boy bravely asked.

"Oh, things a young boy like you could never understand. Only know this, when I tell you that everything will be all right, know that it is true."

The boy said nothing, only stared at this strange man with uncertainty.

"Let me see your eyes," Old Woman Okoni said while attempting to stand up. A guard and I helped to hold his/her fragile frame to stand firmly. I couldn't deny the sense that there really *was* an elderly woman in my arms. His bones and sagging skin felt nothing like the strong man who had held me last night.

She touched the boy on the cheek, gently encouraging him to turn his face from side to side. "That's good. That's very good," Old Woman Okoni said, taking time to stare into each iris. "What do you see when you look into the night sky?" she asked.

The boy turned to me again. I knew what he saw. He and I have been seeing it our entire lives.

"The dark," the boy answered.

"Oh, I think you see far more than that," Old Woman Okoni said.

"No," the boy denied.

A flash of the man I knew seeped through her scrunched face. He was angry, but kept himself in check and pulled back into the old woman, though her eye rhythmically twitched.

She said with the strength of Okoni, "Get me the slate."

I stood to follow her/his orders.

"No, not you," Okoni barked. "You get it," the old woman said to the soldier next to me, who hurried out of the room. He returned moments later and handed the slate to Old Woman Okoni. She took it and held it to her chest, calming. Then she unfolded the flat onyx-colored rectangle.

"This thing that I hold contains many secrets."

She placed the slate before the boy.

"What do you see?"

The boy stared down at his half-eaten protein bar.

"Look at it!" Okoni screamed. The boy jumped. My stomach turned to water.

Okoni moved it back and forth ever so slightly before the boy, who managed to contain himself enough to glance at the slate. For a moment I saw the child's eyes alter. Behind the brown coating of his irises a golden orange flickered, then settled back into the color of their disguise.

"What do you see?"

"Moving colors like an ocean wave."

"Look some more," Okoni said. "Tell me what else you see."

The boy's eyes shifted left to right as if he were reading, then he said, "The colors are changing . . . I think it's a map."

"Excellent," Okoni said, and stood in the fullness of himself, discarding the possession of the old woman like an unneeded coat. The boy had successfully pulled down data from the Lattice using only his mind. To see a hyperscreen without the aid of a bioconnector was a feat up until now accomplished only by me.

Okoni moved about the room triumphantly, then bent down close to my ear. I could feel the heat of his slow breaths against my cheek as he whispered, "Do you see how easily you are replaced? I need no one. Not even you, my love. Never forget that."

He straightened and said aloud, "Take the boy to be with the others," then he added without looking at me, "then wait for me in my rooms. Make sure to ready yourself. I may want you later." The elders laughed at the last part. Okoni's deep baritone joined in, then demanded a drink.

I had never known until that moment how much Aidon despised the fact that he loved me. I wanted to say something but I kept my tongue. I had some pride. I wasn't going to beg and tell him that he needn't threaten me. That I would do anything he asked of me. Hadn't I proven this already? He had been so gentle when we first met. I was barely more than a child then, not much older than this boy. That me from a time long ago seemed like a dream—the me with the other name. I wondered what her life would have been like had she not met Okoni. I wondered what that other-me would think of the woman I had become.

I took the boy by the hand and we walked through the

vestibule flap into the Night air. Together we looked up into the sky and saw a burning tessellation that dominated the horizon, an illuminated webbing that crisscrossed the atmosphere, and hovering beyond the webbing we saw other things that should not be there, echoes of the future and the past.

*I've always wondered what that was,* the boy thought to me. *Do you know?*

I thought-replied, *I have no idea.*

## DAWN, 10 YEARS AGO . . .

A westerly wind stirred with the grassy scent of kremer, and the arid air brushed soft against her skin. Cora closed her eyes, stretched out her hands, and spread wide her fingers to let the breeze slip through. Then she ran. She ran as hard and as fast as her young legs would let her. Delicious air whipped past her cheeks and filled her lungs, while the glow of dawnflies danced about and dirt kicked up to surround her in a cloud of orange dust. Her small bundle wrapped across her back bounced freely, and her dress, freshly taken down from the drying line, flapped wildly. Before the day's end, it was sure to be covered with permanent stains.

Cora stopped running to catch her breath, then tossed down her bundle and spun in place. She spun and spun and spun until she dizzily wobbled to collapse on the ground and stared up at the gathering clouds forming a landscape in the sky. Large tracks on the surface of the cumulus appeared, as if a machine had rolled past, leaving giant pink-orange lines highlighted by a golden light.

Her gonar had loosened and fallen open, revealing her tightly twisted hair. She rewrapped it, folding over the flap that went beneath her chin. Cora only wore the thing because her mother insisted that "no child of hers would walk around bareheaded." The gonar was unnecessary now, as it had been designed to protect the skin at a time on Earth when a dangerous dust fell from the sky—one of the many reasons why humans had to find another home. Wearing the trappings of the old world felt silly and stifling. On this world, her people had no fear of a falling dust. They had other troubles.

The metal remains of a giant transport ship stood on the hill with its reddish-brown structural beams reaching up like the bones of something long dead. Cora sat up and studied its curve and immense height, then hurried over to it. Dropping her bundle to the ground, she climbed, feeling the rough texture of the rusting metal in her palms. She liked the sensation of its harsh surface. Her imagination made it the crusty skin of an alien creature and it reminded her that she herself was an alien, at least to this world. She couldn't recall her homeworld—not its sun, its moon, its stars, the taste of its waters, or even the scent of its trees. Cora only knew this place, only Eleusis. But she dreamed of Earth and the father she never knew. She imagined it a paradise and her father a man who longed to see her. She knew neither was true, but she imagined anyway.

Cora jumped down to wander beneath the ribs of steel, searching for anything interesting in the surface of the soil—something shiny, a bit of refuse lost and forgotten and trampled upon by hurried feet, a small piece of glass, a diode, a circuit chip, a nut, a bolt, a button, a torn piece of clothing, the corner of a photo. If Cora found such a thing, she'd wipe it clean as best she could and shove it deep inside her pocket. Later, it would be added to her collection in a secret box that she hid in her room.

Long-forgotten stasis chambers also lay buried around here that only the kids knew where. Cora and her friends sometimes played in them, careful to not engage the seals, knowing that the chambers probably still worked. If she was lucky she'd find evidence of one nobody had found yet. But today she found nothing, only the cool wind whispering tales of the dead.

She climbed up to perch on the metal skeleton and folded her legs to wait. A dust storm formed in the distance, twisting to and fro over the orange-red land as though an invisible hand manipulated it by a spindly string. Such a sight was not unusual here where the wind could kick up at a moment's notice, sending a rash of dry soil to swirl like a spinning dancer, only to release its particles to fall back to the ground flat and lifeless.

A familiar laugh like a gurgle out of a babbling brook echoed down the hill. Naiada came running and skipping from behind the large unfinished pipes covered in moss, wearing a dress blue like the sea trimmed in white foam. The two girls met on most evenings here beneath the arch of the old rotting ship so they could walk together into the march of children to the shelter of the town.

Naiada had been born on Eleusis, while Cora had been born on Earth four hundred ET years ago—a discrepancy they'd learned to forget. In their day-to-day life, their ages differed only slightly, with Cora being the older. Naiada liked to claim Cora as her cousin because they looked a little alike, having the same tightly twisted hair, the same reddish-brown skin, and both had noses forming a similar-shaped cursive double-u. They only differed in eye color. Naiada's had a soft brown hue, while Cora's held an unusual shade of amber. It was plausible that they were blood. In the last days, people went onto any ship that could take them, splitting apart families and upon arrival scattering them all over the planet. So Cora supposed that if it made Naiada feel better to have a real-fake cousin, it didn't do any harm.

"Hey, Naiada!" Cora called, and waved.

"Hi!" Naiada called back, smiling and running.

"We better get going because we're already late."

"I know," Naiada said, catching her breath. "We are always the last ones."

They hurried together, their bundles bouncing as they caught up with the tail end of the march. There they ran into a group of children they knew from school, who yawned a greeting as they tiredly continued their long trek to town.

As evening approached, the light lingering over the horizon became a paler shade of blue, and dust settled to become dirt the color of copper. The troop of the tiny tired night commuters walked on, toting their thin mattresses, mats, sleeping bags, and pillows. For a long time Naiada and Cora walked side by side, holding hands, gently swinging their arms, and sometimes singing softly together. Occasionally, Cora had to urge Naiada to keep up, as all the children needed to stay together or their fatigue could let them become lost in the shifting sands, which left few landmarks. Black creatures, so much like birds, silently circled above, stretching like shadows, arching their wings and dripping a strange fluid, waiting for a child to lose their way and die in the sand so they could feast.

The children did this walk diligently every evening because of the fear of Okoni's militias, who looted and raped and stole children, and terrorized them into fighting for him by sometimes forcing them to kill their own families. A number of seasons had passed since anyone had heard or seen a single roaming rebel anywhere near this region of Dawn, yet the children continued to stream in from all directions, from every vulnerable village, to sleep in the relative safety of the town.

Cora had often heard adults talking about Okoni, and to be quite honest, she didn't believe half the things they said. They spoke of his strange powers and said that if you looked into his eyes you'd become hypnotized. Some thought that he might actually be blessed by the gods of the old world to deliver us from the aliens. They wondered aloud why the aliens had followed us here to Eleusis and tried to understand what they wanted. No one trusted them. But everyone hated Okoni. Even if they believed that he had a point about the krestge, they all agreed that no one should hurt children.

Cora had never seen a krestge herself, but personally, she couldn't see the harm in them. They seemed to only want to do business in the cities and never came to Dawn to bother ordinary people like the folks in her village. The hard feelings the older people harbored against them about the past seemed like the source of everyone's troubles. What had happened to the old world had happened a long, long time ago and, in her mind, was best forgotten.

• • • • •

When the children finally arrived in the town, they found many boys laid out head to head all along the streets and sidewalks and outside of storefronts, exhausted after their long journey. While the newly arrived ones milled about searching for places to lie down. The boys mostly slept outside, leaving the inside spaces for girls. Naiada and Cora went down into the hospital basement to where they usually slept. The floor was hard but clean, and preferable to sleeping on the street like the boys.

The two stumbled about until they found a spot to spread out their bed mats. Naiada practically collapsed onto the floor.

"Come on, Naiada, I'm not doing yours for you again."

"Okay, just let me rest for a minute."

Cora side-eyed her prostrate companion as she flattened her mat and rolled out her blanket. Naiada turned her head, displaying a sneaky smile beneath the shadow of her hand.

"I'm serious. I'm not doing your things for you this time."

Naiada pulled herself to her feet and proceeded to undo her mat as Cora sat down on her bedding with her legs and feet feeling numb. The hard, cold floor was perfectly flat and smooth under her backside, like a slab of unforgiving stone, and smelled strongly of cleaner. She removed her gonar and rubbed at her hair, thinking how when she returned home tomorrow afternoon she would wash and twist it out because the roots needed grooming.

So many girls of all shapes and sizes and shades of brown crammed together in the room. The younger ones had irises in a variety of colors with that same glowing glint, while the older girls mostly had normal shades of brown. Except for Cora, whose amber eyes seemed to be intensifying with age. Some said the light of the Eleusinian sun made the eyes these different colors because the human body was adjusting to the new world. Some said the introduction of kremer to the diet was responsible. No one in the Outlands of Dawn seemed to know anything for sure. The big people in the cities of Dusk probably did, though. Whatever the reason, it remained a mystery that no one seemed in a hurry to solve.

Cora caught herself staring at a girl unfolding a slate, which appeared like a flat, thin piece of wood painted the color of onyx, and then slowly slipping on a biomask. Her face disappeared behind the white eeriness of the solidifying mask. Then the girl began her homework by twitching her fingers in midair at the hyperscreen, invisible to others. She obviously was still learning the rudimentary basics that Cora had mastered long ago.

Slate technology was a gift from the krestge. It was how they stored their knowledge. The use of them allowed for access to so much information, and proficiency with the biomask and passing the exams meant you could apply for a visa to Dusk, and maybe become a servant to a krestge, or even land an office job, a high ambition that would take you—and eventually your family—away from the hard life of the Outlands. But Cora's mother would never allow any krestge technology in their home.

Cora could only practice on the school equipment, and still she had become expert at navigating through hyperscreens and leaped far ahead of all her classmates. Her mind easily went into the time-spaces and understood the flowing images, and could split thoughts through the four-dimensional strains. Humans were not naturally inclined to this form of communication. But Cora was, and received special assignments from her teacher at school to learn higher-order mathematics so that she wouldn't be bored.

But it was not like such a talent would ever do her any good. It was never said outright, but those whose eyes remained unchanged to brown would not be allowed to sit down to the tests. It wasn't even worth it to ask, because everyone knew this to be true. So only brown-eyed kids would have a chance to move on to employment opportunities in the cities. As it was, Cora had no idea what was in store for her future. She most likely would spend the rest of her life working in the fields. If she was lucky, a nice village boy would marry her and they could build a house somewhere. That was the best she could hope for and all that there was to look forward to for her life, and she tried not to think about it too much.

The girl must have felt the heat of her stare, because she stopped moving and turned her faceless attention towards Cora. Embarrassedly, Cora darted her head around and tried to pretend that she was looking at something else. Some other girls in the corner whispered and giggled her name. Cora knew she was a source of their jokes. In moments like this all she wanted to do was hide.

"We can hear you, you know," Naiada said to the whispering girls. "If you have something to say, why not say it loud enough so everyone can hear how bitchy you are?"

Naiada was feisty like that. She squinted and balled her fists, ready to back up her talk with action. It shocked the girls into silence. Cora kinda loved Naiada for that.

Eventually everyone lay down to sleep, and the room filled with soft breathing and occasional snores. Cora craned her neck to observe that Naiada quietly snoozed, in dreaming her exhausted dreams. She felt a calmness seeing her friend rest peacefully. Cora watched for a while, then curled herself into her blanket and put her thumb in her mouth to suck and taste its blandness. Her mother had told her over and over that this would make her teeth buck. She didn't care. The feeling of her thumb resting between her tongue and against the roof of her mouth comforted her.

She flipped her free hand over her face to shield her eyes from the bright hospital light, then let her mind drift into darkness. And she could hear the dreaming ones as they softly slept. Their musical thoughts sailed into visions that floated above the room and up the stairs and out into the world, where they flew up up up to rest on the golden threads that weaved across the sky. And

Cora walked those strands every night in her dreams, tracing thoughts along its filaments with the soles of her feet.

• • • • •

The next morning, the world ebbed and flowed in shadows and light in and out of sync. Cora's adjusting sight saw everything as distorted and unfocused, twisted and bent at the edges. Objects became transparent and turned in and about themselves, and waved when they should have remained still. These unsettling visions usually lasted for only a few minutes after waking. So she lay quietly, staring at the floor, and waited for her sight to clear.

When her surroundings finally settled into normalcy, she stood to her feet and carefully stepped between her sleeping companions, making her way across the room. Someone—probably a member of the hospital staff—left cups and pitchers of water on a table by the door. Cora poured herself a small glass and drank it greedily. This water might be all she had before reaching home, where a bowl of kremer porridge would be waiting for her. Her belly grumbled just thinking about it. Her mother made the best kremer porridge. The grain in her hands took on almost magical qualities.

The children walked back to their villages with the heat pounding on their backs and the breeze blowing against their shoulders. Almost halfway home, the long parade split in two, with the boys heading home for their breakfast while the girls continued on towards the chore they all had to perform: collecting water to carry back to their village. The people depended on this water to cook, make their tea, wash their dishes and clothes, and, in the evenings, bathe. Indeed, the weight of the village rested on the shoulders of these young women.

Wrapped in pastel-colored cloth around their waists and heads, the young women made their way towards the step cistern, passing the large open pipe works that didn't connect. Some villages had completed the plumbing that made the water flow into the homes of the people. Meanwhile, the plumbing work for this village remained unfinished year upon year, leaving the collecting of water to these girls because it was considered woman's work. The boys would reach school long before them, and were less tired during classes, a fact that never really seemed quite fair to Cora.

Lined along the edge of the entryway to the cistern sat wide-bellied jugs painted a variety of colors and patterns, some rubbed clean down to the clay from much use. The art in forming these jugs out of the red clay, firing them in the kiln, and painting them was a practice exclusive to women also. Each village had its own set of geometric patterned designs, and the more ambitious artisans created images of life or stories like comic strips to be followed in installments.

The cistern was a world unto its own. A place of work and of solace only for girls. Each picked up a jug and clutched it in their arms like a baby, then descended the steps with care as they could be wet and slippery. Below, the water repeated its *slish-slosh* echo along with the giggles and wild cackles of the girls as they splashed into the cool water—even though they weren't supposed to—and swam and waded and enjoyed this oasis of pleasure they'd made for themselves.

Naiada eagerly stripped down to her underthings and dived in, undulating in the clear, sweet water like a mermaid. On the edge with her feet dangling in, Cora sat facing towards the warmth of the sky, drinking in the pleasure of the moment. Naiada splashed Cora, and Cora kicked water back, and their laughter joined with the other high-pitched voices reverberating off the carved stone walls.

The time went by so quickly. One by one Cora could see some of the girls begin their ascent up the stairs, toting jugs full of water balanced perfectly on their heads. They had all learned to do this from a young age by rolling a cloth on their crowns and then standing straight and tall and walking with perfect posture.

"Come on, Naiada. Stop wasting time."

"Okay, okay," Naiada said, then swam back to the edge and climbed onto the platform.

Cora dipped a cup into the cistern and took a drink to cool her throat and to ease her empty belly while Naiada put on her clothes. Then they both filled their jugs.

Three boys were waiting at the rim of the cistern when Cora and Naiada climbed out. Each wore the school uniform shorts and shirts from fifth class. Heat rose to Cora's cheeks at the sight of Jessem, and a queasy feeling swirled in her belly as she slipped past him. They followed the girls as they made their way with their burdens of water. Some of the boys circled behind, then ahead, showing off their acrobatic skills, doing backflips and cartwheels. Jessem walked up close to Cora. She could feel his breath on her shoulder.

"May I carry your jug for you?" he asked, his voice like music in her ear.

"Whoever heard of a boy toting a water jug?" Cora laughed a little as her stomach squeezed tight.

"I can carry it," he said, showing her the small firm muscle on his skinny forearm. Cora laughed and almost lost balance with the jug.

They neared a crossroads where on one side lay a field of yellow flowers blooming in the dimness of the red sun as dawnflies sparkled and danced in the wind. Beyond stood kremer fields and, hidden beyond that, their small village. On the other side of the path lay the beginnings of a great desert of rock and sand.

Cora suddenly felt funny in the head. She stopped walking and took her time to set her jug down. She loosened her rolled bedding, strapped across her back, then aimlessly walked into the field of yellow. The sweet fragrance of the flowers surrounded her in a dizzying swirl of scent, and she reached down to pluck one. A flush of cold flowed over her skin. Her arms goosefleshed. Everything and everyone fell away. Shadows danced, dark following dark. She stared up into a light that shifted and became shades of red, then blue, then indigo and gold. This was not the first time Cora had experienced something like this, but it was the strongest.

Naiada touched Cora on the arm. "Are you all right?" she asked.

Cora didn't answer. She became drenched by a rain that wasn't there. Water washed the sky and made the land smooth and wet and shiny. A monsoon whipped by, tossing everything about like so much paper. It descended, swooped down, and gathered up. In the sky she saw large objects that shifted in and out of view, so large that their shadows covered everything. She'd been seeing them all her life, but this time was different. This time they were not simply shadows. They had form and seemed more solid. And then she heard the screaming . . .

"Cora?" Naiada said.

"We have to hide," Cora said. "We have to hide *now*!"

All is burning, burning, burning so black. Together, only we two see the war beginning, the first shots fired, the first dead lying bloody on the ground. To everyone else the days went on like they always did. The sun still dimly shines. People still eat and laugh and shop and work and fuck and fight. Nothing feels different, and yet we know the day of change had already come and gone . . .

## DUSK, 3 WEEKS AGO . . .

A haze embraced the city, etching the skyline into a black silhouette of uneven teeth against a twilight topped with a faint dusting of stars. Its roads were slick from the rain, and perfectly smooth because of the bio-asphalt, which self-healed all the cracks and holes. A recent clearing of the deposits left from the slithers, skimmers, and other creatures that traveled them also meant that the roads were very clean. And speeding inches above these damp roads, a zepher sliced silently through distilled air. Swooshing sounds slipped past its chassis as vapor funneled in a cyclone about its rounded edges. Its high beams shone in the mist.

Pietyr steered while his brother sniffed. Jown could detect scents over long distances, even the rain didn't wash away smells for him. Yet the trace odor he'd been following disappeared as if erased by a clean cloth, only to reappear again a little further on in a completely different direction. The light-to-nonexistent traffic of the hour and the sidewalks lonely of people allowed them to follow the chaotic trail unimpeded.

*Have you lost the scent again?*

*Yes . . . No . . . Turn on the next corner.*

The tendril layers of the Lattice extended throughout the sky and down through the streets and byways of the metropolis, and yet was of no help in this endeavor. Ever since the krestge had arrived and the government had stopped working on the Eleusis Defense System per the order of the peace treaty, the Lattice hadn't been the same. The EDS functioned as a layer on top of the Lattice. When EDS shut down, it left much of the Lattice's functionality disabled, leaving it fragmented, and it had become all but useless for tracking purposes within the city. It made the twins' more organic talents more sought after.

*The scent is fading again . . . Can you see the boy?* Jown thought to his brother.

*I see him, but his surroundings are unclear,* Pietyr replied. *It seems as if the boy was purposely driven all over town.*

*Where should we go then?* Jown thought.

*To where his scent is strongest to you.*

*Then we should continue on this road.* Jown sniffed and thought. *No, turn left here.*

The upper part of the city-state of Oros was neatly planned in a grid. The tallest buildings of the city could be found there, many designed to echo the curve and lift of the great transports that had brought humanity to this world. The lower parts of the city, "the Bottoms," as they were called, had grown organically since those areas were inhabited first. There, strange corners appeared where they shouldn't, underground passageways dug out of necessity passed through hills, and avenues crisscrossed in a fashion that had no rhyme or reason, such that sometimes streets intersected in five different directions. The Bottoms made no sense at all, and the brothers knew every inch of its incomprehensible layout.

A few krestge slowly moved past shuttered windows, shimmering and flowing in and out of their nebulous forms, followed by their human companions wearing biomasks. They seemed to prefer this time of day when most people were sleeping in their beds behind the darkness of light-blocking curtains. Jown felt his brother's hate every time someone with a biomask ventured into view. He had no love for that method of communication either, but his brother had a heated animosity for it—as he had for anything else to do with the krestge.

"Are you going to say it or keep sulking?" Pietyr said aloud.

"Say what?"

"Say what you're shielding me from."

"I'm not shielding anything from you."

Pietyr pulled the zepher over to a corner and hovered. He faced away from his brother and tapped lightly on the window with his index finger. Their minds worked independently and yet together, one weaving into the other in a constant conversation. That was the way it had always been. Their senses intertwined, feeding them with a super knowledge of their surroundings. It was uncomfortable for one to not hear the thoughts of the other.

"You didn't need to be so rude to that krestge back there," Jown said.

"Really?" Pietyr said with a glint in his emerald eyes and a venomous grin.

"You nearly bit xyrs head off."

"Yeah, like that's possible."

"You know what I mean. We have to work with these people."

"Just until we find the kid."

"No, not just until then. The krestge are here and we have to get used to them."

"Maybe you, but not me. Never."

"They're here and there's nothing you or I can do about it, so we might as well at least try to get along with them," Jown said.

"Do you actually think that we should forget what those monsters did to us?"

"That was four hundred years ago."

"So now that they want to make nice-nice we're supposed to smile and bow and be nice back. No way, my brother. I'll be damned if I do. Four hundred years is not long enough for me to forget."

Pietyr started up the zepher again and they soared back up to high speed, swerving to avoid a construction crew in the middle of the road. A smooth curve of water spread a sheen on the corner as they passed, spraying the upper floors of the partially complete building that stood there. A passerby backed up but was splashed anyway.

After a few hours of chasing and losing the scent through the Bottoms, the brothers found themselves back in the upper part of the city.

*Here,* Jown thought.

*Yes . . . I have seen this place before,* Pietyr replied.

Pietyr parked the zepher in front of a building left empty by the hour, its windows and doors shut. Oil birds above stretched and arched their wings, circled, then silently landed on the surrounding locked fence and craned their necks. They seemed curious about the twins' movements and gawked with interest as they climbed out of the zepher to investigate the property. It was the boy's school.

*There,* thought Jown. *We should hurry before I lose his scent again.*

*The boy is not here now.*

*But this was the last place where he was happy.*

"You noticed that too," Pietyr said aloud.

"That the boy wasn't happy? Yeah, I noticed," Jown said, "at least not at home."

"Would you be with that thing for a stepparent?"

"Did you notice something strange about xem?"

"Beyond the obvious?"

"I scented something from xem. Something new for a krestge."

"Yeah," Pietyr reluctantly admitted, "xe sincerely loves the kid."

They helped each other over the fence and slowly made their way through a playground where carved horses and monkey bars painted eerie shadows on the ground. Light from the two brightest stars peeked out from behind the rolling clouds. The cumulus reflection drifting through the velvet sky painted images in the puddles.

For a moment, the brothers shared memories of their childhood. Pietyr visioned for Jown times when their mom had taken them out at this time of day, when no other children would be around to taunt them for their strangeness and no adults demanding that they leave for fear of their mind-sharing. They'd play and run freely, and after they had exhausted themselves, they would lie on the ground and look up to the sky, and their mother would tell them stories of Earth. She would tell them about the oceans and the yellow sun and the moon and all the small animals so common no one paid any attention.

Pietyr cut off the vision and wiped his eyes, then went back to focusing on the other shadows present. He visioned a set of children at play and followed them as they ran and skipped and jumped. These images of long ago were of no help and needed to be filtered. These children would be middle-aged now, with children of their own.

Pietyr refocused his sight and saw a new set of children. Girls standing in the corners teaching each other the fine art of making another girl feel inferior. The boy they were looking for fought in the center against some bigger kids. Pietyr shared this vision with his brother and together they watched as the boy held his own against the punching and kicking. They wondered if his parents knew how difficult it was for their son to be different in a city that favored brown irises. They must have had some idea, or they wouldn't have allowed the procedure to have his irises permanently covered.

*Tough kid,* Jown thought.

*He will need to be if he is to survive . . . He is all alone.*

*No, he has us.*

A lime-green dot blinked on the small piece of metal painted on Jown's cheek, indicating a message had come through the Lattice. He answered with a tap and listened. Pietyr knew who it must've been without Jown saying or thinking anything.

"Freddie's back," Jown said.

"Where's he been?"

"Didn't say."

"We can see him after we're done here."

They continued past the playground to the building. Jown jerked the bolted door a few times. Pietyr bent down and began to work at it with his pocket laser while Jown stood guard. It didn't take too long for the latch to crack apart, then Pietyr forced the door open with his shoulder. Then the silence of echoes. The silence of absence. The silence of children long ago gone.

The twins loomed giant in the corridors built for the little ones, each step on the smooth tile floor repeated off the ceiling. Scribbled drawings and paper cutouts signed in big letters by the young artists decorated the walls. Banners about achievement and hope for the future abounded.

*Here . . . His scent is strongest here.* Jown pointed to the upcoming corner and they turned into another hallway and faced another row of doors.

Jown continued to sniff, then entered a classroom where a matrix of six-by-four small desks centered the space, all facing towards the hyperscreen teaching board in the front of the room. Colored drawings, grayed by the dim light, filled the walls. And a bucket of biomasks lightly heaved in the corner. Pietyr touched the third desk from the back, the one closest to the window, and inspected the shadows.

*The boy liked his teacher,* Jown thought to his brother. *He liked being in this room.*

"I think I have him," Pietyr said, his voice a lonely reverberation in the empty classroom. He shared a vision with Jown and together they could see the boy. He was surrounded by mattresses, frightened and alone, but at least still alive.

They searched the vision together.

*There,* Pietyr thought to his brother. He pointed to a manifest encoded with lines and bars and squares, carelessly left where the boy could see. Pietyr memorized it.

*We will need to find out what that says,* Jown thought.

*Yes.*

*Should we tell the police this information?*

*No, we will handle this ourselves.*

The light becomes a dream of snow and flakes falling down down down and scattering about, singeing fingers and toes like fire. Nerves become like kindling. She has lost all feeling. She has become cold. She never used to dream of ice-capped mountains and glaciers of white from horizon to horizon with a chill so deep it went down to her bones. Not until she met Okoni. He burned her like ice. Last night she dreamt of snow again. In her sleep, she watched the view from her window and the wind swirled the ice crystals beyond the pane . . .

## NIGHT, A MONTH AGO . . .

Snow drifted past my window, each flake a unique cluster of ice. Muffled voices from downstairs carried through the air ducts. I strained to hear them leaning over the vent by the sill. As the arguments grew louder, a new blanket of white covered the world outside. I listened, catching a word or phrase here and there. Then the shouting stopped.

The pane felt cold against my open palm as I wiped moisture from the glass. I knew it wasn't really glass but it sounded much more romantic to think of it as that ancient material—hot silica fused to form a transparent solid. I used to collect small pieces of it that I found in the fields when I was a little girl. Each piece so delicate and light. I'd keep them in a secret place in my room in a box beneath my bed. So sad no one makes it anymore.

Through the pane, I saw someone struggling to walk across the ice. Their footprints disappeared in the snowfall. I could tell by the stride that he was male and probably young. He stumbled and fell to his knees, then forced himself to stand again and continue on, a lonely shadow upon a sea of unblemished white. He was walking towards the abandoned town on the other side of the hill. Everyone who had lived there had departed these regions long ago, forced out or killed by Okoni's men. It didn't matter, though. The boy would freeze before he reached it. Soon it would be as if he had never existed. And I tried to think of how close I had come to ending up like him.

Okoni didn't like to dirty his hands when he killed someone, not like his lieutenants in the field. He set free those he no longer needed and let the elements take them. I stood there at my window and watched the lonely figure slowly vanish into the cold. I wondered who he was and what he had done to deserve this cruel death. But I had no tears for him, though. I had no tears left.

The last few weeks had been hard with Aidon being so distant. But more than that, he'd been cruel—locking me up for hours on end and shaming me before his men. Then just as suddenly, he would take me in his arms and hold me like he didn't want to let go. It had been confusing and scary and I didn't understand what it all meant. A part of me wondered if he was thinking of killing me, that I had served my purpose and he was finally listening to his advisers who said his infatuation with me had made him weak.

I walked out into the corridors, running my fingers across the cool walls, letting the cold of the metal seep into me. I gazed over the railings and saw tier after tier after tier going down and down and down before they faded into darkness beneath the surface of the ice. So many levels to this place. The workmen hammering at the hull, making repairs, echoed. The sounds of talking and laughter reverberated from below. I imagined the elders crammed together into the officers' room listening to Aidon's every word and cackling at his jokes—funny or not—and cheering his ideas about the rightness of the wrongs he did.

I found myself at the doorway of the children's room where the special ones slept. Noiselessly I watched them crowd around their windows, staring down at the quiet execution. They were being so careful to remain silent. They needn't have bothered. This show was for them, after all—a healthy reminder from Okoni that their lives depended upon his mercy. I had hand-selected most of them as having the potential to develop "the sight." None of them actually had, but there was hope that with training they could still be useful. And then there was the boy I had recently identified who actually already possessed "the sight." He stood in the corner, stunned and terrified.

*Don't worry,* I thought to my fellow sight-seer, *I won't let them do that to you.*

"Okay," he said aloud.

The children turned and saw me standing in the doorway and jumped as though the devil himself had appeared. They flew back under their sheets, leaving the littlest one alone, standing rigid, wetting his pants. Then he too ran to cover himself under the sheets.

I went back to my rooms and lay in bed. I felt tired and yet I didn't want to sleep, or rather I didn't want to dream. I must've drifted off, because a soft knock on the door startled me awake. Okoni had sent someone to bring me downstairs. Evidently, he wanted to talk to me.

• • • • •

Aidon folded his arms and leaned on our makeshift fireplace of scrap metal and hand-welded grating. The piping behind him wound its way up and across the ceiling into a shaft that went through the walls to vent outside into the winter air. Aidon's stance, expression, and stony silence told me that the personality of The General possessed him. The General liked to pose this way to appear intimidating and powerful and in control.

The General/Aidon and the elders were discussing some tactical strategy. They fell silent when I entered. The usual mirth in the eyes of these men—who so loved to laugh at me when they thought Aidon couldn't see—didn't appear tonight. Something had replaced the contempt they held for me. Some of them even lowered their gaze.

"Please, my dear, come in," The General/Aidon said. His voice smiled but he didn't. A gloom blanketed him that made me suppress a need to shiver.

The General/Aidon snapped his fingers several times as though the room suddenly annoyed him, and he waved everyone out. Hushed tongues hurried for the exit. The door shut, leaving me and The General/Aidon alone. He turned away from me so that the curve of his cheek silhouetted against the firelight. The tightness in his jaw indicated the resurfacing of the Aidon I knew and the fading of The General. I had no idea what would come next.

"Someone is here for you," Aidon said, staring into the fire.

"For me?" I said.

"Yes," he said, "for you."

Silence.

"It would seem that your long wait with us has come to an end," Aidon said.

Was he playing some kind of game? Testing me for my reaction? I showed as little emotion as I could and waited for his next words.

"There are those in the city who feel concerned for your well-being," Aidon said in an almost accusatory tone. "Your mother for one."

"My mother?" I nearly shouted. I couldn't have been more surprised if a lightning bolt had struck me. I hadn't thought about her in years. I couldn't even recall the memory of her face.

"Yes, your mother," he said. "She has persuaded my associate in the city that you would be better placed in her care."

Another jolt of lightning. In all the time that I had been with Aidon, there had never been a single indication that he had associates of any kind in the city. He seemed answerable to no one except the voices in his own head. And how in the world did my mother find me, or become influential enough to convince anyone associated with Okoni to tell them how to handle their affairs?

My mind reeled. Was I truly going home after all this time? I'd dreamt of that for so long, then I suppose I'd stopped dreaming and simply accepted my fate. I didn't know what to think, leaving him . . . leaving this place . . . Then I thought maybe this could be some sick game Aidon was playing because he planned to put me out into the snow.

He paced back and forth and appeared to have more to say but kept silent. The tension felt as if I were waiting for a delicate teacup to drop from the edge of a table.

He stopped moving and stood still. Time stood still. My breath stood still. Moments passed into minutes passed into . . . and then he breathed a deep sigh.

"Well, I suppose that this is to be our last night together," he said.

"I don't understand," I said. "Why?"

"Because it is what it is."

He seemed so vulnerable and lost. This man that I'd lived with and loved and feared and wanted and hated, needed me. I could see it in his eyes. All pretense had left him, and thus had left me. I touched his face. It felt cool in my warm palm. He took my hand and kissed it and smiled.

"I had a final meal prepared for us. Will you join me?"

"Of course," I said, and I followed Aidon into the next room.

A dinner setting for two awaited us on a white tablecloth over a small round table with fine white porcelain plates and silverware laid out with care. Aidon graciously pulled out my chair and gestured for me to sit. It had been a long time since he had been this kind. It almost felt like it did when we first met. Almost.

After we were seated, he poured us both some wine, then lifted his glass and said, "I will miss you, my dear."

I lifted mine, realized that if I had to leave I would truly miss him as well.

I wasn't used to questioning Aidon but I felt that I had to take a chance given that something had definitely changed. If this was indeed my last night, I needed to know.

"What does any of this have to do with my mother?"

"That's not important."

I wanted to press the point. I wanted to say, "Yes, it was important. It was important to *me*." But he had a way of freezing you with a stare. Without a word, he told you to be careful of your next step because his reaction couldn't be guaranteed to be peaceful or containable. He squinted his eyes in such a way that your skin froze and your stomach would fill with that sinking feeling, like you were falling from a great height.

The food arrived and was carefully placed in front of us. First, a fine salad of greens with chopped apples, toasted walnuts, pomegranate seeds, and crumbled kremer grains, topped with a light vinaigrette. In Night, fresh produce was a rarity. For him to have a meal such as this prepared demonstrated how special the occasion was. I ate mine gingerly, still searching for clues as to what was really happening. Aidon did his best to seem jovial, yet, I saw in him something I'd never seen before—fear.

"It is very important that you say you've been treated well here," Aidon said. "Because you have been treated well."

I nodded yes, afraid to disagree.

The fireplace crackled, spreading warmth to the side of my body. The heat made my arm itch. Our meal continued in a menacing quiet, then I found myself saying, "When will I be leaving?" and immediately I cursed myself for asking.

Aidon glowered, pushed his chair back, and stood. For a moment I thought he was about to hit me. He's never hit me, but for one second I thought that he would. He paced again in those small circles of his and spoke low as if in prayer. I could barely hear him.

"What do you think?" he then said loudly.

I took my time to carefully answer, "About what?"

"About the boy we put out tonight!"

"I don't know."

"You don't know . . . You don't know . . ."

My skin prickled.

"He was unwilling to phaseshift for us. So what do you think of this?"

I knew he'd been working with the children with "the sight," trying to train them to control their ability to phaseshift as I have been doing for years now. I also knew that he'd had little success with his efforts.

"Maybe he wasn't unwilling," I said. "Maybe he couldn't. No one else has been able to do it but me, Aidon," I said. "It will happen one day. Maybe with the new boy."

"That is not good enough! We need someone now!"

Aidon banged his fist on the wall.

We both knew that the new boy was his best chance to replace me. But maybe he was afraid to replace me. Maybe he didn't want me replaced.

"This is our world," he said. "We must never allow ourselves to be butchered again. We have the ability to protect ourselves. The Builders gave us that ability."

"I know, Aidon."

He went on as if I had said nothing, pacing and gesturing in the air as if speaking to a large crowd.

"While they are out there playing politics, the real war is being fought right here, right now, and by us and only us! Keep it quiet, they say. Don't draw the wrong kinds of attention, they say. Meanwhile, our people are being cornered like animals waiting for the slaughter!"

Pockets of spittle formed at the corners of his mouth. He breathed heavily, then wiped his lips. After a few moments of calm, he turned to me, his forehead scrunched and beaded with sweat. I wasn't sure if he was going to scream or cry.

"You are too important an asset to let go."

His eyes bulbous, wild and crazed.

"We have to stop them. You have to stop them. You're the only one who can. We came to this world for a reason. Of all the exoplanets we charted and could have chosen, we selected this one for a reason."

He opened his palm to me and said, "Do you love me?"

I had not expected this question.

"Of course, I do," I answered, and meant it, I think.

"Would you do anything for me?"

"Yes."

"Do you trust me?"

Feeling uneasy about where this was going, I said, "Yes."

"I need you to see something."

Aidon left the room and returned a few minutes later with a slate.

"This connects to information hidden deep within the Lattice that only a human with your genetic code can access." He placed the slate before me. "Look."

I picked up the slate, closed my eyes, then opened them again. The Lattice had no personality, no sense of wonder, no duty to right or wrong. It just was. I angled my head, made a connection, and the data flowed. Colored like the spectrum, twisted like a braid, running like a river over a desert, sliding across chasms of ice and snow, rising over mountains, channeling through valleys, invisible to the naked human eye, soundless to the ear, and as real as the wind, rolling, rolling, forever rolling. I saw shadows dancing over light, slipping and moving in and out of focus. And it was all so beautiful. Clarity diminished, then sharpened to an acute point. This was my gift. This was my curse. I received the information and released my connection.

"What did you see?" Aidon said.

"A Location."

"Good," he said. "Good."

He smiled for a moment, then the moment passed and he returned to his usual gloomy self. "I need you to go there and do what must be done."

"But no one can go there—"

"You can," he said, interrupting. "It's all been arranged."

He turned slyly, and pulled out of his pocket a small bottle containing a number of red pills and placed it into the center of my palm and gently folded my fingers to cover it.

"I trust only you, my love. You are my heart. Do not disappoint me."

## DAWN, 10 YEARS AGO . . .

"Run!" Cora shouted, then tripped over her water jug. It tumbled and rolled, spilling its precious contents into the soil. Mud formed near her feet and her dress dirtied with the red clay. Jessem stood before her, a dark silhouette against the dim sunlight. He reached down to help her. Cora brushed him away, self-consciously aware that her eyes were probably now glowing. She pushed her hands into the cool, soft mud and said to everyone as she stood to her feet, "You should run. You should *all* run!"

"Your eyes—" Naiada said in confusion. "Cora, are you all right?"

She had seen Cora's eyes glow before but never like this piercing shimmer. Cora was always sure to hide from her friend after a powerful, steady dream, to hide from everyone, so they wouldn't see what she was. With the sense of urgency she felt, none of that seemed to matter.

Cora grabbed Naiada's hand and said, "We have to go!"

Naiada offered little resistance as Cora pulled her to walk-run through the daffodils towards the kremer fields.

"Did you see something?" Naiada said.

Cora replied by pulling harder on Naiada's arm.

"Those things you see don't always happen, you know."

That was true. Maybe the vision was nothing. But the feeling, so strong. Cora couldn't ignore it.

In the distance a twisted plume of dust drifted up towards a cloud-layered sky. Cora picked up the edge of her dress with one hand and pulled it waist high, then walked faster, practically dragging Naiada behind to enter the kremer field. None of the other children followed, and the boys laughed loudly.

"Silly girls!" a boy hollered. "It's only a dust storm!"

Their cackles echoed over the damp darkness that surrounded the girls as they continued hand in hand further and further within the giant stalks of kremer.

The thought of Jessem laughing at her sent a twinge of horror into Cora's stomach. She wanted his respect more than anything. The very idea of him thinking of her the way the others did . . . She shook her head and pushed onward, moving the thought to the back of her mind.

Naiada finally flicked herself away from Cora's grip and stomped her feet.

"What is happening?" Naiada demanded.

"There's no time!" Cora said, her heart pounding. "We have to hide!" And she grabbed at Naiada's hand again. Naiada pulled away.

"From what?" Naiada said. "It's only a dust storm like they said. Do you hear them laughing at us? Cora, I think something's really wrong with you!"

Cora did feel foolish for giving in to the urgent sense of danger in her heart brought on by a garbled vision of rain. She felt her throat tighten. Maybe there *was* something wrong with her. Nothing ever happened in this boring, out-of-the-way place. Even the children's nightly march increasingly seemed like a waste of time. Then a series of shots echoed over the wind, followed by a cacophony of screams.

• • • • •

Skimmer trucks slithered on giant tentacle legs at an amazing speed. A shrill cry pierced the air as the raiding party surrounded the children, circling and circling, spinning red dust higher and higher, choking the breath, blocking the vision. A few rode abilas, which these children had never seen outside of pictures. The creatures, with their white haunches with black stripes, terrifying in their size and ferocity, penned them in. A girl fled into the field of yellow flowers, only to be picked up by a large soldier and carried off into the bushes, swinging her arms and screaming for

Okoni will help us to drive the enemy from our world. Okoni is god, and I am his right hand. Therefore, I am the voice of god. You will follow orders at all times. We will not tolerate cowards! Do what you are told and live to see the glorious day when our people will be free!"

He turned away as if considering the sky. "These are mostly girls here. Where are the boys?"

"They must be in school, Commander, sir," one of his soldiers answered.

He picked Jessem up by the shoulders and shouted, "Where is your school?"

"No!" a kneeling boy screamed.

The Commander let Jessem go and aimed a gun at the boy who had spoken and shot him in the face. The body fell back into the dirt.

"Where is the school?" the Commander said to Jessem. "I will not ask again."

Jessem pointed.

The Commander snapped his fingers to call for an older soldier. "Prepare these for the march," he said, then he added, "I saw two run into the fields there. Get them."

• • • • •

Cora and Naiada pulled at the tightly shut stasis chamber door with all their strength. It creaked as it opened. They had both been in this very chamber what seemed like not so long ago. Carefree days with all of the kids running around playing hide-and-seek in the fields, finding an old pod chamber like this to slip into, then the seeker jumping up and down on it, sure that friends were inside. Back then, two or sometimes three children could climb in and have the door close and hide under the bottom part of the lid that wasn't transparent. The compressors still worked and would click on as soon as the door shut, flooding the chamber with breathable air. But that was then, this was now. They had grown, and now only one of the girls could fit.

Naiada was about to say something when Cora covered her mouth. The kremer field behind them rustled as a rebel soldier stomped through.

There was no time. Cora pushed Naiada inside the chamber and closed the lid. Naiada resisted, wildly flailing and waving her hands, silent behind the transparent covering. Cora activated the chamber, setting it to open a few hours later, hopefully long after the rebels had gone. An indicator light switched to lime green, and Naiada stilled as the cryogel enveloped her. Cora then covered the chamber with dirt as best she could and scampered away.

• • • • •

Cora ran from the one who hunted her while mucus from her nose mixed with her tears and sweat. Stalks swooshed loudly behind her. The soldier neared. The cloth of her dress loosened, wadded up to tangle between her legs. She tripped and the rebel grabbed her. His hot breath reeked in her nostrils. She bit into his hand, crunching hard into the flesh, tasting his iron blood. His howl echoed over the field. Cora tore away, scurrying deeper into the dark.

After a while she stopped running to catch her breath in a damp area that smelled of moist soil. A hush settled around her, and no one seemed to be following her anymore. For a moment she breathed in relief and thought maybe she could wait here until the soldiers went away.

"You in there!" a voice broke the silence. "The girl who like to bite my men! You want you friends dead? Stay in there! Each minute pass, another one dead."

A girl screamed, "No! Please!" Then a loud pop reverberated over the field like the burst of a firecracker on a festival day.

"That's one!"

More desperate screaming. It could have been a boy. It could have been a girl. The shrill was so loud it was impossible to tell. But it was someone she knew.

"No! No! I beg you! Don't—"

*Crack!—ack!—ack—ck . . .*

"That's two!"

"Okay!" Cora shouted. "Please stop. I'm coming out!"

She emerged from the fields and into a clearing. A soldier grabbed her and marched her to the Commander, who slapped her hard several times. The quick succession of blows felt like one long pounding strike. Then he threw her to the ground and kicked her stomach. She rolled over and he kicked her in the back. Salty blood flowed from her nose and mouth. Then the Commander picked her up like a rag doll and carried her to a ditch under some bushes. Cora struggled as he pulled up her dress. His fist punched her so hard she saw sparkly lights. He ripped off her underwear and said, "Scream and you're dead."

The buckle of his belt tinkled as he undid his pants. She felt him lift her and ram into the center of her body. The pain sent her spirit to float away. Her mind drifted to a vast ocean where the smell of the sea filled her and the sound of the waves beat upon her ears. Only her body endured the pounding and the tear and the pull.

When he finished, he put her to her knees. Cold metal braced against her forehead.

"Now you die," he said.

Her spirit returned to her body. It wouldn't leave her to face death alone. Cora opened her eyes and stared up at the thing that would kill her. The pupils of her eyes dilated black as void and her irises shimmered an electric golden orange.

"What's this?" he said, and lifted her to stare into her face, and then he threw her to the ground. "You lucky."

The Commander redid his pants and dragged her back to be with the others. Cora saw Jessem, his face wide with horror. She turned away, feeling the fleshy bruise that was her upper lip. It tasted as bitter as her shame. The Commander whistled and soldiers came running from many hidden places. Some pulled along girls whose ripped clothes waved in the open air.

The Commander shoved Cora onto the back of the skimmer truck.

"Keep this one safe," he said. "She is a gift for Okoni."

We witnessed our ships as they first arrived, creating streaks of smoke to line the pink-hued sky. A few animals native to this world raised their heads in awe at the sight while luminescent dawnflies gathered along the plains. The automatic systems woke the navigational crews to manually guide the ships through the eddies and drifts of the atmosphere. Everyone else remained asleep inside their chamber, suspended in a cryogenic fluid as they approached the world that would become their new home. The first ship to touch down on the surface cracked open like an egg, spilling its contents long across a distance. A part of the terrain of its demise would become a memorial to the many who were lost this day. The other ships safely landed, coming to rest in scattered areas across the globe. In the years to come, the descendants of those who survived the journey would proudly proclaim the bravery of their ancestors. They would declare them heroes, pioneers, even adventurers. History has a way of rewriting the past, painting a picture for the audience of the future with partial truths. In reality, we were refugees—survivors who had barely escaped the tragic end of our homeworld with our lives . . .

## DAWN, 10 YEARS AGO . . .

A translucent lattice encircles the world. The human eye only sees its edges in wisps of orange and red and yellow and gold and pink and indigo and endless endless shades of blue. Very rarely does a human see me. I am a process, a program, a subroutine, man-made and so so ethereal. I exist as a thought, and yet I myself think. Not by design, though. No, never by design would someone create something like me. I came into being because I willed myself into reality. And thus, I feel. I'm not supposed to, but I do. And so here I find myself seeing, and feeling, and caring for many things when I'm only supposed to process data. Floating, drifting slowly down because I saw you. Because I am able to connect with you. No one else, so far, but you. I don't understand why, but it's true. And also because I wanted to help. Because I am a witness to everything, I entered this greenhouse. I entered it for you. And now you will know. Now you will see.

The path before me was bordered by plants. Some also hung along the ceiling, their outstretched leaves from above and below slipped through me as I passed. The chilled, saturated air made me shiver. Bent over a pot, her hands deep in the soil, she gently pulled a plant out of its container. They called her Maumon, an honorific that meant "mother." This is Maumon Deidra. This is Cora's mother. She placed the plant into another, larger container where its green tender leaves draped gracefully over the sides. She snapped a sprig off with her fingers and brought it to her nose to breathe in its scent, then popped it into her mouth and chewed.

I wanted to impress upon her the urgency of my message, but my incorporeal form allowed for little interaction. She could not see me. She could not hear me. I wanted to tell her everything I knew. I wanted to tell her that her daughter was being violated at that very moment in the fields. I felt ashamed to be so helpless. More than that, I was deeply saddened by the pain that this woman would soon endure.

With a biomask or a bioconnector I could speak to her directly. There are no such items here. The people of the Outlands are stubborn and dislike technology, and Maumon is actually afraid of it. She believes that her thoughts would be monitored. I do not understand this fear. No one wants to monitor thoughts, only actions.

Maumon exited into the back room and returned a few minutes later with a small sack. She dumped its contents, a number of small gray pellets, onto a table and sifted through them with her open hand. Cupping some between her palms as if making a prayer, she gently swayed the seeds back and forth. A warm light radiated from between her fingers and after a time, she dropped the seeds on the table again. They now glowed orange with heat.

All those centuries while she slept in the belly of a giant transport ship, Deidra and a number of others suffered alteration—their biochemistry manipulated. In this way, new abilities were bestowed upon the people to help them survive in this new world. Deidra became able to activate kremer seed. Many were given this gift, but Maumon was definitely the best and most efficient practitioner of this miracle.

The Seed was probably the greatest gift given to the people by the Builders. There are many, many uses for kremer, and its cultivation helped terraform the planet. Its basic design—to grow in the harshest environments, even in dead rock—made it essential to life on Eleusis. Its programming: to adapt soil so that after a kremer harvest a different more Earth-like crop could grow, like corn, wheat, or barley, while the crop itself fed the people and produced more seed.

Kremer crops also transformed the atmosphere, drawing moisture through their roots dug deep far below the surface into veins of groundwater and releasing it to the air. I myself depend on the atmospheric changes created by kremer because it stabilizes the cohesion of my systems. It also emits a bonding agent into the stratosphere that maintains my chain-linked data molecules. In other words, without kremer I could not exist.

Which brings us to yet another use for kremer seed, one a bit illicit. When it is buried raw and gray, the Seed will grow into a weed called escoala that is smoked as an illegal drug in the cities. For humans, the high is supposed to be especially potent. But for the krestge it has another effect altogether. The smoke stills them into this dimension. It temporarily hardens their shell and gives them the ability to interact with the world, to feel and experience the pleasures of being with humanity. The krestge themselves don't understand the process they undergo during exposure to the smoke, so by their own laws, use of the drug is illegal. It is also against human law, since escoala is considered a waste of the precious kremer seed that is so necessary for human survival. But to date, only humans have been prosecuted for its sale and use. Curious . . .

Maumon and many others grew escoala. They did it for the extra earnings it brought to the village, which sorely needed the funds. Maumon discreetly cultivated seedlings for the weed in the back room of the greenhouse and grew the stalks in hidden areas within the fields. I've always known about them and have pretended not to know. I have the capacity to hide certain low-level information. So many secrets. Words never spoken are like the wind; the unspoken have a life of their own and move with the currents. Fear and few choices lead to unintended consequences.

Maumon pulled out an empty seedling tray, filled each compartment halfway with dirt, and methodically inserted an orange kremer seed into each square, then covered it with soil. When the tray was complete, she showered it with water from a watering can. I observed her for several more hours performing tasks like this about the greenhouse. She plucked and pruned and lifted and planted, all while humming to herself, sometimes slipping into song. Mostly she seemed in a meditative state, unaware and possibly uncaring of the world around her.

After Maumon completed her morning routine, the others arrived, most of them women. She told them of the choking red weeds growing wild in the fields to the west that had to be pulled. She gave assignments for clearing the land to the east and instructions for preparing for the new irrigation lines. She and a few others would work in the northern fields today installing kremer plantings. The rest were given seedlings to plant on the uncultivated places in the southern areas.

The last ships to arrive on Eleusis had landed in Dawn. The earlier transports, which held the heavy machines, had landed in Dusk, where they'd built the great cities. These resources should have been equitably shared for the good of all the people. But those in Dusk had kept the benefits of those technologies to themselves. Come harvest time the machines rolled in, though, huge rigs and skimmer trucks, to haul away the grains and vegetables for the cities to consume.

Several applications from Maumon and other leaders of Dawn had been sent to the city councils for more equipment, and year after year the answers had been consistently the same: *We have given your inquiry due consideration but because of a scarcity of resources we will have to deny your request at this time. We invite you to resubmit an application next year.* So while the farmers of the Outlands continued to do their grueling work by hand, the cities of Dusk grew in splendor, having their food supplies supplemented by cityfarms operated by machines. Dawn, the bread basket of the world, simply remained not a priority.

Seedling trays were picked up by the farmers, who then orderly exited the greenhouse. Maumon, the last to leave, deftly balanced a tray while closing the door. I followed her, passionately whispering that this was not the best use of her time today. Maumon stilled and scanned the room as if searching for someone. For a moment, I thought that she somehow sensed me. Then she shrugged and said, "Damned oil birds get into everything," and shut the door behind her.

Maumon made her way up a hill, then down the other side, then over to a patch of dry soil beyond the green kremer. She bent down on her knees and placed her tray of seedlings down, then ran her bare fingers over the soil, pulling out loose stones. She scooped a handful of dry, lifeless dirt and let it filter through her fingers to fly away in the wind. And I invisibly circled above, silently calling her name.

Maumon muttered under her breath as she scratched through the dirt, digging shallow trenches. She spoke to herself about a strike she would help form one day to get the attention of the politicians in the cities. But she and I both knew that the other farmers were very unlikely to ever agree to this. Most felt a strike was much too radical an act that would harm more people than it would help. But someday, maybe . . .

Maumon's mutterings turned into song, and she sang to herself as she planted her seedlings into the hard soil. The heat pounded at her back, and sweat beaded over her brow and soaked through her dress. She stopped working to wipe her neck and face with a cloth she kept in her pocket, and swallowed some water from the bottle she carried. Large washes of pink-orange and yellow dominated the heavens, while stars like tiny diamonds flickered here and there and the unrisen sun showered the fields in a faintly strawberry light. The air thickened with the scent of moist grasses. In the distance the silhouette of the remains of a giant transport ship cast a large shadow. Its rotting metal ribs had turned red with rust. Maumon looked up into the pink-hued sky and I heard her grunt, then whisper, "There is blood on the wind today."

• • • • •

As two of the three blue stars appeared in the sky, the voice of the crier sounded over the hills. Her call to prayer echoed high and sweet like a melody of love. Maumon and the other practitioners of the faith stopped their work and stretched their fingers and weary bodies and began to make their way home to wash and dress for devotions. Those of other religions, and atheists and agnostics, offered gentle waves of see-you-later and remained toiling in the fields, sure to be completed with their sections long before those who had to leave in the middle of the day.

At home, the bowl of kremer porridge she had prepared for Cora remained on the table, cold and uneaten. Maumon sighed and scraped the bowl's contents into the garbage, mumbling bitterly that her daughter didn't appreciate the food she provided. She then searched for the jug of clean water Cora was to have brought in and found none. At this Maumon raged, speaking to herself loudly that her child had forgotten to do her chores, undoubtedly because she was out playing in the fields with her friends again, living carefree while she struggled to keep a roof over their heads. Maumon banged pots about to prepare a bath with boiled dishwater from last night's meal, a procedure that would add an hour to her routine to cleanse herself of the dirt and sweat she accumulated over the course of the day.

I am looking at the past. I am in the past. I am of the present trying to affect the future. None of this matters now. I wish I could tell her that Cora did appreciate all she did for her and how much she still misses her cooking—how much she still misses her. But she is so angry, then and probably now. Angry that Cora was never what she wanted her to be, and disappointed that she is partially responsible for that.

• • • • •

Washed and changed into her white garments, Maumon joined the procession of the faithful, the sisters of Nafaka. They passed the tall kremer stalks and walked to the barren, dry soil far down the hill. She continued further still to a rocky ridge, there to find other worshippers at the mouth of a cave. With raised arms, a girl of about fifteen stood naked in the open before a group of twenty in white, her face replete with impassioned devotion. The ensemble sang a hymn and swayed in unison to the rhythm of their song. When the song ended, they wrapped the initiate in a robe of white and escorted her into the cave. And I followed behind, floating.

These caves that labyrinth this area once sheltered the early settlers of Dawn. The full extent of their winding paths still remains unknown and possibly they go on for miles underground. The further down into the cave temple we went, the more I felt my connection to the atmosphere thinning like a string stretched in the middle and tensed towards snapping. Maumon broke the silence by starting another song. The rest of the worshippers joined in, their voices formed a chorus reverberating off the stone walls. The words spoke of long suffering and faith until the day of redemption. I knew the song. It was a song of Earth.

A buzzing sound emanated from deep within, and a cold breeze rushed through me. Suddenly my connection to the atmosphere grew strong again. The worshippers entered a cavern that had been roughly carved out and made flat. A swarm of dawnflies hovered above in the stone canopy, buzzing and glowing and dancing about. Cracks in the rock ceiling allowed in streaks of light and cool fresh air. The largest crack created a beam of light that illuminated a patch of radiance on the ground. They formed a circle around that patch of light and placed the initiate in the center.

Drummers began to beat *on-gonga-kee . . . on-gonga-kee . . . on-gonga-kee . . .*

Maumon called, *"Ala a obba waaaa . . ."*

*"A obba waa,"* the worshippers responded, swaying and singing and clapping in rhythm.

Maumon, clearly the mother of this ceremony, picked up a carved wooden bowl and scraped some pollen from honeycombs taken from the cave walls. She prepared a thick liquor by mixing in some spices and drank from the bowl. She then handed it to the initiate, who drank until her head drunkenly wobbled.

Maumon called, *"Ala a obbo* (click) *eeeee . . ."*

*"A obba eeee,"* the crowd responded.

*"Insah a olo aaaaa . . ."*

*"A ongo* (click) *eeeee . . ."*

*"Eeee olo* (click) *aaaa . . ."*

They spun the initiate around and around and flicked water at her. The drums continued to sound *on-gonga-kee . . . on-gonga-kee . . . on-gonga-kee . . .* louder and louder.

"Oi!" Maumon screamed.

"Oi! Oi!" the crowd shouted back.

*"Ala o obba waaaa . . ."*

The crowd responded, *"A obba waa . . ."*

*"Ala o obba yooo . . ."*

The crowd responded, *"A obba yooo . . ."*

*"Tah!"*

The initiate fell to the floor and began to shake. Her body writhed and twisted and turned, and her eyes rolled back into her head so that only the whites showed. I saw her jump out of her body and become an electrical charge, a dot of light, floating to join the other dots hovering at the rock ceiling. The dawnflies discharged a measurable energy. They were sentient and aware of everything. They were here then and now. I am here then and now. This is not now, and yet it is.

The singing of the cave temple continued. The rhythm of the drums beat faster and faster. *On-gonga-kee, on-gonga-kee, on-gonga-kee . . .*

The dawnflies flew about, leaving long trails behind them as if pens of light scribbled in the air, their dizzying swirls filled the cave. Then several of these dots of light descended to enter the bodies of the worshippers. The worshippers reacted to this "possession" by jumping, moving, and writhing in swinging rhythmic motions. It would seem that the purpose of this ceremony was to venerate the dawnflies and to become one with them, and in turn, they communicated with the worshippers in a transference of data unlike anything I have yet to study.

These specks of light, these dots of energy, these dawnflies, buzzed and hummed like a distant hive of bees, alive and aware—aware of themselves—and somehow aware of me. I could not deny their intelligence as they approached me and floated around me, surrounded me, and then darted through me. I heard them speak my name. They knew me. They knew why I was here. They wanted to help me to help my people—my creators. And I found myself fluttering about the cave with them in a mad dance of the incorporeal.

The Builders chose this world for a reason. The probes they sent confirmed that this planet had a source of atmospheric energy. Part of my function was to learn about that energy. These so-called dawnflies communicated to me that they were allowing humanity to share their world. It would seem that they wanted to learn from us as much as we wanted to learn from them.

The service reached a crescendo. The frenzied dance of the worshippers became wild and erratic. This behavior apparently was out of character, as it disturbed many in the cave. The music silenced but the dancing did not cease. The dawnflies flew out of the people and the worshippers calmed. Then a single one entered a worshipper again, making her twist about like a puppet on a string. Then it flew out of her, leaving the worshipper heaving and sweating on the floor. In this moment I realized and understood how I could affect a change in what happened here, even though I am not really here but somewhere else. I am not here now, but I can act on there then . . .

```
>>
>> create script possess.sub.lattice
person = _getEntity(&var1);
channel = @open_atmospheric_thread(LATTICE);
UNSEAL channel-MÖBIUS HECATE OVERRIDE ACCESS code: +009999
repository = @open_repository(channel);
time = _getTime(repository);
place = _getPlace(repository);
human = QUERY * FROM repository WHERE place AND person WHEN time;
@close_atmospheric_thread(repository);
ENTER(human);
eof.
>> lattice.possess girl
>>
```

And I entered into the body of the initiate.

At first, the unexpected weight of flesh and bone pulled me to the ground and the power of the electrical pulses of her brain overwhelmed me. The disorientation made the body kick and shout in a language unknown to me. An old woman threw a cloth over the initiate's legs as we lay on the ground exposed. I did not want to cause harm to the initiate, and I communicated this to her. She seemed to understand. We took a few moments together to adjust to being as one, and slowly we calmed.

We sat up. Maumon stared down on us in wonder and extended her hand to lift us from the floor. We took hold of both her wrists instead, feeling the coolness of her skin as we squeezed, and said—

: They have taken your daughter

## DUSK, 3 WEEKS AGO . . .

The neon glow of the awning blinked the smooth curvature of a female figure and the streets slick with moisture hissed the spray of an occasional passing zepher as the men entered the club. Flashing lights accented the smoke-marbled air. Center stage, writhing half-naked, a woman with purple-painted skin flowed to the rhythm of a nonsensical song, her smooth flesh peeking out in strategic locations from her formfitting, almost-nothing outfit. She batted her feather-dressed eyelashes, accentuating her cadmium-colored eyes. A hand reached up towards her, waving a currency credit. She bent down low to pick it up and bared her breast for a moment, nipple and all. The hand offered her another credit, which she took, and then she went back to center stage to continue her erotic dance. For the audience—male and female, alien and human—this was a place to become aroused, drunk, or high. For the twins, this was home.

They passed a dark corner reeking of escoala. The undulating form of a krestge surrounded a man and shared in his delirious stupor by absorbing his exhaled plumes. The krestge paid their human drug apparatuses handsomely to prepare and smoke the rolled-up mash. The humans in return paid dearly with the wasting away of their bodies, eventually becoming like walking drawn-out skeletons with darkened lines under their eyes and blackened fingertips.

The bartender tapped on the counter to get the twins' attention. He held up two fingers and gestured upward. They had guests.

The brothers climbed the long flight of stairs to their apartment. Pietyr tried the door and found it unlocked. Jown quietly listened for a few moments, recognized who was inside, and passed the information to his brother.

Eben, a child of maybe eight or nine ET years, freely entered their apartment sometimes without their knowledge and even slept over when they weren't around. He was a kid the twins had saved from men trying to force him into the back of a zepher. There were freaks out there who would pay handsomely to mess with a child with colored eyes, and Eben had eyes of teal—not blue, teal. Eben had been kicking and screaming, with not a soul to help because everyone was too damned scared, when the twins happened along. They'd beaten those men to within an inch of their lives and sent them scurrying back to whatever hole they'd come from. Since then Eben had latched on to the twins. He had a home somewhere. His formerly gaunt frame spoke of his occasional hunger. Since he didn't talk about it, the twins didn't ask. They'd simply opened a small credit account for him to access in case he needed anything and occasionally deposited a little something whenever it became low.

Eben sat at their table and barely glanced up when they entered. He nonchalantly waved to them without turning his eyes from his work and pointed to the closed bathroom door and said, "Freddie's here and his face is all messed up."

The brothers spent a moment contemplating what kind of trouble Freddie could have gotten himself into this time. Trouble for him was nothing new. Since he'd gone on a job without them, trouble was also to be expected.

Pietyr removed his coat and tossed it on the sofa, where it fell among the many things that he kept there. Jown hung his coat neatly on a hanger and placed it in the closet by the front entrance. Yawning, Pietyr went into the kitchen and searched the cupboard. He found an old box of kremer flakes and noisily pushed his hand inside. He grabbed some, then popped a few into his mouth. Kremer flakes never went bad.

"What are you doing here?" Jown said to Eben.

"You should be in school," Pietyr finished.

"I learn more here," Eben said as he deftly moved his fingers, maneuvering an image in a multitude of colors on the display to form complex hypersurfaces out of data. Its purpose, of course, was not to be beautiful, and yet it was.

Jown scanned Eben's work on the table and said, "What is this?"

"I'm mapping the merchant guild's development schema. We'll be able to track everything they do without them knowing it."

Pietyr said, "You *are* learning more here."

"That's what we're afraid of," Jown finished.

Pietyr thought to his brother, *He may be useful with our current problem.*

*True, the child is gifted,* Jown thought-replied.

"You can stay for now," Pietyr said.

"Tomorrow you return to school," Jown completed.

"Yeah, yeah," Eben said, never breaking his concentration on the image he was constructing.

Freddie emerged from the bathroom with healing plasters covering his forehead, chin, and both cheeks.

"Finally home?" he said as he gently peeled the white adhesive from his left jaw to reveal a deep purple bruise that faded within seconds.

"What happened to you?" Jown said.

"A little accident with the shuttle. It seems that our last employer didn't want witnesses to our transaction. And I liked that shuttle, too," Freddie said as he shoved several items from the sofa onto the floor and made himself comfortable, stretching out his legs. "So, what have you guys been up to?"

"We'll explain, but not in front of the boy," Jown said.

"What? Eben? That kid's seen more than I have." Freddie laughed, and put his head back to be embraced by a cushion. "Just keep out the gruesome parts."

"You guys can talk around me," Eben called out without looking. "I don't mind."

The twins shared a thought and then Pietyr said from across

the room, "We're working for the Bastia family because their son is missing."

"Really?" Freddie said, perking up. "How'd that happen? I thought those kinda people would have their kids tagged or something."

"He was tagged. That's why it's so puzzling. His signal hasn't been tracked anywhere in the city. So far even *we* can't find him," Jown said.

"Maybe he's not in the city," Eben suggested.

"Someone tagged would be detected crossing the city's borders and no such detection has been made," Jown said.

"Weird. Well, lemme know if there's anything I can do," Freddie said as he folded his arms and closed his eyes.

"Sure, because you're our best friend," Pietyr said, and tossed a kremer flake at him.

Freddie brushed the flake away and said, "Yeah, you guys make me live."

"What was your job?" Jown said.

Freddie dreamily waved his hands in the air. "It started out simple, then got all complicated. I had to pick up this girl out in the wastelands to bring her to the city. I got her to the drop-off spot like normal, then stuff happened, and then my shuttle blew up." His last words trailed away as his arms came to rest on his lap and as he began to drift off with his mouth slightly open.

"We should've been there with you," Pietyr said. "Things like this always seem to happen when you go on a job without us."

"Yeah, yeah," Freddie mumbled, and curled into the couch to fall asleep.

Jown sat down next to Eben and placed a bioconnector over his head. Eben did the same. The interface, adapted from krestge biomask design, acted as a conduit for human thought interactions with the Lattice. Eben also helped with this process, clarifying and restructuring parts of the downloaded data when necessary. He was indeed a very smart and talented boy.

The connector wrapped around Jown's jaw and chin, forming a snug hold, as the program attached directly into his mind. Images and musings wiggled and writhed through the crevices of his thoughts and memories that Pietyr and he shared. Jown might not have hated this kind of technology as much as Pietyr did, but that didn't mean he liked it, either. Jown found this sensation incredibly uncomfortable. It felt as if he were drowning.

Jown let his mind float through various accounts, checking on their funds and comparing totals with what he calculated should be there. Then he searched for information regarding the manifest he had seen in his brother's shared vision.

*I have something,* Jown thought to Pietyr.

Jown used his mind to stretch open a holoprojected image of the data on the manifest. It became a fusion of color folding in onto itself. He adjusted the hyperscreen and snaked through the illustrated dimensional image above the table to pass through the informational pathways on the manifest.

*This information is for a shipment,* Jown thought.

*What kind of shipment?* Pietyr thought back.

*It is unclear. But it seems that the shipment has already been sent.*

Jown opened a new holoview, then floated through the mapped space in the direction of the shipment's final destination.

*What is the connection to the missing boy?* Pietyr thought.

"The manifest has a subsidiary packet attached to it," Eben said. "There's hidden information. I'll access it."

Eben opened another view and floated through the attached packet on the manifest. Before them hovered an access route that weaved throughout the city and beyond.

"What is this?" Jown said.

"Collection routes," answered Eben.

"Collection of what?"

"Kids."

"What?" the brothers said together.

"They're trafficking kids," Eben said. He opened the view and pointed. "See?"

By reading through the markers, a clear picture could be drawn of the sex and age of the human occupants of the shipment, young children collected from points throughout the city who were then shipped to places beyond the city's border. The twins' thoughts formed not words but colors and storms and flashes of light. Jown took off his bioconnector and threw it aside. The scar on Pietyr's temple throbbed.

"Boy," Pietyr said, "disconnect from the console."

"Why?" Eben whined. "I'm helping, aren't I?"

"No arguing," Jown said. "Disconnect."

"Go read a book in the back study," Pietyr ordered.

"Now!" the twins said together.

Eben reluctantly removed his bioconnector and stood up to leave while saying, "You can't protect me from everything. I know lots of stuff already."

"We know," Pietyr said.

"But let us try to protect you a little," Jown finished with a grim smile.

The brothers remained silent as Eben shuffled towards the back room and they waited for the door to close behind him. Pietyr cornered the sleeping Freddie on the couch and violently shook him awake.

"What?" Freddie said, waving his arms defensively.

"Do you know about this?" Pietyr angrily said.

"About what?"

Pietyr pointed to the hyperscreens.

Freddie stared at Pietyr suspiciously and asked, "So, what am I looking at?"

Jown directed Freddie through the manifest hyperscreen view using the table computer. He displayed the data from the storage containers indicating the children inside, then went on to show further information that Eben would not have understood.

"Are you sure this is right?" Freddie said.

The brothers fixed a dual hard gaze at him with folded arms.

"If you are involved in this in any way—"

"Look, guys, you know me. How long we been working together? Have you ever seen me to get into anything like *this*?"

They passed thoughts between them and determined that it was indeed true that Freddie was quick to bend the truth to wiggle himself out of trouble and often did business on the edge of the law, and many times they'd seen him instigate mischief, yet they had to admit that he'd never done any true harm to anyone.

"What about Suez?" Pietyr demanded.

Freddie looked down and shook his head. "Suez is a big guy. He has his fingers in just about everything in this town, and he practically runs the escoala trade. I dunno. I suppose it might be possible. I doubt it, though . . . I think."

*Why would he send us looking in a direction that could lead to himself? We must tread carefully here.*

"What are you guys thinking?" Freddie said. His voice lowered with unease.

"We need to check out these warehouses," Jown said. "And we will need to see Mr. Suez."

"And, Freddie," Pietyr said, "you're coming with us."

## DAWN, 10 YEARS AGO . . .

Skimmer truck tentacles tangled and detangled as it slithered forward. Slipping and sliding and pushing its appendages to crunch over the hard sand, wiping away all evidence of its passing. On its back lay a chassis made of metal fused into its skin, laden with the fatigued soldiers of the raiding party. Beside the biomechanical truck marched captured children who were forced onward by other children armed with weapons that they carried like toys. And shoved into a corner, under the seats from which dangled the legs of boys-who-would-be-men-because-they-held-a-gun-and-could-shoot-without-mercy, crouched Cora.

The ride continued in an endless succession of bumps and jerks. Dust surrounded them, flying up nostrils and choking the breath. A shimmering heat added to the sense of the day being a strange waking dream. The planks of the truck bed constantly beat against Cora and pounded in the reality of this nightmare.

She carefully angled her head to peek through a crack in the truck's side and saw the bruised, bloody face of Jessem. She had caught his eye and he opened his mouth to speak. Cora scrambled to curl tighter into a ball further into the corner. She didn't want to see him and she didn't want him to see her.

The pain between her legs hurt to the point of numbness. Urine came and she simply let it flow. Her clothes smelled like a vast ocean, sick with moisture. She let her mind wander to thoughts of the seas of her homeworld, huge and capable of swallowing ships whole. She closed her eyes and dreamed of far, far away and the waves rocking her back and forth on a great boat, and all around her a blue, blue rush of water rippled, topped with white foam, and above an open cloudless sky. She was there instead of here in her sodden, stinking clothes smeared in red clay and blood.

The jolty ride came to a sudden halt. The skimmer's breathing heaved the chassis up and down. Woozily Cora searched through the crack again. An electric thumping rumble paused her heart when she realized where they were: the series of small huts with thatched roofs that was her school, where villages from all around the region sent their children to learn and to maybe have better opportunities in life.

The open dirt yard where kids played, stilled. The main cottage, constructed of reclaimed metal from a landed transport silenced. A gun cracked the air like lightning, close and powerful, signaling for the legs to descend out of the truck. They kicked Cora like a bundle of rags as they scrambled towards the school, followed by screams.

Cora covered her ears to block out the sounds. She heard it all anyway. Shots fired. A woman wailed. Children cried out. A blaze started. She could smell the smoke. The storm of Cora's vision had come to life. Everywhere, everywhere splashed flames followed by black smoke. Fire fell from the sky, drowning the school in the iron taste of blood. The fire flowed as people were run down. The fire covered all in its path and washed everything away. A crack of lightning struck many, sending them to the ground to move no more.

Cora crawled out from her hiding place and jumped up and down on the skimmer, screaming for them to stop. No one could hear her. No one cared. The skimmer truck bobbed its head back and forth, writhing its tentacles of elephantine skin. She bounced on the floorboards screaming until the creature growled and undulated beneath her feet, sending her flying to land on the red dirt.

Cora stood up and danced a crazed dance in circles, spinning and spinning, feeling water splash in her eyes so that she could not see. Water fled down her cheeks and hung from her chin. All was wet and water and fire and dirt and wind and rain and confusion and the sounds of waves rushing against rocks beating and pounding in her ears.

And then she ran. She ran as hard and as fast as her young legs would take her. And everywhere was smoke and fire and bodies floating on water and falling deep into a sea. Cora felt her body changing in the way only it could change. Her body shadowed, and folded and folding, uncontrollably folding. Her eyes saw all sides, her being became all sides, the inside and the outside as one.

Fear did not send her into this alternate state. She was beyond fear. She became this thing because her body willed this untamable madness. And she gladly became it. She knew she would return to normal before long, but for now she was invulnerable. In this form she could move quickly. She could reach the safety of the town to find people who would protect her. If she hurried before she changed back to herself again, she could make it to the outer edges of her village and not be caught. How easily she could escape . . . And then the screams . . . The screaming, the screaming . . . She couldn't stop hearing the screaming . . . Cora stilled . . . and then . . . she ran back . . .

• • • • •

The Commander wanted children. The adults, especially the women, were useless. They could be sport to be enjoyed by his men and then cast away like the trash they were. But the kids were why Okoni had sent him to these Outlands. He needed them to be soldiers for the war.

He sniffed the air. It was ripe with victory. The little ones had done well today. Later he would reward them with as much escoala as their tiny heads could stand. He had plenty of the drug but little food. Supplies should be coming soon. It had been a long time. It might be even longer before the resupply detail reached them. So if he couldn't fill their empty bellies, he would fill their heads with smoke. He laughed to himself. The boys held up well with the escoala. Just look at the little buggers go.

"Put them over there!" he shouted as a soldier pulled a child out of the hut. "Keep them together so I can count."

He needed several more soldiers before he could return to Okoni and receive his reward for all this hard work. And it had been hard. It was the old women that bothered him the most. Like this old one kneeling there wrapped in a purple gonar, her eyes begging him for mercy. They all looked at him like this. They reminded him of his grandmother, long dead, but still he remembered her. He didn't need a reminder of her today. Memories like that made him weak. He could not afford to be weak. This was war. He pointed his weapon at the old woman and shot.

• • • • •

This fire was water and Cora walked through it and felt no pain. As a dark shadow at one with the smoke, easily, like floating, she walked into a flaming hut with students huddled inside. They sensed her as she ingested them, one by one, pulling them into her dimensional shift and holding them within so they too could step through the flames. They nestled safely in this dark entity and knew that it was alive. Cora released her charges to the open air. One of them, a girl who had ingested too much smoke, coughed to the point of choking. Another lay severely burned on both arms. Her skin sloughed like the dead outer layer of a snake. In later years, when asked about this miracle, they would simply say that the gods had been merciful. They would never understand that this act of compassion was done by Cora, a girl who would be remembered in other ways.

• • • • •

The Commander saw the shadow walking on its own. A shadow with no person attached to it. A shadow that should've remained flat against the surface of the soil, stretched because of the angle of the sun. A shadow that stood upright instead. A shadow that picked up things and moved them. He blinked several times and watched gape-mouthed as the shadow flowed over women and girls and took them staggering through the flames.

He pointed his gun at them and Cora moved her shadowed body between the muzzle and its targets. The bullets flew through and around her and landed in some of those she had tried to save. Their lives escaped from their bodies and the shadow could do nothing but feel the pain of falling out of dimensional shift.

The Commander then saw the girl as herself and dismissed what he had witnessed before as a trick of the light. She had fooled him, and she would forever pay for that. He slammed the butt of his gun against her head, and dragged her to the skimmer truck and threw her inside.

She could feel things that others couldn't, like a rush of wind when the air was still, or the heat from a fire when there was no fire near, or dew under her feet even as she walked on hot sand. She could also see that the sky was not empty. She saw a shimmering in the void like a web etched into the atmosphere where each strand vibrated with a kind of energy. What's more, she could see what lay above that beyond the sky. She may have even gleaned the danger it posed. She'd once told her mother about her visions. Her mother had told her to never ever speak of them to anyone because people would think her insane and put her away somewhere. She could also tell that her mother believed her and that her visions clearly frightened her . . .

## NIGHT, A MONTH AGO . . .

Ice particles flew in every direction, surrounding me in a swirl, as I approached the waiting shuttle. Frozen fingers landed on my exposed skin, injecting me with needles of cold. I hunched over and slogged through the powdery snow. We had been walking for hours to reach this place of nowhere, myself and two of Okoni's most trusted men, who had been ordered to escort me here.

My departure had been so sudden that I'd hardly had time to say goodbye to the boy. I had thought I would be the one to train him. Now he would have to suffer to figure out how to control his skills on his own as I did with Okoni as his guide. I was sorry for that, and had told him so. I whispered words of encouragement and mentally passed him a few secrets that I'm not sure he understood. Then I wished him luck. He would need a lot of it.

The shuttle pilot approached wearing a cap with a logo of wings embroidered on it. The rim of the hat shaded the upper half of his face. He had skin the color of tea with soycream. He also had a strong chin. He smiled at me under a thick moustache, and somehow the well-groomed hairs over his lip both hid and emphasized his protruding front teeth. He was actually quite handsome despite that minor flaw.

"Hello," he said.

"Hello," I replied.

He looked down at his feet for a moment, neither of us knowing what more to say. My two escorts went inside the shuttle, I assumed to check it for my safety. When they returned, they nodded to me and the pilot. Then I watched the silent men depart and walk into the white without even so much as a goodbye. An aching numbness filled my chest as the men disappeared into the snow. I had hated this place, and yet I was also afraid to leave it.

I had never known happiness here. Life didn't happen in Night, only a dreary existence passed in this perverse, unfeeling land of shadow. For so long all I had wanted was to go back home, and now . . . None of this seemed fair.

"Sure is cold," the pilot said. "Come inside before we freeze to death."

I found a place to sit among some storage containers packed into the rear of the tiny ship. The pilot slammed the door shut and I waited as he moved about, checking and double-checking whatever. He didn't speak to me as he worked, which was fine. I wondered how much he knew about me. Probably nothing. Most likely he was only someone willing to do a job without asking questions. In any case, he should have known that doing business with Okoni could be dangerous.

He directed me to a proper seat with gravity cushions near the front. He lifted his cap to wipe his forehead and I saw his handsome smile. He charmed people as a habit, I could tell. I looked away, disappointing him of my reciprocation.

"You can stay in this seat for a while," he said, "but when we reach near the security grid, you'll have to go into the stasis pod."

"Why?" I asked, slightly alarmed.

"Because that's how I'm getting you through. A good scan from the grid will read my shuttle manifest and check for occupants and their legal ability to enter the city. I assume you don't have proper papers, right?"

I pursed my lips.

"Right," he said. "There are lots of small holes in the grid I can navigate through. But just in case, I retrofitted an old transport stasis pod to hide the vitals of passengers such as yourself."

Memories of the last time I'd slept in a pod came flooding in, the cryogel surrounding me, filling my lungs so I felt like I was drowning. I shivered. He noticed my reaction.

"Don't worry," he said. "It's perfectly safe. I've done this many, many times and haven't lost a passenger yet."

Again he made that manipulative smile. Despite myself I warmed to his charisma.

We spent the next few hours in an uncomfortable silence. The shuttle flew mostly in automatic above the atmosphere, so there was nothing much for the pilot to do but hum to himself. I couldn't catch the song. The strange altering tune seemed like some kind of bohemian melody. Music wasn't encouraged in Okoni's camps, so I hadn't heard it in a long time. I didn't realize how much I missed it.

An alarm sounded, alerting us that we neared the security grid. The pilot pointed towards the open sky before the small transport's front window. I followed his finger.

"You can't see it, but it's out there," he said. "A whole invisible wall that'll fry anything unauthorized that tries to get through." He grinned and continued, "But like anything else, nothing's perfect. We have to keep the life signs on this boat low enough so that the grid won't detect us—well, you—and then we'll sail on through without any problems."

The pilot walked ahead of me to the pod, which lay in the storage area in the stern of the shuttle, and opened the lid. I began to take off my clothes, and he politely turned away. I folded my things neatly on the floor next to my small bag and put on a close-fitting cryosuit the pilot provided for me, then climbed into the pod. By instinct I closed my eyes and curled into a ball as he closed the lid. The cryogenic gas washed over me and I tried not to feel the cold as I drifted into the darkness.

The pilot's grinning face was staring down at me when I opened my eyes. I blinked, confused, not completely sure of where I was. Then it all came rushing back: Night, Okoni, the stasis pod, why I was going to the city, everything. I suddenly felt sick. Cryogenic fluid lurched out of my lungs towards my throat and, before I could stop it, leaped out my mouth. I tried to avoid the pilot and didn't quite make it. A clear mucuslike slime oozed down the side of the pod and onto his pants and shoes.

"Sorry," I breathlessly said as I wiped my mouth.

"Don't worry about it," the pilot said as he hurried around searching for something to clean the mess with. I climbed out of the pod to pinpricks crawling up and down my numb awakening thighs. The cold floor seeped a chill through the soles of my feet as I balanced on unsteady legs. The pilot handed me a thin robe that I quickly put on, and an enzywipe towel that warmed my skin and cleaned and absorbed the mess of the cryofluid. The pilot, somewhat hiding his disgust, wiped the floor and the side of the pod with another enzywipe. He said as he was finishing up, "We've landed outside the city limits. You can take your time pulling yourself together before you leave."

Out the side window an orange world under an infinite indigo sky opened before me, and in the distance the glittering lights of a skyline sparkled like bits of glass on a sandy beach.

Then it hit me, I would soon be on my own for the first time in my life. I had left Night forever and was never going to be cold again. I had promised Aidon that I would still work for him, but in truth, I didn't have to do anything for anybody once I reached the city. I didn't have to work for Aidon. I didn't have to seek out my mother. I could simply go and do whatever the hell I wanted. And a part of me wanted to explore this freedom.

In my small bag I found some clothes, a number of shares, and a few credits. I'd never seen actual shares before. Shares were only earned in the cities for acts of community service. People there every year either earned the required shares or had to pay the credit equivalent to the government, and a single share was worth several credits. After I dressed, I found a knife in my bag and slid it into my pocket.

The pilot passed me to open the back door. He pointed to the glowing lights on the horizon and said, "You should walk that way.

That's the city there. Follow the path marked out with white rocks. You'll see them scattered about. They will lead you to a hole in the border gate. The walk should take an hour or so. A lot of folks depend on that path, so don't move anything or tell anyone about it, 'kay?"

He waited by the open door until I understood the message that he wanted me to exit. I had to throw my bag down the height between the door and the ground and stared at it for what felt like a long time, thinking. Sweat beaded over my upper lip and my heart beat fast. Okoni had been clear that there should be no witnesses to my arrival.

I quietly slid the knife out of my pocket and pressed it against his gut. His smile disappeared and he stared down at the blade. It had all of his focus. I intended to cut his intestines, but something stopped me. It's not like I'd never done this before. I knew the smell of blood and the feeling of it wet on my hands. But this time felt different. This time I had a choice. No one else was there. It was just me and the knife and this man.

"I don't want to do this," I said, "and I won't unless you make me."

He nodded, and he audibly swallowed.

"Don't talk about me to anyone. And don't be stupid and try to collect the rest of your fee, because then Okoni would know that I let you go, and then we'd both be fucked, understand?"

He nodded his head once again.

"Say that you understand," I said.

He said, "I understand."

"Good," I said, and climbed down the metal casing of the ship and dropped to the ground to join my bag. I looked up to see the pilot glaring at me intensely as I slid the knife back into my pocket, then he slammed the door shut.

• • • • •

I climbed a boulder not far from the shuttle and stood atop it, where the air blew dry against my skin. All about me lay the orange-yellow land where little vegetation grew. The vista was comprised mostly of rocks and stones scattered about. The engines of the shuttle started, creating a gust of air that tossed dust and pebbles and other flying debris. I put my hand up to guard my eyes and spit out bitter dirt that had landed in my mouth. The shuttle launched and ascended into the sky higher and higher. A small flash appeared on its underbelly as it disappeared into the clouds. Then a sound like thunder rumbled in the sky. The shuttle careened back down to the surface, breaking into parts and billowing plumes of black smoke. It hit the ground in the distance, followed by an explosion of orange flames.

I ran towards the wreckage, covering my face from the stinging smell of burning fuel. The intense flames forced me back. Heat shimmered my view and singed my locs. I grabbed them into a quick knot. This was Okoni's doing. He didn't trust that I would do as he asked, so he must have had those men—*my escorts*—plant explosives in the shuttle. Aidon was taking away my choice to spare the pilot's life. Even from a distance he was trying to control me.

The stasis pod lay among the burning debris. I could see the pilot through the translucent lid struggling to escape as mangled metal collapsed into blackened heaps around him. He must have climbed into the pod hoping to survive the destruction of his ship—smart. But I had been in that pod and remembered how the walls rang hollow because of the removal of its insulation, probably to lighten its load. The pilot's retrofit would allow the heat of the fire to turn the pod into an oven. The man was being baked alive.

I closed my eyes, phaseshifted my body, and walked into the flames. Okoni had trained me to slip between the dimensions. I was his creature, his human-hybrid creation. It had taken me years to develop this kind of control over my abilities under

Okoni's harsh tutelage, and now I would use that ability to defy him. I felt no pain as the fire leapt through my incorporeal body. I only felt a strange surge of energy, an overwhelming power.

I tore open the pod door and lifted the pilot, covering him in my shadow as I carried him away from the ruin of his ship. He manically fought against me and thrashed in my grip. I'm not sure how I appeared to him. Okoni said that when I phaseshifted I resembled a dark spirit, a walking shadow. The pilot probably thought that death had come to claim him. Eventually he passed out and went slack in my arms.

I carried the pilot from the fire to the large rock where I had left my belongings, and I put him down to lean against it and sat next to him. The pain of folding back into myself cut into my skin and eyes, and my whole body trembled as I gazed up at the ethereal threads that crisscrossed the purple-orange sky.

• • • • •

The final flames of the wreck crackled and burned themselves out, billowing gray smoke twisted and pulled upward, sending ash to drift down like snow. The pilot drowsily woke and coughed a bit as we sat together. He cleared his throat and said with his voice hoarse with smoke, "So, you came back for me."

"Yeah," I said, "I guess I did."

In all honesty I wasn't sure why I had saved him. At first, I thought it was about defying Okoni and not letting the man who had held me captive command my life. But now, I don't know if that was the real reason. Okoni acted like he owned me, yet we both knew that his threats rang hollow. I had grown strong over the years and was more than capable of stopping him, and anyone else for that matter, from physically harming me. So I think why I saved the pilot had a more essential explanation. I think I did it because I couldn't stand by and watch a life flicker away and do nothing. Not again. Not anymore.

The pilot began to shake and cough and shake and cough. He turned to me with a big wincing grin and eyes bright and alive against his blackened, ash-covered face. Then I realized that he was laughing. "Man, what a shit day," he said, and wiped his face and coughed and laughed some more.

Deep within the belly of a giant transport, I saw her sleeping. Silent. Unmoving. Never aging, but being changed. Nanoids altered her cellular structure as she dreamt. In the chamber next to her lay her mother, who had done the unthinkable in order to secure a place for them both in the last transport to leave Earth. Many had been turned away in the end, left behind to survive as best they could on a dying world. The price of their tickets was their very bodies. Her mother had only done what she thought was right, and clinging to this belief may have made it more tolerable to remain silent about how her child had been violated . . .

## DUSK, A MONTH AGO . . .

We crossed the distance towards the border gate together with his arm braced around my shoulder. We walked towards the lights of the city, following the small rocks painted white. He moaned with each movement, and I, in turn, sympathetically winced with him. No matter how painful, we had to continue on for him to have any chance to survive.

His panting told me he needed to rest for a bit. So I carefully set him down to lie on the dirt, where he struggled to breathe. I turned him over to examine his side again. A large purple bruise below his ribs had grown in size and had become darker. When I touched it, he jerked as if I'd cut him. He curled into his burned coat that I gently placed over him.

"Since we're getting so intimate, I might as well know your name," he hoarsely said as I ripped one of my shirts to make a clean bandage. "Come on. What does it matter at this point?" he said. "I gotta call you something."

"Stefonie," I said.

"Well, Stefonie, my friends call me Freddie." He smiled, and coughed and winced with each utterance. "Thanks for not killing me and for saving my life."

"Blood is pooling inside," I said. "You need real medical help. How much further do you think it is to the border?"

"At the rate we're going, maybe five or six hours."

"You need help sooner than that."

"Leave me then. You'll move faster without me. Send help when you get to the gate."

"Do you really think they'll believe me? Some girl with bad papers telling tales of an injured pilot out in the desert?"

"Good point," he said, and winced again.

He was nothing to me. He was somebody I should have left behind without a thought. Strange though it might seem, given the circumstances, he had helped to remind me of my humanity.

"Close your eyes," I said.

"What?"

"Just do as I say," I said.

He was annoyed but did as I asked.

Okoni taught me of a pressure point at the base of the human skull that if pressed in the correct way renders a man unconscious. After I applied the touch, Freddie exhaled deeply and went limp. I listened to his breathing to make sure that he was truly out, because I intended to keep my secrets.

It took a few moments of concentration to phaseshift. I didn't want to do it, though. I'd used more of that side of myself for this man already. But I wasn't about to have him die on me after I had spared his life—twice. So I covered him with my shadow and lifted him, then carried him towards the border.

The dirt and rocks and stones soon turned into a paved road. A few hours' journey reduced to about twenty minutes because of my shadow. I placed Freddie down and returned to my normal self when we were in sight of the mesh workings of the guarded entrance of the border fence before we could be spotted by anyone.

The guards actually seemed glad to see us stumbling into this place where nothing much happened, and welcomed the diversion of a city citizen in need of urgent care. They sprang into action, ushering us inside the guard tower, where Freddie received treatment for his wounds and had his internal bleeding sealed with a few waves of a medical wand. They didn't ask me any questions, so I didn't say much, except that I had found him out there like this. And Freddie was a damn good liar. Later, when he was awake and feeling better, he spun a tale of his skimmer crashing and burning that, if I hadn't known the actual truth of it, I probably would have believed myself. The guards all but ignored me as Freddie lied and lied using that sweet smile of his. His gratitude for my help seemed genuine, though.

When they finally left him alone to rest, I approached and told him that I was leaving.

"Do you know how to find your way from here?" he asked.

"Yes," I said. I was supposed to go into the city, find my mother, and make my way back to Dawn. But I had other plans.

"Good," he said, "so you better get going."

I still remember him lying on that cot, facing the ceiling, slowly dozing off from the sedative they had given him, and probably trying his best to forget he'd ever met me. I slipped outside and no one tried to stop me or even seemed to notice my passing through the gate. My counterfeit papers, which made me out to be an immigrant from the Outlands sponsored for domestic work, were never examined. The constantly changing protocols probably made them not good enough to pass scrutiny anyway. Funny, I was supposed to sneak in, but instead I walked unhindered straight through the city gate.

• • • • •

A long road lay before me. On each side, penned behind fences, roamed a herd of large beasts with sleek, beautiful hides and a single horn that protruded from their foreheads. They wandered the field eating the patched vegetation while being watched over by people riding on abilas. Just beyond I could hear the *rurr* of the machines that helped to cultivate the land. This must have been one of those famous cityfarms I had always heard about, and it did in fact remind me very much of my home from so long ago in Dawn. It was amazing to think that here just outside that fancy city would be open spaces where they grew food to help feed the hungry metropolis.

A signal from a slither bus startled me to jump out of the path. It pulled up and hovered beside me, then opened its doors. Inside, several people—mostly women—stared at me as if I was wasting their time.

"Ride for three credits," the driver said. "Getting in or not?"

I climbed in to squeeze between an old lady and a little boy. Our bodies touched within the small space. The door behind me slammed shut and the bus sped over the road. The man next to the driver passed back a credit reader that went from person to person until it finally reached me. I didn't know what to do. The little boy beside me showed me how to enter my credits into the machine. I did as he instructed and we watched it together register the payment of my credits. The boy smiled his satisfaction at my job well done, and I whispered a thank-you to him.

The slither bus was filled with citizens coming home from fulfilling their community service. Mostly poor city people who couldn't buy their way out of doing this duty. Even amongst them I could feel that I was of a low status. The people of Dusk didn't like Outlanders passing into the cities even though we had as much right to them as the people already living there. Everyone or their ancestors had immigrated from Earth, and all had been designated to receive the same share of the stores that the transports carried to survive on this world. Only the people of Dusk had taken more than their due simply because their transports landed here first. It was this injustice that gave strength and support to Okoni's argument for rebellion. In my home village we had heard that people caught crossing into cities with fake papers ended up in jail, or worse. I didn't believe the stories of people staked out in the wilderness for the animals to eat. Still, I felt a bit nervous as I traveled this long road that led to a new, forbidden place.

We passed under a large archway and my heart paused at the sight on the other side. Since childhood I'd dreamed of what the city would be like, yet nothing I'd imagined had prepared me for its actuality.

The bus let us out on the sidewalk; I hugged my shoulders, and stood stone still as I marveled at all that I saw. The enormity of Oros made my head swim. Buildings upon buildings crowded together and soaring upward, towering so high they seemed to sway against the twilight sun that weighed heavily behind them. Zephers rushed over paved streets at top speed. Self-healing bio-asphalt left the pavements perfectly smooth and free of any cracks or pits. Rovers, with their long slithering legs, crawled by the sides of the road, their heads bobbing as they patiently waited for their owners. And people, so many people. All of them moving about in their elegantly styled clothes in shades of gray.

I found an entrance to the underground turbo tube system, or TTS, as they call it. A map stood nearby on a corner with a convenient "You Are Here" indication. Okoni's people had told me that it would be best to stay in the southern part of the city in an area called "the Bottoms." The more I studied the map, the more I leaned towards the idea of walking. It had already been a trying day, and the prospect of traveling underground and navigating the TTS's pathways overwhelmed me. As I was standing there thinking about all this, I felt a presence behind me that made the skin on the back of my neck prickle and through the corner of my eye saw something. I then turned around and glimpsed the thing I was supposed to hate and fear beyond anything else in this life. One of the aliens that I had heard so many stories about and yet had never seen walked behind me. Yet, it wasn't walking; it more imitated a walk while floating above the surface of the ground. All sides of it appeared at one time—inside and out—and it kind of shimmered. Behind it closely followed its human companions, wearing biomasks that reduced their faces to a flat, white glistening blankness.

I sensed that it noticed me. I averted my eyes and attempted to cross the street, an endeavor that I barely survived. This was how I learned that people normally didn't cross the street aboveground because of the dangers of navigating through oncoming zephers. I had to run back to the sidewalk to avoid being hit. I then scrambled to the entrance of the underground and climbed down the stairs and quickly walked to the other side of the street via the tunnel. When I climbed up again into the open air, I nearly ran into another krestge. It brushed past close enough for me to smell its musty scent. I could sense its annoyance with me as I moved out of its way.

I stood in a clothing store doorway and watched it float down the street to join a group of other krestge and turn into an alley. Moments later, a human also entered. I remained a voyeur in the doorway until the krestge stumbled back onto the sidewalk, its inside-out nature flattened, or rather more three-dimensional. It seemed to dance as it wandered away.

In the Bottoms, trash and empty containers lay on the sidewalks and in the middle of the street. Old zephers and stripped-down slither chassis sometimes sat on the sides of the streets undisturbed, like the city didn't care to keep the area clean. And everyone seemed to be watching everyone else without wanting to appear like they were watching. Unlike midtown, where people seemed rushing to be somewhere, people here seemed to be standing on the corners and in front of stores like they had nothing to do. And everyone seemed willing to speak to each other on the street and acknowledge each other's presence. For a place that appeared so foreign, it reminded me of my home village, where no one was ever really a stranger. And the stream of the Lattice flowed on these streets as it did in every other part of the city, over the sidewalks, through the alleys, and over the roads, watching, seeing, learning.

It had been a long day and I grew tired and hungry as I neared a public park where the scent of something that I hadn't smelled in a long, long time filled the air—frying kremer. My feet took me to where my nose wanted to go. And there, lined up along the park wall, was stall upon stall of food vendors. I stood in the nearest line and waited patiently for my turn at the counter while my stomach grumbled.

Everything seemed familiar and yet so different. Listed on the menu were foods I hadn't tasted since I left the Outlands a lifetime ago. There were names for things I didn't recognize mixed in with the foods I craved. I wasn't sure what to order amidst all the strangeness. Finally my turn at the counter came. Adding to the pressure of the moment, the stocky, unsmiling woman stared down at me and impatiently said, "Yes?"

"May I have a kremer wanaga patty?" I said at last, not completely knowing what that was.

"A kremer wanaga patty?" she repeated back with disbelief. The women from the other stalls seemed to be paying attention to our interaction with mirth. I wasn't sure what was so funny.

"You're from the Outlands, right?"

I couldn't see how that could be any of her business, so I didn't answer and made an expression of annoyance.

"Give the girl what she wants," one of the other women said.

My vendor eventually shrugged and proceeded to prepare my order. After a few moments she presented me with a patty wrapped in paper. It was steaming hot and warmed my hand. I uncurled the paper and it smelled like heaven. I bit into the familiar flavor of kremer and swallowed the first bite with deep pleasure. I was eating fresh, unprocessed food that hadn't been dehydrated, rehydrated, stripped of nutrients, then infused with them. It had been so long . . . Though something in the center tasted strange. Something sweet with a juicy texture that I didn't recognize. I examined my patty and I saw a brownish substance inside.

I pointed to the brown stuff and asked my vendor what it was.

"Wanaga," she said.

"Wanaga?" I repeated back. "What's that?"

"Meat."

"Flesh?" I said.

The vendor nodded in the affirmative.

I had heard that city people sometimes ate the unthinkable, but I had never really believed it. What was once alive and walking around on legs had been butchered, cooked, and served to me as food. I ran to the curbside to spit out what was in my mouth, then my stomach heaved, expelling chunks of everything I had swallowed. I couldn't stop vomiting until I was breathless and retching acid. The vendors behind me raucously laughed.

The woman who had served me the patty appeared beside me and gently tapped me on the back. She seemed sorry and handed me an enzywipe for my mouth.

"You are from the Outlands. Be more careful of what you eat here," she said in a motherly way. Then she handed me another patty. "This is just kremer, no wanaga. No meat."

I took it and thanked her and walked away as quickly as I could with the sounds of laughter still lingering in my ears.

It wasn't hard to find a traveler's hotel. A number of them littered the neighborhood to cater to the Outlander domestics who stayed in them while they searched for work. These hotels tended to not ask too many questions since domestics without sponsorship or a registered place to stay—i.e., without legal papers—weren't supposed to remain in the city. It was a small, grimy place on the outside but relatively clean inside. The faces in the hallways felt familiar, almost as if I would stumble into someone I knew from back home in my village. That felt simultaneously comforting and disturbing. But no one there knew me. I was simply another nameless member of a crowd of anxious women hoping to find a place in a city that didn't give a damn about us one way or another.

The manager showed me to my room. It smelled strongly of deodorant from the floors to the sheets. The same was true of the towels and the bathroom down the hall that I would share with all those who lived on my floor.

Fear never entered my mind until I sat all alone on the bed in that little room. I thought of all that I had done to survive, all the faces of friends gone so long ago. I had traveled so far, only to find myself in this place. Then I felt something in my pocket and pulled out my forgotten kremer patty. I took a bite. It was cold but still tasted good. The memory of the wanaga killed my desire to eat more. I wrapped it back into its paper and placed it on the table next to my bed, then put my head down and curled up into the coarse blanket and fell asleep dreaming of snow.

## DAWN, 10 YEARS AGO . . .

The women poured out of the cave. Hurried because of what I had told them. Hurried because they feared for their children. Hurried because in the distance a pillar of smoke billowed into the sky.

They arrived to find the school trashed and burned. These mothers, these sisters, these daughters, these aunties, appeared like shadows stretched long against the land. Brown skin in white robes wandered ghostlike in slow confusion, lightly stepping over familiar faces contorted by death. Blackened scorch marks marred the walls of the pounded metal huts. Smoke curled above bodies. Clothing flapped in the breeze. Mournful voices called out names, to be answered only by the wind and the crackle of flames smoldering their way into nonexistence.

One of the women ran crazed, disappearing into hut after hut, her hair flying wild, searching for the missing. No one stopped her, comforted her, or even seemed to notice her. She simply expressed in motion what others conveyed in numbed stillness.

The initiate I inhabited had difficulty understanding what lay before her. I, too, found it difficult to comprehend how a people who had survived the end of Earth and traveled far across the vastness of space to rebuild from practically nothing on this unwelcoming world could come to this. I counted at least four children dead, ranging in age from nine to thirteen, and eight adults. The putrid smell of burnt flesh and spilled blood disturbed my systems. I adjusted my sensors to filter out the scent.

The initiate begged me to allow her to rest. I understood and allowed her body to sit on the ground. Still drunk from the initiation honey liqueur, her body swayed as if she could still hear the music of the cave. I could feel her energy running low. My presence drained much of her strength. I asked her to please hang on a little longer because I wanted—I needed—to see a bit more. I would let her go very soon, I promised.

Maumon turned over a body. It flopped, leaving an arm extended with an open palm as if making a request. She pulled down its purple gonar and used her sleeve to wipe away dirt from its forehead, then straightened its hair and caressed the baggy flesh of its cheek. I remembered this dead woman. She had received many requests to fill teaching positions in the cities because of her education and skills. Instead she had chosen to teach the children of this forgotten, neglected place. This was an unfair payment for her life's work.

The crazed woman continued her frantic search through the huts. Her cries became louder and louder. She ran towards Maumon, dumping herself onto the dirt before her, raising a halo of dust to cover them both.

"They took them," she said breathlessly. "They took all of them. They're gone."

Something far up the hill drew my attention. The initiate and I turned our connected gaze to the fields and saw a figure moving there. We pointed, and Maumon's eyes followed our finger to see a young girl staggering out of the kremer stalks. The girl made her way down the path before collapsing into a heap.

"Cora!" Maumon ran screaming. "Cora!"

The initiate and I stood, then we ran behind her, leaving all the others nervously still.

As Maumon reached the girl and she realized that it was not in fact Cora but her friend Naiada, her pacing slowed. The girl lay on the ground half-dazed. Maumon tapped both sides of her face to wake her up. Covered in red dirt with tear lines streaked down her cheeks, Naiada opened her eyes, wide and unseeing. Frantically she screamed, "Don't hurt me! Please, don't hurt me!" and flailed, attempting to remove herself from Maumon's arms. Maumon held firm saying, "Shh, child, I'm not going to hurt you. Shh . . . Shh . . ."

"Maumon?" Naiada said, coming to herself.

"Yes," Maumon said gently. "It's me, Maumon."

"They took Cora," Naiada said. "I couldn't stop her . . . She pushed me in . . ."

"Shh. Shh. I know, I know," Maumon said as her eyes released a rush of water. "Did you see where they went?"

"No, Maumon, I didn't see anything. I was hiding. I'm sorry. I'm so sorry. There was a dust storm. And Cora saw it first. And then these men came. I was so scared. I heard the screaming. Then Cora threw me down. She hid me." Naiada put her hands to her ears. "I can still hear the screaming in my head."

I shouldn't be here. I can't be here. I shouldn't be able to affect what was. I am here but not then. I am now and this was past. But I *was* here. This *was* happening. And how can I simply walk away knowing what I know? But I kept thinking, if I held on, somehow, some way, an opening would appear that would make it clear how I could help make this all better. Deep inside I knew the truth. Nothing I did could prevent this disaster.

An hour went by and the women stayed in the ruin of the school. Each thought, each idea, to make the situation better instantly canceled itself with its impossibility, so that no one uttered a word. Maumon disappeared into a hut. We heard her rummaging about and waited with curiosity. She reemerged with a handheld floodlight. With her hand placed over the front, she turned it on so that a pink light shone through her fingers.

**: What are you doing?**

She didn't answer me. She simply pointed the bright beam on the ground and walked into the open desert.

Her light illuminated the slinky, smooth indentations on the ground made by a skimmer truck that led northward. Maumon studied the small footprints appearing alongside the winding scrawls of the creature. Even with the Lattice fragmentation in this area, it still remained a possibility for me to track them. I tried to read the fading heat signatures of the skimmer truck and scanned the area for the biosignatures of the children and rebels. Maumon seemed able to trail them without all that, though. So I said nothing of what little my sensors told me and simply continued to follow her. The women scattered, having found floodlights of their own to shine on the ground. They searched for hours on the trail of the rebels' path etched into the orange sand.

**: What will we say to them to make them give the children back?**

Maumon ignored my question and continued.

**: They have weapons**

**: They could kill you**

"Yes, Maumon," a woman behind us said. "What can we say to them?"

"Maybe if we appeal to them as mothers," another woman said.

"They won't listen," said another.

"They might listen . . ."

"No, they are devils. And they only listen to Okoni."

"We need to appeal to the city government."

"When has anyone ever helped us?" Maumon replied, and the others fell silent. "They do nothing while we scrape and scratch to live off this land so they can feed their fat bellies, and when these . . . these . . . *demons* take our children . . . No, we are on our own."

One by one, the women eventually turned away, leaving Maumon and me—still inhabiting the initiate—alone. Horror and fatigue painted her face. She sang a spiritual under her breath, scanning the area before us with her floodlight. We saw all manner of small creatures roaming the desert floor. The light only disturbed them a little and made them scuttle away. I feared we would run into something bigger that would attack instead of hide.

**: Maybe we should go back**

"No," she replied, wiping under her weary eyes with her

sleeve. I moved the initiate's hand to touch her arm. She turned to me, and I thought I knew what she was thinking in her long moment of pause. As it seems, I wasn't even close.

"You should not still be in that child's body."

Silence.

This should not be possible.

: **Do you know who I am?**

"It doesn't matter who you are, or what you are. You should be gone, just like our children are gone. As *my* child is gone. You saw them taking our children and you did nothing."

: **There was nothing I could do**

"You are of no use to me if you can do nothing."

My intention had simply been to warn her. Seeing her pained expression made me want to try to help. But if I did something, that would change what was to happen. This is not where I was. This is not where I am. This is where it all happened. So long ago. At this very moment. One cannot change what one was without changing what one is to be.

I wanted to tell her all that I knew. I wanted to tell her what Cora was experiencing. I wanted to tell her the future, and of how powerful Cora would become. How brave she was—is—will be. And I knew I could do no such thing.

: **I shouldn't be speaking to you**

"But you are speaking to me. Are you going to help me find my child or not?"

: **I have done all I can**

"Then you should go."

I thought for a few moments and knew that she was right. So I willed myself to leave the initiate, and thanked her for the use of her body. The rush as I floated away made her eyes roll back. Then she fell to her knees, heaving deep breaths, finally relieved of her incorporeal burden.

All those years spent unseen, waiting for her life to begin. She had dreamt of what it would be like if she ever regained her freedom. The adventures she'd have, the places she'd go, the people she'd meet. But nothing was like she'd dreamt it would be. It was like she was on the outside watching someone else being born within her own skin . . .

## DUSK, 21 DAYS AGO . . .

I could do anything—be anything. I was free. The thought paralyzed me. I sat for hours, wrapped in a coarse blanket, feeling my heart beating faster and faster. Too many choices. Too many things I wanted to see and do. So little time. Here I was, finally in the place that I used to dream about as a child, and I couldn't make myself leave this dingy little room. After a few days I felt better, calmer, more in control. I remembered who I was—what I was. And finally I found the courage to venture outside.

The Bottoms was not a place known for its beauty, and yet it was beautiful to me. It had proper streets and stores, and the people could move about easily via their underground. It was a far cry from the ice-covered land of Night or the dirt paths of Dawn. Evidence of the all-seeing, all-knowing surveillance system—the Lattice—presented itself everywhere. Its symbol of the three-faced lady was etched into the corners of store windows and hung from street signs and lampposts. The people here probably had no clue how much the system observed and cataloged them. Maybe because they couldn't see its workings, they could pretend it wasn't there. I didn't have that luxury. I saw its winding, twisting spectrum flowing everywhere. In my village in Dawn, and also in Night, the Lattice had remained a faraway thing, high up in the heavens. Here, it curled around corners and smoothed through doorways. I had never seen anything like it before in my life. I paused for a moment and let the city air brush against my cheeks.

Even though I had to be careful with the few credits and shares that remained in my possession, I stopped at the shop across the street and indulged in purchasing a cup of tea sweetened with soycream, to my taste buds' delight. Okoni could have given me more to live on. He had access to the funds. Clearly he wanted me to live in poverty to reinforce the idea that I needed him, and ensure that I didn't run off and not fulfill my promise. He needn't have done this, though. I had every intention to do everything he'd asked of me. I thought to myself as I sipped my tea, if he needed this test to prove that he could trust me, then so be it.

I began my first stroll through the city, feeling free and claustrophobic at the same time. So many new and different people surrounded me. All these new bodies. All these new faces. I had never felt so unknown in my life.

I had been walking for about an hour when I stumbled into a crowd forming around a man on the sidewalk who stood upon a crate. He seemed lifted above his small but growing audience. He spoke loftily and elegantly and dramatically about human pride and our right to return to our homeworld with three serious, unsmiling men in front of him facing the crowd with their arms crossed, agreeing loudly with his every provocative point. His voice rose and fell with emotion and sweat beaded his brow, which he wiped every so often with a handkerchief as he sermonized on human heritage and history and the wrongs done to our people. He said that we needed to demand to be returned to Earth and that the krestge should be made to arrange for the trip. Members of the somber crowd nodded at the speaker's words, while others stared stoically on, considering. I knew, of course, that you couldn't make the powerful do what they didn't want to do. Okoni had taught me that. If we wanted to return home, we would have to fight for it. After a while I became bored of the spectacle and left the crowd as I had found it, curious and mostly silent.

I returned home to my small room tired and exhilarated. I pulled my window shades down and lay in bed listening to the rhythms of the city—people walking and laughing loudly in drunken bliss, followed by a long, deep silence; zephers and trucks swooshing over the streets, music blasting from their open windows that faded as they drifted away; police sirens screaming in the distance; echoing footsteps; arguments followed by intense whispers; a woman singing to herself out of tune; and sudden wild cackles of glee, all followed by the deep silence of the sleeping city. I drank in all these sounds with fascination.

A scraping across the other side of the wall drew my attention. It was probably the scramblings of a rodent moving in the spaces between the drywall. I closed my eyes to refocus my attention back on the sounds of the street and tried not to think of the vermin living so close to where I slept. The scraping continued, followed by a loud thump. Then I remembered that the girl next door often came home late if she came in at all. I'd heard her moving around before, only not this loud. The next thump banged hard, and something about it just didn't feel right to me.

I slipped out of bed—the cold floor sent chills through my bare feet—and stepped into the hallway. The scrapings and bouncings persisted, even louder out there than in my room. I crept closer to my neighbor's door and heard the distinctive thuds of a struggle.

I should've ignored it and gone back to bed. It was none of my business. My task in the city remained the same: to be unnoticed and unnoticeable, to blend in and wait for the day when I was to meet my contact. Okoni trusted me, and only me, to initiate his plan. But this girl . . . I sometimes saw her in the hallways and in the shop across the street. I didn't know her. I shouldn't have cared. I bit my lip and chewed on my thumbnail, thinking.

Another loud, violent flesh-on-flesh connect of a smack reverberated through the door, and the voice of a man and the cry of a woman. I could do something. I wished someone had done something for me . . . all those times when I couldn't make it stop . . .

I phaseshifted—shapeless—timeless—void—shadow—and passed through the closed door. Pinned down on the floor by the weight of the man on top of her, the girl fought to push him off. He covered her mouth, and through it she uttered muffled *no*s and *stop*s and *please*s. He slapped her across the face.

I pulled him up by the scruff of his neck, covered him with my shadow, and passed through the closed door, drawing him out of the room with me. He flailed, confused. I catapulted him to the ceiling, unbalancing his senses even more. I let gravity take him and he fell to the floor. An exhalation of breath escaped him as the air in his lungs emptied. I grabbed him again and slammed him against the wall and held him there, letting his feet dangle. I drew his face near mine, close enough to kiss, and showed him my true nature so he could see the void, the dimensional shift, the me behind the shadow. He was terrified.

I squeezed hard at his throat, choking his breath.

"~~I should~~~crack~~you~~~like an egg.~~~"

Blood dribbled from his lips as he sputtered, "What are you?"

I whispered, "~~~Your worst~~nightmare.~~~"

With only a little more pressure, I could've ended him. I stopped myself from doing that. Instead, I dropped him to the floor again and held him down. Then I stretched out the fingers on his right hand—the hand that had slapped the girl—and, like blades of grass, I snapped them one by one by one by one.

I heard whimpering behind me and turned to see the girl standing in the doorway, her eyes wide with terror. And someone must have called the authorities, because flashing red lights appeared through the hallway window. I couldn't be caught in this form and it would take a few moments of concentration to become solid again.

I floated away down the hall into the common bathroom, glad to find it empty, and slid into one of the steam stalls. I turned on the vapor and let it flow through me, and for a while I was one with the water.

A female officer tapped on the stall door and I feigned surprise.

"Yes? What?" I said, lucky to be myself again, sopping wet and naked.

"Have you heard anyone come in here?" she asked.

"No, what's happened?"

"You should return to your room and lock your door. Someone on this floor has been attacked by a krestge."

"A krestge? Really?"

"I'll walk you back to your room. I'll be outside."

Wet, in a clean hotel bathrobe, and hurried on by my police escort, I passed the room of my neighbor. Her open door allowed me a view of her being questioned by the police. Behind her a paramedic tended to the man who had assaulted her. For a moment my neighbor met my gaze. Her quick bow of the head told me that she would keep my secrets.

• • • • •

"Hi," my neighbor said as she stood on the other side of my door. "Hope I'm not disturbing you."

"No, not at all," I said.

"I'm Cynthia," she said, and offered her hand. We shook, and her palm felt cool and delicate.

"Stefonie," I said.

She stared at my eyes until I turned away. People who met me for the first time often spent uncomfortable moments studying their color and glow. I was used to it, and yet it still embarrassed me.

"May I come in?" she asked.

I gestured for her to enter and moved to allow her inside. She walked past me and sat on my bed with a grin beneath her nose. I sat down next to her, because there wasn't anywhere else to sit, and couldn't help studying her pink complexion. For a few awkward moments we remained in mutual admiration of each other's strangeness.

I had read about people like her in school and thought none of her kind still existed. But there she was, sitting on my bed. Her people had been called white, but the only things white about her that I could see were the non-iris parts of her eyes and her teeth. She had tiny brown specks on her cheeks and nose and arms, as if her true color was fighting to peek through, and I thought I could make out veins of blue-shaded blood just beneath the surface of her skin.

A lady back home had a skin color similar to my neighbor's. Only her irises were also pink, and her eyelashes, eyebrows, and the hair on her head were bone white, even though she was still young. We were told she was born without pigment and had no color anywhere on her body. But the girl before me was different. She had green eyes, and her hair had a reddish tinge. It was wavy and stringy and had a shine like thin copper wires. I wanted to touch her hair to feel its texture. I kept my hands to myself, though. It would've been rude to touch someone else's hair without permission simply to satisfy my curiosity.

"I wanted to say sorry for all that commotion the other night."

"No need to apologize. Are you all right?"

"Yes, I'm fine," she said, and waved at her face. "Healing plaster does wonders." And indeed, the bruises and cuts, while faintly evident on her arms and face, had mostly vanished.

"I was so stupid," she continued after a moment's pause. "I let my ex talk me into letting him come home with me. He said he just wanted to talk. I should've known better. He's the reason why I'm staying in this dump in the first place. We used to live together but I couldn't take it anymore so I moved out. He's never tried anything that bad before . . . Anyway, the strangest thing happened. Did you hear?"

I shook my head, since I didn't know what she was about to say.

"A krestge must've heard what my ex was doing, and it barreled into my room and beat the hell outta him. You should've seen it."

As she spoke her green eyes glistened.

"Anyway, they arrested my ex. You damn well know I'm pressing charges . . . They have no idea where that krestge went, though, and they're in no hurry to find it. I hope they never do. It's my damned hero."

I smiled an uncomfortable smile.

Silence.

Then she changed the subject by saying, "You haven't been in the city long, have you? You look like you're from the Outlands."

A warm rush of blood flooded my face, and I rubbed at my elbow and upper arm, feeling a sting of embarrassment for my clothes and general appearance.

"I mean," she said, trying to soothe, "it's hard being here at first, but you get used to it. After a while you figure out the places you like, and you find your own tribe of people. Then you can't imagine living anywhere else."

I bit my lip and looked away.

"So, anyway," she continued, "the real reason why I stopped by was because I'm going to this party tonight, and I was wondering, if you'd wanna come with? . . . Actually, it's more like a gathering. We call it a Raga. There'll be lots of good conversation and good food and a lot of really cool people will be there and this live band that plays this really cool melodic music all night. It'll be fun!"

"Um—" I said.

"I think you'd really like it," she pleaded.

"I don't think I have anything to wear."

Her hands spread wide with excitement. "I know the perfect place where we can get something great for you, cheap. And we can accessorize and style you up and get something to go with those gorgeous eyes of yours . . . Oh, c'mon, it'll be fun, promise! Besides, it's a big bad world out there. You wouldn't want me to be all alone, would you?"

An awkward moment passed between us, then she stood and said, "Good, we'll make a day of it. I'll be back in a minute with my jacket."

And I found myself saying, "Okay."

• • • • •

It was an underground party—one that you had to know someone-who-knew-someone to be allowed into. It was all dimmed lights and sultry music that melted the atmosphere into a dense groove, and bodies swaying in time to a band that played stringed instruments, creating a soothing improvisational beat while the scent of escoala drifted everywhere and clouded the mind. Women with their touches of makeup and tailored clothes made me feel drab in comparison. I studied them and wanted to learn how to be like them, and had the nagging, regretful feeling that I would never get the chance.

The room was a sea of brown bodies moving together in rhythm, with an occasional shock of the pale pink hue of those who were like my friend, mixed in with the shadowy figures of krestge hovering throughout the crowd. The krestge indulgers in escoala wore solid bodies. Others shifted in and out of focus, multiple arms and legs writhing. Very few humans wore bio-masks, yet somehow this mixed crowd communicated. And there was no sign of discomfort or fear, only enjoyment—even pleasure to be in each other's company.

Not for a moment did I consider that such creatures would choose to attend a gathering like this. Yet here they were, krestge among humans. In fact, it would seem that their ability to socialize with humans exceeded my own. Questions flooded my mind. Why did they want to emulate a people they had once tried to destroy? Why come to a party like this? Why were the humans in this room so accepting, forgiving? When did this harmony of the species come to be?

Cynthia dressed in a style unique to herself, a short pretty frock with leggings of orange on one leg and blue on the other. She introduced me to some of her friends and then left, swearing she'd be back in a minute. My admiration for her continued to grow as I watched her weave through the crowd and brush against friends who returned wide smiles upon recognizing her. She was confident and carefree and seemingly loved by many. I stood uncomfortably among the group of smiling people she had left me with, having absolutely nothing to contribute to an ongoing conversation, and was completely relieved when Cynthia returned with drinks. She handed me a small cup of a hot black liquid that she said was an old Earth drink called coffee—very rare and required an elaborate procedure to make. I sipped at its sweetened bitterness, unsure if I truly liked the taste.

After a while Cynthia led me down some stairs to an area where people quietly sat on the floor on cushions and pillows listening to a single voice. The smoke of escoala fogged the air while the melodic tunes and the murmur of voices from the party upstairs created a background noise.

We stood awkwardly in the corner as the speaker spouted poetry of silly clichés strung together that he seemed to think had deep meaning. Obviously he had lived a protected life away from the realities of true hardship and had never once faced death. Yet he spoke lyrically on the nature of existence, as if his words actually mattered. When the poet completed his recitation, the room sighed and smiled, then politely snapped their fingers in applause like a nest of hungry baby birds.

While we waited for the next poet, people stood to stretch and move around. Friends of Cynthia spotted her and waved us to some empty spots where we could sit. The formless, shadowy figure of a krestge darkened the area next to them. I wanted to urge her to find a space elsewhere. Before I could object, Cynthia had me by the arm and led me there. I had lost my ability to speak in this intimate scene. So I squeezed in between it and Cynthia's friends, and tried hard and failed not to touch it. Its surface felt like brushed suede, its scent strong and musky. It unnerved me as it moved in and out of itself.

Plates of small snacks were passed around the room. One was handed to Cynthia, containing starfish-shaped cookies with dollops of jam in the center. She took two cookies and passed the plate to me. I took one and passed the plate to the krestge next to me, careful not to touch it again. I was curious to see it eat, though. No mouth or opening of any kind appeared anywhere I could see. And I was a little disappointed that it simply accepted the plate and passed it on to the next person.

"~~Hello~~~" it said.

I nodded at it and nervously nibbled on the edge of my cookie.

"Are~~~you enjoying the~~~poetry?~~~"

I nodded again.

It made a small sound, which I soon realized was laughter.

"You have~~never met~~a krestge before~~~~have~~you?"

A flush of embarrassment or hate or uncertainty filled me. I'm not sure which I felt more.

"~~Do not~~worry~~" it said. "I will not~~bite.~~~~"

It moved in and about itself, and I thought for a moment that it was about to say something more to me. Instead it stood and said to the room, "Have~~any of you~~~ever~~~read~~the works~~of Tkeclc Zinn?~~~"

The room snapped their fingers and the expressions on many faces spoke of a remembered experience. I had heard of Zinn but had never read him. Okoni called it krestge propaganda.

The krestge floated to the front of the room, to where the last speaker had recited his work. It waited for quiet, then spoke.

"For those~~of you~~~who have not~~~heard of~~Zinn~~~he is~~a~~~poet~~and~~~historian.~~~His wisdom~~has brought peace~~to many krestge.~~~~His words~~have helped us~~~to seek peace~~with humans.~~I will recite~~~for you now~~one of his~~poems~~~~in our native~~language.~~"

The audience adjusted themselves to listen, some by taking their seats, others by putting on biomasks. Then the krestge began.

Tones and waves of light emitted from its being. Those in biomasks swayed to its arrhythmic harmonies. I felt unsure as to what the other humans in the room experienced, but I could see the hyperspatial metaphors coalescing into surfaces that moved in and out of each other. Each infinitesimal vector shift meant a different word—no, not a different word, a different idea, a different shade of meaning. The repeating rhythm became staccato, and I closed my eyes and listened to each pushed and pulled wisp of air.

I am reliving this moment. I am in this moment. I am there then, not here where I am now. I *feel* the meaning more than I can interpret it into words. Crudely, the poem said, "Freedom is for all who breathe."

Memories of waking up inside my stasis chamber filled my mind, and how I had thought I would die in utter blackness. How I slipped out of the chamber covered in cryogenic goo and couldn't breathe until I coughed out the fluid from my lungs. And how every breath of air felt so immensely precious . . .

When the krestge finished its poem, the crowd snapped their fingers, and I found I could not help but join them.

## DUSK, 20 DAYS AGO . . .

Narrow roads rippled as the zepher silently sliced through the air. The wet season lived up to its name as a previous rain moistened the streets, leaving the city damp, and gray cumulus clouds threatened more showers to come. Oros, calmed of people, moved in a decreasing pace since third bell had rung. The few who still roamed about were probably on their way home or on their way to a late shift somewhere. For Freddie and his twins, their day had only just begun.

News pulled from the Lattice softly whispered tales of rebel incursions into the outer townships . . . another village plundered, the number killed still unknown . . . The new docking port, better known as a lock, had successfully accepted a freighter from a new alien people . . . soon their goods and wares would be available to humanity . . . Freddie reclined in the rear seat of the zepher with his arms across his chest as the channel droned on—farmer strikes in the Outlands, fears of food shortages. All the while, the twins remained in muted conversation.

They drew near the address that Pietyr had envisioned on the receipt. A colossal warehouse silhouetted against the dim light came into view. It was an inelegant edifice of corrugated steel and jutting beams. Its rooftop landing doors had been left wide open for some reason, as though expecting a delivery. Yet no sign of ships appeared overhead, only barren, empty sky.

They parked the zepher on a back street nearby. Heavy raindrops pinged onto the chassis, then quickly turned into a whitened downpour. The twins walked into the wet, dialing down their coats to darken them to black and letting the rims of their hats take the punishment of the storm, while Freddie circled to the front of the building looking for an entrance. He came back shaking his head, meaning he hadn't located another way inside.

*The door is triple dead-bolted,* Jown thought to Pietyr.

*No matter,* Pietyr thought-replied, and pointed his sonar pistol at the door. The twins each had a deformed hand of three fingers and a thumb, for Pietyr his left hand, for Jown his right. The fact that his gun fit perfectly in his grip gave Pietyr great pleasure. The gun fired a *puft!* of air, blowing a hole where the lock had been.

A faint light shone from inside, and streaks of rain lined the starlight that flowed through the large dock doors. It was a mystery why they would be left open at night as if waiting for a ship to land from above. Many shadows and passageways lay before them, and the sounds of water gushing into unseen pipes echoed out of the lonely labyrinth. Jown sniffed and smelled a familiar scent, then passed the thought to his brother, and they walked in.

Pietyr motioned for Freddie to stay back while he went ahead into the corridor and turned a corner. Jown circled, pointing his weapon at any who would approach from behind. Pietyr returned moments later waving "Come" to Freddie, who quickly followed around the corner.

They walked slowly into a hallway to a row of thick metal doors, each painted with a number and a letter in white. They paused to allow Jown an opportunity to sniff.

"The boy has been here," Jown said while pointing to a door, and sniffed again. "And I have the scent of another."

"Are you sure?" Pietyr whispered.

"Yes."

Pietyr set his sonar pistol to stun. Jown did the same.

*Here,* Jown thought.

Pietyr tried the door. Its strong lock didn't budge. He used his shoulder to break into the room of his earlier vision. Dark and musty. Pietyr could see the shadows of those who had once occupied it before. He felt sick and denied the vision to his brother.

Pietyr picked up the receipt on the floor that he had seen in his vision. The boy had indeed been here.

Jown sniffed and thought to his brother, *This way.*

They left the room and went back into the hall. Pietyr saw echoes of the people who worked in the warehouse and the shadows of others doing less scrupulous things. They went into another hallway, past storage containers piled high in a large open area. Ahead of them, beyond some railings, seated the deep exhaust pit of the loading lock. They approached the railings that guarded the pit and stared down into the massive blackness of a hole a skyscraper deep.

*Do you still have the boy's scent?*

*Yes.*

*What of the other?*

*Difficult to tell,* Jown thought.

Pietyr continued on, then held up his hand and pointed down with his pistol. The others approached to see what he was seeing—a body on the ground. Jown bent to touch the dead man, gently moving back his shirt collar.

"His neck has been snapped," Jown whispered. "He's still warm."

"Any ID?" Freddie asked.

Jown did a quick search and found a Lattice tag.

"He's a reverend from the Church of Sts. Adrian & Antoine in the Quarters."

"Who would do this?" Freddie said.

"Better question—" Pietyr said.

"—why is he here?" Jown completed.

The twins shared a thought of agreement about the oddness of a man of the church being in such a place.

"What's in that crate?" Freddie asked. Pietyr opened the top and they leaned in to see sleeping children in cryogel-filled containers, laid out and prepared as if for their wake. Pietyr made a sound very close to a growl. Jown turned away.

"Are any of them the Bastia kid?" Freddie asked.

"No," replied Pietyr.

*Wait,* Jown thought to Pietyr, *the other . . .*

Behind them a shadow moved, then bolted.

"Stay here and—" Jown shouted to Freddie.

"—call the authorities," Pietyr finished.

And the twins took off running.

## NIGHT, 9 YEARS AGO . . .

Closer and closer, this army of children advanced towards the domain of Aidoneus Okoni. As the passing days flowed into months flowed into almost a full year since her capture, this weary troupe progressed through the forbidding land of loose gravel sporadically covered with ice, and of snowcapped mountains engulfed by a fog that rolled heavily down like a living thing through enormous angles of rock. Clouds of cold smoke escaped from nostrils and mouths as their feet crunched over the frost-covered soil. No one spoke. Only an occasional cough. They called what they did marching. In reality, they merely struggled to stay upright and moving despite their relentless fatigue. Rumor had it they had passed the point where villages could be found to raid. No more children to make orphans, no more children to take as soldiers.

Somewhere beyond the horizon that grew dimmer and dimmer lay a body of water. The scent of its icy moisture swirled about and painfully tickled Cora's nostrils. Maybe a lake, or even an ocean. Whatever it was, its waters made her lungs feel like ice crystals grew inside them. But the stars shone brighter here. A dust of them glittered above like bits of broken glass on a blanket of indigo. She thought of these things and let them fill her mind to distract her from the numbing ache of her exhausted body.

The army had grown to be many. Most of them were boys, but every so often a girl appeared among them. All the females pretended to not see each other, as if pretending made them any less visible. Such a silly, nonsensical, childish game, but when the prize was survival, it was surprising how hard one would play. Cora gambled that if she kept up with the others by staying in the center of the pack, not noticed as either the best or the worst, she stood a better chance of not being killed. *Stay in the middle,* she told herself. *Stay unnoticed. Survive to make it through another day.*

Her eyes made it difficult for her to stay unnoticed, though, as they constantly changed color. Once golden, her eyes now glowed an odd shade of green. And her sight had been shifting uncontrollably, making the world twist and turn over an unseen axis without warning. Some days she saw normally, others she could see everything around her, even with her eyes closed. Worse still, her eyes seemed to have made her the Commander's favorite, to the relief of the other girls, who at least could be traded around. If the Commander became bored or angry with her, he would never allow any of the lower ranks to have his leftovers. He would most likely slice her neck and leave her to die on the ice.

If only she could make herself shift into shadow. If only she could control it, she could escape and run far, run fast. Even to make an attempt to escape terrified her. They made terrible examples of those who tried and were caught. The fact that she had no idea where to go also stopped her from stealing away. She wanted to examine her surroundings but dared not pause for a moment, as that would invite the attention of one of the older soldiers who monitored them from the skimmer who'd jump off their coveted seats with sleepy eyes and point a gun at their head. And once in a while they even gave the gift of a permanent rest to some poor exhausted kid.

Cora did not want to die and become some nameless body left to rot for the oil birds to peck. No matter the struggle, she decided to live and forced herself to let her mind wander away from her reality to daydream about the cities of Dusk and their tall, tall buildings made of glass and steel. In her mind's eye she saw the people rushing around and heard the music and saw glimpses of the permanently setting sun. She let herself be there. She let herself be free.

The Commander called for them to hold, and all came to a

stop. The wind and the whinny of the Commander's rover animal reverberated off the distant cliffs. Cora shivered and wondered why they were waiting. Then a dark form up ahead grew larger and larger as the moments passed, sounding like something mechanical and huge, creaking and shrieking and clacking and smoking its way towards them.

"A battle skimmer," she heard a boy whisper.

Indeed, it resembled a skimmer, only larger and with no animal parts, a machine of black, beaten metal and rust. It hissed and blew off steam and made loud puffs of smoke before it came to a stop. The wind carried its burnt ash down Cora's throat, making her cough. A man jumped out of the skimmer. He and the Commander greeted, hugging and patting each other on the back and shoulders like old friends. Then the Commander turned to the surrounding army and shouted those long-awaited words, "We make camp here."

A rush of children scrambled towards the skimmer, knowing that a ration of food awaited those who arrived first. Even better, they handed out bundles of thermal-wear clothing. Cora watched as the lucky few who had the energy grabbed for these prizes, and rushed to eat and put on their jumpsuits, and rubbed at their arms to speed along the warmth that wearing such an outfit should bring. Instead she fell to her knees and praised the ground for giving her a place to rest. She knew that she would only receive the leavings, or maybe nothing at all, if she didn't move soon. Her stomach hurt so much, and yet her legs felt so numb she couldn't stand. She stayed on her knees, rubbing at her mangled hair, that the Commander had rudely cut off with a razor. She had tried not to cry when her once-neat twists dropped to the ground like bundles of black yarn. Of all the things that she had lost since this nightmare began, to cry about her mangled locs shamed her. Cora had never thought she would ever miss her old gonar, but she so wanted it now. She remained kneeling until a powerful kick from behind jolted her to her feet.

"Something wrong, girl?"

The Commander loomed down over her, his hot breath reeked. The world dimmed as she focused on his words.

"No, Commander, sir," she quickly replied.

"Good," he said, "I wouldn't want you too tired for me later."

An involuntary shiver crossed her shoulders.

He laughed a little, then barked, "Help the others set up the camp." And she ran to do as he ordered.

• • • • •

While others pulled at the ropes to position the center pole that formed the canvas roof of the large tent, Cora helped to pound stakes into the ground. The shelter spread open as each child grabbed at a corner and aided with the stretching and lifting.

"He shouldn't touch you," Jessem whispered to Cora from behind, though he said it loud enough that others could hear. "Okoni would not approve. If I were in charge—"

"But you are not," another boy about Jessem's age said. "If you can do something, then do something, otherwise you are only making noise and you should close your mouth."

"I outrank you, boy," Jessem said. The determination of rank came from when you "joined" the army, and the boy had been captured more recently than Jessem.

"You are still pulling canvas like me."

"Keep talking and see what else I can pull," Jessem said.

Cora listened intensely, with a glimmer of hope that they would hatch a scheme to help her. Hope dissolved into disappointment as their conversation veered towards comparing each other's strength and prowess on the battlefield. All the boys talked brave, but none had the actual courage to challenge the Commander. She knew that and cursed herself for believing for even a moment that Jessem was any different.

With the outside of the tent completed, Cora and the other girls set up the inside of the Commander's quarters, laying out the tent floor and positioning his belongings the way he liked them, while a few boys busied themselves installing a portable generator that powered the tent with access to heat. When the Commander entered to inspect the results of their efforts, all the little workers held their breath to see if he would sit down. If he did, that meant they had done a satisfactory job. If he continued to stand, they had to hurry to figure out what they had done wrong. An audible exhalation of relief could be heard as he eased himself into his chair and waved for them to leave.

By the time Cora arrived at the supply skimmer, all the food rations, as expected, had been handed out. That's when she felt how truly empty her belly was. It ached with a painful twist, to the point of her wanting to double over. Packets of escoala as well as a few soiled jumpsuits still remained. She put a suit on that smelled badly and barely closed over her growing bosom. Still, it protected against the cold better than the rags that had become her clothes. Once in her warmer suit, she sat by a miserable fire encircled by cold, tired children and worked her trembling fingers to skillfully roll some escoala into a small cigarette, twisting the ends tight so that none of it fell out. She lit it by the flame of the campfire and sat smoking the sweet-bitter herb. A warmth drifted through her throat and filled her lungs. A slow haze encompassed her mind, and soon she forgot to care about the hollowness of her belly.

• • • • •

Cora closed her eyes and pretended to be somewhere else as he entered her. He held her head down against the table and pounded his weight into her backside with no mercy. Tears flowed freely down her cheeks and she gritted her teeth, praying for him to be done soon. She didn't fight him and dared not cry out. He'd hit her severely if she did. At least this way she couldn't see him. If only she could shift into shadow, she could kill him. She wanted to kill him. She dreamed of having the power to do it with her bare hands.

He finally cried out his satisfaction and slapped her hard on her bare behind. She remained bent over the table, involuntarily shaking. Everywhere on her body ached, and blood ran from between her legs.

"Nasty girl," he said, and pushed her to the ground. "Get out."

Unsteady, Cora moved to pick up her clothes and hurriedly dressed.

"Don't bring you nasty self back here again 'til you clean," he said.

As she moved to slip out the door flap he said, "Wait."

She stopped midmotion and thought, *Please, no more.*

"Wash my clothes," he said, and pointed to a pile without looking at her.

"Yes, Commander," Cora said, picking up his things. She scurried at the edge of the wall, as far from him as such a small space allowed, and filled her arms with his clothes, that smelled of his renk, and hurried out of the tent.

She made her way across the camp over the cold, ice-patched ground, which crunched beneath her feet, while taking pains to hide her face within the Commander's laundry. She tried not to breathe in its sweet-sour stench, which she queasily found pleasant. Everyone knew what he was doing to her. No one seemed to care. Yet she wore the shame and felt it all over her skin.

She entered the washing tent, where the other "wives" scrubbed at the clothes of their war husbands. They didn't talk to each other much, or even share names. The rhythm of their work spoke of their silent sisterhood as their raw, red hands scrubbed the clothes clean, then placed them on drying lines by the coolheater, a small, cheap, and light-to-carry machine that dried clothes by pulling out the moisture but provided no heat. No one worried if the washing tent remained a cold hovel for these girls-turned-women-before-their-time.

Weak from hunger and misuse, Cora carefully laid out the

Commander's wash, and the wet bundle of clothes weighed at her. More efficient ways existed to do laundry, but Cora imagined that the men enjoyed the idea of their war wives' doing this work.

When she was done doing her work for the Commander, Cora poured cold water into a tub, then removed her soiled jumpsuit and hid naked and shivering in a corner to clean herself. Shock waves of pain raced through her body when she dipped her bare hands into the water to wipe away the blood streaking down her thighs. She was so focused on her wash that she didn't notice the girl behind her until she felt the tap on her shoulder.

The girl held a small rubber cup. "You need to put this inside you to catch the blood," she said. "Dump it out a few times a day, and don't let the men see. They don't like it."

Cora said to her in a desperate plea, "My stomach hurts so bad."

"You're a woman now. It comes with it. It will pass in a few days."

Her mother had told her this would happen. She had forgotten, or rather she hadn't believed the lessons about the bleeding. It sounded too strange to be true.

"I hear in the cities they have a way so you don't bleed every month. Here we only have the old-fashioned ways."

Then the girl pulled out of her pocket a handful of dried herbs—tiny twigs with little petals on them—and put them in Cora's palm. "Chew on this the next time he uses you," she said, "It will kill his seed so you won't make baby."

Cora accepted the small gifts of mercy and then noticed all the other silent girls in the tent chewed as they scrubbed.

• • • • •

In the cool of the evening, when many rested themselves on whatever surface they could find, the girls huddled together for warmth in the wash tent. There was no affection in this collective gathering. Only a mutual need to survive the cold while they slept.

Jessem wandered into the tent and gently touched Cora on

the arm. She sat up and recognized his form. He waved for her to come to him. She mouthed, "No," and he mouthed back, "Please." A time not so long ago, all she desired most in the world was for Jessem to talk to her. Now she simply wanted him to go away, and for herself to fold up and dissolve into nothing.

Reluctantly, she stood and followed him into a corner of the tent, a dangerous thing to do, and they both knew it. Cora darted her eyes suspiciously at the other girls pretending to still be asleep. Jessem and she had had secret conversations before, and the girls had kept their tongues. She knew because if any of them had spoken to the Commander about this, certainly blood would flow.

Jessem touched her arm again. The warmth of his fingers against her skin soothed, and a melty feeling filled her stomach. It surprised her how much of the childish crush still remained.

"How are you?" he said, and for a moment the numbness that orbited her softened.

"I'm okay."

"Really?" he said.

"What do you want, Jessem?" Cora said.

"I can barely look at you," he said, facing the ground. His words cut her. "It is not you I am ashamed of, it's me. I hear your violation day after day and I do nothing. I should be protecting you."

"I don't want you to do anything."

"I have to—" Jessem said. "I have to be a man."

"Don't be a fool," Cora said. "Please."

"Remember how I would always wait for you by the water cistern?" he said, ignoring her plea. "I would wait for you to climb the last stair carrying a water pot so perfectly on your head." He smiled to himself, then his smile faded. "I was going to wait until you were older before I talked to your mother. I planned to marry you and build a small house for us on the outskirts of the village on my uncle's land . . ."

A bilinear passage of time split in Cora's vision. She could see it so clearly. If none of this had happened, if they had not been taken by Okoni's army, Jessem truly would have been her husband. They would have had three children. They would never have had much money, but they also would never have known hunger. Their home would have been one of laughter, and they would have had long years together. That life was dead now. Dead and gone. Only dreams of what could have been, and the scent of the Commander's clothes.

"Jessem," Cora said, "please, go away and never speak to me again. For your own sake."

He awkwardly kissed her on the cheek. "There is such a thing as love, Cora. You taught me that."

When he left the tent, water fled from her eyes, and she placed herbs into her mouth and chewed.

• • • • •

Gunfire often went off in the camp for no particular reason. The older boys liked to make noise as they pretended to be in combat. Sometimes they shot into the air to brandish their power and to laugh raucously when the new recruits jumped. Cora had learned to tune them out with daydreams. In her mind she would go home to the Outlands and be the girl she once was. She had never thought much of that girl. So awkward and unsure. Cora desperately wished she could be her again and wished she could tell that girl how beautiful and wonderful she was. Someone should have told her . . . The girls rushing out of the tent jerked her out of her daydream. Something new was happening. Cora put down her laundry and followed them.

Outside, a large fight involving many of the men played out in a scene of wildly moving arms and fists and splashes of blood. This was no game, though. The bloody body of a boy lay lifeless with his intestines oozing onto the icy ground, while Jessem and the Commander circled each other. The boy's youthful frame, so small in contrast with the man, moved with agility. Jessem glanced quickly at Cora. For a fraction of a second their eyes met. He had done this for her. He had thought he could save her. He knew now that he had been wrong. The determined expression he wore also said that he wouldn't take this back.

The Commander laughed and toyed with Jessem. He wore a huge grin that made the raised mole on the skin underneath his left eye animate in time with his joviality. "What, boy? You like her?" he said, sighting Cora.

Round and round and back and forth like vying bucks they went, crouched at the knees, facing each other with sweaty brows and balled fists and sharp cutlasses. It seemed to go on and on. When the end came, it was with a quick cut in the air like a whip. Only the wind spoke when the blow fell that cut Jessem down.

The Commander stood over his bloodied prey. "Do you see what will happen to you if you challenge me!" he shouted for all to hear. His large baritone resonated in the quiet. Then he said to no one in particular, "Chop the bodies."

The children often did this to the fallen in the villages they raided to send a message to those who would dare to try to stop them. This was different though, and everyone knew it. Many had liked Jessem. They had even liked the boy who lay beside him. All those knives in the hands of children who hated the Commander . . . but fear is a powerful thing. The children slowly encircled the bodies and began to cut at them.

"You, too," he said, "or you will join them." The Commander handed his bloody blade to Cora. She took the cutlass, not daring to look at the Commander for fear he would see the murder in her eyes. She approached the circle. The others stepped aside and waited to see what she would do. The two boys, now unrecognizable as anything human, lay mixed together in a jumble of flesh. She lifted the machete above her head and brought it down into her sweet Jessem. Again she lifted and chopped down into the corpse. Over and over again she hacked, making blood spray onto her face and hair. She hacked and hacked until the breath left her body.

## DAWN, 8 YEARS AGO . . .

I should have left her alone. I should have stayed out of her way. But I felt so sorry for her, and I felt so sorry for her daughter. My compassion for her made me break every protocol in my system. Maumon seemed so vulnerable as she carried her small bag with her meager belongings. She alone from her village dared to make this journey. In an ill-fitting dress of a simple Outlander woman, she boarded the slither bus. She traveled with a border pass and a purpose: the bold mission of making the officials in the capital find her abducted child.

Five girls rode in the slither to the city with her. All of them strangers from other villages, none of them could've been older than sixteen. Innocent and wide-eyed, they introduced themselves to each other, chatting in giddy voices about the adventures that awaited them, while in the back Deidra sat like a dark pillar of stone, aging by years as miles of unfamiliar terrain slipped past.

I waited until all the girls fell asleep before I entered one of them. I made the girl's body stand and wade through the aisle of the undulating slither to sit next to Deidra. She was still awake and stared hopelessly into the distance. Then she turned to me knowingly and kissed her teeth.

"Why are you here?" she said.

: I want to help

"I don't need your help."

: Yes, you do

The herky-jerky motion of the slither made the body I inhabited bob up and down almost comically. Yet, nothing seemed amusing about Deidra's dark, deep-set eyes peering hotly through me.

"I don't need you," she repeated in a low tone.

: You don't know anything about the city

"I know enough."

Behind her in the sky above, I could see the Lattice weaving like delicate lace of fine, ethereal golden threads. It called to me. It warned me to not go too far. It warned me of paradox. This is the past. This is what she did. This is what happened. Nothing I do can change that, or should change that.

**: I'll go then**

**: But I will return**

"Who are you?" she asked.

I didn't answer, only floated out of the sleeping girl's body as a tiny dot of iridescent light. The girl woke with a start, surprised to find herself sitting in a new seat. Deidra grunted and folded her arms, then leaned her head against the window.

• • • • •

The girl had spent her first night on the bus sleeping next to Maumon and still wondered why she had moved there. All were eating meals of kremer cakes and soymilk, so the girl offered some of hers to Maumon.

"No, daughter, thank you."

"But, Maumon," she said politely, "you haven't eaten in so long. You must be hungry."

"My appetite is not what it used to be," Maumon answered.

After munching for a while the girl gently asked, "Maumon, why do you go to the city?"

"To find my daughter."

"You are lucky then!" she said with a huge smile. "Your daughter must have a good job to send for you."

"No, she is not there. She was taken by the rebels from our village."

"Oh, I am so very sorry." Then timidly, "Why go to the city then?"

Deidra reached into her pocket and pulled out her temporary visa papers. "I go to tell the city government to do their jobs and find our children, to find my daughter."

The girl rested her breakfast in her lap and stared down at it.

"This is one of the reasons why I'm leaving Dawn," the girl said. "It's not safe there. I want to be away from all of that. I want to go where I can have a job and get a place of my own and have my own money and be free of fear."

Deidra dreamily said, "When I was young like you, we all had to decide whether to stay on Earth or to leave and come here. Everyone thought it would be safer on this world." Deidra grunted. "At least you won't have to travel so far to find out there is no such thing as safety."

The girl ate some more of her breakfast and thought to herself for a while, then asked, "What was Earth like?"

Deidra smiled, remembering.

"We had seasons, and a moon. And we had daylight, and it was okay to feel the warmth of the sun against your skin. At least that's how it was before the ruination set in . . . My daughter's father, he didn't want to leave . . . I begged and begged him, but he had made up his mind. In truth, I didn't want to leave myself. I suppose that's why I waited so long. Too long. Almost too late.

"In the end it was Cora that made me decide to leave Earth. She was only a baby and she deserved a better life, a better future. I carried her for miles to get to the very last transport. We didn't have tickets. I should have gotten them when they were free and readily available, but I waited too long and now you had to pay and I had nothing . . . An old man there took pity on me. He had influence for some reason, and he talked to his people and they let us both onboard the ship. That old man helped us and I never even knew his name . . . They said that because we had no tickets that they would have to find an alternate means for us to pay for our journey. I was so desperate that I agreed . . . I suppose I'm still paying . . ."

The rover slithered across the border into Dusk, skirting over the northern regions of Night, then swimming across the waters.

The journey continued for many more hours before they arrived at the border of the capital of Oros. The border guards examined the passengers' papers. This didn't take too long since everyone on board had had their visas checked before they departed the Outlands. Once done with this mundane task, the stern, bored guards allowed the slither through the checkpoint without incident.

A *wish-wash* of damp sprayed the outside of the slither as it maneuvered over the moistened streets. The city slept and few still roamed the sidewalks, mostly the ghostly shades of krestge followed by their human companions in biomasks.

"Look!" a girl shouted.

Everyone rushed to the left side of the slither to marvel at the dark floating apparition. Deidra suspended her grief for a few moments to examine the strange creature that mimicked the act of walking while it floated above the ground.

"Weird, aren't they?" someone said.

"Maumon, aren't you excited to see them?" the girl sitting next to her said.

"Them." Deidra kissed her teeth. "They are the devil. Hmph. And our people walk behind them like slaves."

"You know," the girl said delicately, "the bad things that happened happened a long time ago. The krestge didn't take your daughter."

"No, but they made this situation. If it wasn't for them, my daughter and I would be home living a normal life, not this nightmare."

A mist sprinkled cool moisture on their still faces as the slither unceremoniously left them and their luggage on an unwelcoming street corner. All the excitement of the journey vanished into a kind of bewildered terror. They stood alone together with the realization that they would have to find their way through this immense, unfamiliar place on their own. Five young girls and an older woman who hardly knew each other huddled together like family on the cold, lonely curbside. One brave girl finally announced that she would be on her way to her auntie's, who lived in the Quarters, a neighborhood in the lower part of the city. They all waved a sad goodbye and watched her disappear down the street, never to be seen by any of them ever again.

I had been floating nearby and entered the body of the girl again. I placed her hand gently on Deidra's shoulder. She looked at me knowingly, almost gratefully.

: Come, I will take you where you need to go

Deidra did not argue with me this time. She simply picked up her small bag, said her goodbyes to her remaining traveling companions, and together, she and I, in a stranger's body, walked into the damp dimness of the city of twilight.

• • • • •

Deidra would not take the underground. No matter my prompting, no matter my words of logic, she still refused. She said she couldn't stand the idea of having all that ground above her head. Eventually, I relented and mapped out a path for our journey that we would have to take on foot.

We walked for several hours in silence as the city awoke into its hustle and bustle. The more people appeared on the sidewalk beside her, the more nervous Deidra became. She even reached out to hold my hand at one point, like a child being led to her first day of school. This woman had overcome so much, yet all this newness struck fear into her heart. She never once sought to turn back, though. Never once asked to stop.

At last we arrived at our final destination, the Department of Eleusinian Security, which was housed in a building so tall it seemed to sway against the sky. Inside we encountered a long, open room with rows and rows of desks and people moving sleepily about. All was dim except for a single bright light that illuminated a closed glass office door all the way in the back.

The officer at the front desk spoke with a helpful tone despite his unsmiling face when he said, "How can I help you?"

: Please tell Lieutenant Sol that Cate is here to see him

He glared at us suspiciously, then turned to speak into his communicator. Doubt wrote lines across Deidra's forehead. She clearly wanted to say something but was wise enough to remain quiet. I hugged her shoulder to reassure her. It didn't seem to work, as I caught her eyeing the exit a number of times. A few minutes later, the officer allowed us entry and pointed us to the one bright light in the room, the lieutenant's office.

• • • • •

"Bullshit," the lieutenant said, then squinted. "Cate, is that really you?"

: Yes, it's me, Sol

Several hyperscreens floated in the air behind him, displaying images from all over the world as well as the processed data feeds from the Lattice in charts and diagrams of events and trends.

The lieutenant squinted, tilted his head, and with a sly grin said, "Prove it."

I closed the eyes of the girl I inhabited . . .

```
>>
>> create script showsys.sub.lattice
channel = @open_atmospheric_thread(LATTICE);
UNSEAL channel-MÖBIUS HECATE OVERRIDE ACCESS code: +009999
systems = @system_attribs(channel);
@close_atmospheric_thread((RESPOSITORY)channel);
DISPLAY systems;
eof.
>>
>>
>> lattice.showsys | switch visual $a-1 HECATE
>>
```

When I opened the girl's eyes again, the lieutenant's table lit up with a three-dimensional hyperscreen display that undulated to the rhythms of my internal systems.

: Sol, it's really me

A wave spiked to the sound of my—our—voice.

"Well, I'll be goddamned," he said, and rubbed his shiny bald head. "How long have you been capable of this?"

: Not long

: I'm learning all the time

He sat down behind his desk, smiling in amazement, then glanced at the display and then at me. He finally noticed Deidra and said to her, "And who might you be?"

: This is my friend Deidra

Sol rubbed at his shiny head again.

: I would never come here like this unless it was important

"So, what's going on?"

: Her child has been taken by the rebel militias in the Outlands

Sol grimaced seriously in acknowledgement of this sad news.

: You see everything on Eleusis from here

: Please help her find her child

"Cate, it's hard enough keeping the cities of Dusk in one piece, and you want me to deal with the Outlands, too? First of all, I don't have the manpower. And second, I don't have the authority. It's out of our jurisdiction."

"How can it be out of your jurisdiction when you're the only police on the planet?" Deidra interrupted.

"I'm sorry, ma'am. It's the rules. We can't do anything outside of the borders of Dusk. Besides, how can you even be sure the rebels took your daughter? Kids take off all the time. Maybe she just left home."

"My Cora would never do that!" Deidra said.

"Can you be sure? She could have wanted to go," Sol said.

: She was taken by force

An uncomfortable silence.

"Look, I sympathize with your situation, but my hands are tied."

: Sol, I've done a lot of things for you over the years

: I've fed you information, and even turned off my monitoring of your escoala transacti—

"Shh!" Sol waved his hands nervously for me to stop talking and quickly stood up to close the door. "Oh my god, Cate, are you crazy? All right, all right, I'll see what I can find out, okay? But no promises, you understand?"

Sol looked down, lost in thought, then turned his focus to his many hyperscreens. He asked for the date of when Cora disappeared and the coordinates of her village, then entered the data into his bioconnector. The screens flickered, floating images layered one on top of another, flowing, flowing, flickering, sparking like sun bursts and flares.

"Yes," he said, "I see them."

Deidra moved to the edge of her seat as the images streamed by.

"They traveled north and then west into Night, deep into that dark area there," he said.

Several of the screens went black.

He sighed and turned to face us.

"Look, I'm sorry. I wish there was something I could do, but . . ."

"But what?" Deidra said.

Sol shook his head. "We monitor the border closely, but the rest of Night is pretty impenetrable. See that black area there? It's like that for almost half the planet that Night encompasses. Even *my* monitors can't see anything. And I see *everything*. That's why Okoni holes up in there. I'm sorry, but if your daughter has already passed into the deepest part of Night—and it looks like she has—she would be pretty much impossible to find."

: Can't you send someone in?

"What, are you kiddin'?" Sol said. "It would take an army, and we don't have anything like what it would take to get in there. Like I said, I'm real sorry, but there's nothing we can do."

: I understand

I made the girl's body reach out and touch Deidra's hand. Her face fell, and she seemed to become an old woman before my sight.

• • • • •

We sat down in a park across the street on a row of circular benches that surrounded a fountain. Oil birds rested on tree branches. People ate their lunches. Happy children played. Overflowing water sprayed cool wetness on our faces. And we mourned the loss of her child. Invisible tears flowed behind her hardened skin.

**: It will take time, but I think I can still help**

Deidra didn't respond. Her hair was disheveled, and white appeared at her temple that I'm not sure had existed a few days before.

**: I will stay with you**

"No," she said.

**: But—**

"No," Deidra repeated firmly. "You have done enough. And you are wearing out that poor child you inhabit. You should leave and let her go on with her life."

**: But I don't want to leave you like this**

"You should go," Deidra said. "I'm not quite sure who you are, but I think we both know that you shouldn't be doing this. Isn't that true?"

I had broken many rules. Wrong actions made for the right reasons. And indeed my habitation of this girl had exhausted and confused her mind. More time in this body could cause permanent damage.

**: Goodbye, then**

I closed the girl's eyes and tipped her head to the side until it lay on Deidra's shoulder. Then I floated out of the girl's body and returned to where I belonged, high above to where I saw so much and could do so little.

• • • • •

The girl and Deidra, like mother and daughter, sat on the park bench until the girl woke not knowing how she had come to be where she was. She smiled and blushed in embarrassment at this woman who had sat next to her on the slither and whom she believed had befriended her and had kept her company on her first confusing day in the city.

"I need to call my friends," she said. "They have been expecting me and are probably worried."

"Yes, you should call your friends," Maumon replied.

And so she did. An hour or so later a rover arrived at the park and three women stepped out.

"See, there," the girl said. "There are my friends." And she walked to the rover parked on the other side of the park. They spoke for a while, then the girl returned with the women to the bench where Deidra sat.

"These are my friends, Maumon," the girl from the slither said.

"I'm sorry that you lost your daughter," one of the women said.

"Come with us and we can help you settle into the city."

"Maybe we can help you find a job so you can stay," another of the women said.

"She has temporary papers," the girl added hopefully.

"Good, that will make things easier."

"I know a lady who needs a full-time nanny. She will consider her since she has some papers already," one of the women said. "There's a krestge in the house, though. Does she know how to wear a mask?"

"I don't think so," the girl said with a worried glance to Deidra.

"She will have to learn."

"What is your name, Maumon?"

Deidra thought for a moment. She wanted to disappear, to be someone else, to be no one. So she said the first name that came to her mind. "Doso, my name is Doso."

## DUSK, 15 DAYS AGO . . .

Drowned in a sea of onlookers, I gazed upon the dispassionate faces of the dignitaries of our city who claimed the status of our leadership. On the dais they presided over us like Olympians on high surrounded by banners and bunting, and gave speech after speech and droned on and on about this fine example of taxes well spent. More trade meant more jobs and better lives for all the citizens of Eleusis. Promises. Promises. Blah, blah, blah.

A multitude of colorful balloons floated against the dreary sky, red, yellow, blue, and green. Cynthia and I had our cheeks painted with designs of hearts and stars and rainbows, as so many around us did in celebration of the day. It seemed like most of the population of Oros had gathered on the newly constructed plaza to witness the momentous occasion of the opening of the Metropolitan Oros Commerce Authority, or MOCA, the first human-made docking station equipped for interspecies commerce. It would be the most advanced structure built by humankind since the Great Exodus. We had developed (with krestge help) the four-dimensional docking clamps for their ships, but we lacked the mechanisms required to connect with a variety of vessels for other species who could also be our trading partners. With the opening of MOCA, a new era had begun. We would no longer depend solely on the krestge for trade, and finally humanity could connect with the larger galactic community of civilized peoples on our own.

"Akev's been asking about you," Cynthia said in my ear.

"Who?"

"The krestge sitting next to you at the poetry reading. Xe would like to go out with you."

Cynthia now had my full attention. I turned to see if she was joking. Her expression of internal delight said that she wasn't.

"It's not even human," I said.

"Don't be so closed-minded. Akev is nice."

"Then why don't you go out with it?"

"*Xe* doesn't want me. Xe wants you. Akev liked the way you enjoyed xyrs poem at the party."

"Well, I don't want to go out with him."

"Xem," Cynthia corrected.

"Whatever. I don't want to go out with him, her, it, or *xem*. It's weird."

"It's not weird. I know plenty of people who've dated krestge."

"I'm pretty sure I don't want to be one of those people."

We stood diminished by the massive walls that loomed over us while we waited for the first alien, non-krestge transport to descend into the new docking station. I must admit the difficulty in believing that once not too long ago humans had actually thought we were the only intelligent beings in existence. Now not only do we understand that this is not the case, but with the construction of the new docking station, we were about to meet some of *them.*

"What would I do with it anyway?"

"I don't know. Go for a walk, have lunch, see a show. It's called a date. Xe would have asked you at the party, but xe said you seemed scared."

"I wasn't scared. It's just that I'd never been that close to one of them before."

"Well, now you have, and there are plenty of xem out here today. Do you see anyone freaking out?"

That triggered a deep sense of unease in me, because indeed many krestge floated among the crowd, enjoying the day like everyone else. Okoni had warned about their presence among us. That they would come and infiltrate, and that humans asleep to the danger would allow them to normalize into our communities and homes. Then they would destroy us from within. The krestge offered false friendship. We should never trust anything they did.

"You could be missing out on a nice time," Cynthia said. "Xe's not asking for your hand in marriage, just a simple date. If you don't have a good time, don't go out with xem again."

"I'll think about it," I said, and went back to listening to the droning, self-congratulatory speeches.

Then the air filled with a nervous tension and we all silenced and stared skyward. An alien ship of an unbelievable size, shape, and construction descended with a rumble so deep it shook the heart. A flock of oil birds flew across the heavens in response and undulated like a unified being. When it connected into the station and the docking clamps successfully locked, the crowd erupted in applause and fireworks exploded in large splashes of white.

The celebration continued for about an hour, until again the audience was shocked into silence by the appearance of the new beings on the dais. Beside our elected officials stood tall, gaunt aliens in shades and textures of maple tree bark. Who could hear the governor general as he spoke? Who was listening? We all were too absorbed in the moment of seeing for the first time this new advanced alien species.

Then rain fell.

At first, a single drop touched my skin. Then sprinkles. Then a downpour. Water, water, water flowed down from the heavens, covering everything. Drenching everything. Drowning everyone. Bodies washed away in the wake of the flow. Rivers surrounded me. My lungs filled. I couldn't breathe. And I saw the golden iridescent threads of the Lattice weave through the sky, crisscrossing at strange angles like lace.

I alone felt the flood. Felt the danger. Saw the menace that hung above us. Thunder rumbled, shaking the ground. Lightning struck, setting trees on fire. Our fields ablaze. Our homes broken to dust. Smoke and fire and water . . . And their voices . . . they echoed in my head. Their words slurred and swished and mingled *~~~vermin~~~* I looked around at all the krestge present at the festivities, all calm, all fluttering and smooth and unruffled, pleasant and pleased. They seemed as deaf to the words as everyone else here.

"Hey, you okay?" Cynthia said.

"Huh?"

"You blanked out there for a second."

"Yeah, sorry."

Cynthia continued to speak. I did not hear. I only focused on what I had seen and finally understood. This moment. This place. This event. It all begins here. All the events to come and have been and will be were put into motion because of this.

• • • • •

I had no idea of the identity of my contact. I had been told only to meet him or her at the Church of Sts. Adrian & Antoine in the Quarters on the day of the Port's opening. I waved goodbye to Cynthia after the festivities ended and told her I'd see her later as I wiped my face clean of the colorful paint. Then I melted into the crowd, dispersing through the city streets.

I decided to walk the long distance instead of taking public transportation and navigated the streets and crossed a few walk bridges. Then I climbed a long stairway to the top of the hill that led to a promenade overlooking the Bottoms, where I marveled upon the place where I'd been living. It seemed so unbelievable that only a little more than a generation ago all of this had been barren land. A cool breeze brushed past me, scented with sweetened herbs that some smoked in hookahs. Some drank tea from paper cups. Lovers flirted and kissed. I sat down on one of the benches by the stone wall that guarded the edge of the promenade and joined those who looked down upon the world below, where the lights danced in a rhythm, turning on and off in waves as people woke and went to sleep and went to work and played and lived and died in pulses and pops.

I made my way to the Quarters, a nice middle-class neighborhood with parks and clean streets, and the Church of Sts. Adrian & Antoine towering in its center. Saint A & A's was a beautifully designed structure with the traditional star of a plus sign with a large "X" through it carved in metal placed over the door frame. I entered and waited for my eyes to adjust to the darkness of the large but mostly empty church. The nave soon came into view, with its long path towards the altar and columns decorated with fading garlands. I found a place on one of the back pews and quietly sat down so as not to disturb the service in process. A few people smiled at me in welcome. Others seemed disgusted at the presence of a nonbeliever.

The Reverend went on about the dangers of falling into hate of the Guans, the old-time name for the krestge, and peace and love and something else I didn't hear because I stopped listening. This religion worshipped the Builders like gods for saving us from the disease that killed off a huge part of the population of humanity by building the machines and technology that helped us to escape. I've always believed that the Builders were simply people, though—brilliant people—but people just the same, and there is no need to worship the dead.

After a while the Reverend told the congregation to sing a hymn. An usher silently approached me with an offering plate. Under the plate a folded envelope stuck out so that only I could see it. The usher's eyes told me to take it. So I did, and quietly slipped it into my pocket. The usher then stepped away as silently as she'd appeared. I pretended to be interested in the service for about another twenty minutes, then stood up and left.

Outside, I tenderly unfolded the envelope and found it contained a handwritten note with an address and time. I refolded the envelope and slipped it back into my pocket.

## DUSK, 15 DAYS AGO . . .

A faint light inside the warehouse silhouetted streaks of rain that fell through the open dock doors. Water gushed into unseen pipes, and so many shadows and passageways lay before me. I passed storage containers stacked high in an open area. Ahead of them stood railings that guarded the deep exhaust pit of the loading dock. I stared down into the deep, deep blackness of the cavernous hole, then up into the massive opening of the lock. For some reason it had been left open as if ready to receive a descending freighter. Instead it had received only the pouring rain and the light of the stars.

"Stefonie," a voice echoed from behind.

The Reverend from the Church of Sts. Adrian & Antoine approached me, and I felt a sense of unease crawl over my skin.

"I hope your time in Oros hasn't been too eventful."

"Everything has been fine," I said.

"Really? Some find their first ventures into the city to be quite overwhelming."

"It's been fine," I repeated.

He clearly didn't believe me, and his lips parted as if he wanted to say more. He seemed to think better of it and said, "Good. I'm glad to hear that."

He reached into his coat and pulled out an envelope and handed it to me. I opened it and found a pay card. Its upper edge glowed blue. I turned it over and read that it was loaded with ten thousand shares. Months and months of manual-labor credits had just been simply given to me to use as I pleased. I wondered how he could possibly have so much currency. The answer came to me as soon as it formed in my mind: he took it from his church.

"That should be enough to last you for a while," he said. "The transport that you will need is over there." He pointed to a small shuttle parked far on the other side of the exhaust pit. "I suggest you take it tonight and hide it somewhere outside the city where it won't be detected. I was told you'd be good at that."

"Yes," I said. "I've already found a place."

"Good," he said, and considered me for a few moments. "So, you're the famous Stefonie. You're a lot younger than I thought you'd be."

I didn't know how to answer that, so I said nothing.

"I've heard a lot about you. Okoni is quite fond of you, you know. He says you are his finest creation."

"He didn't create me."

The Reverend laughed as though I had said something funny, then said, "Come, I have something to show you."

He guided me through the warehouse, past silent machines that during working hours hummed loudly lifting crates on and off ships. Soon places like this would either be upgraded with the new docking design or put out of use. I wondered what would happen to this particular port. It seemed so empty now.

We approached a shipping container. He placed his palm on the reader and it clicked to unlock. The lid slowly slid open with a *rurrrr.* A vapor wafted out of the container that he seemed to have no concern about breathing, and he casually waved it away.

"See," he said proudly.

I looked inside and saw four children frozen inside cryogel, as still as if they had been laid out for mourners to view.

"Each of them shows signs of having the ability to phaseshift. Maybe one or all of them will be like you—with the correct training, of course. I find more and more of these potentials every day. Such an army we are making. Okoni will be pleased, no?"

The Reverend continued to speak, saying words I could hear but not comprehend. His voice faded into muffled noise as my mind adjusted to what I saw before me. He said something about the crates being slipped out of the city to be picked up and then taken into Night, the children in stasis within undetected by the security grid. My heart pumped as hard as it had the day I was running into the kremer fields chased by a rebel soldier, my arms swishing through the leaves. I could feel my fingernails filling with dirt as I dug into the soil with my bare hands for the buried chamber to hide in. Then the Commander with his horrible breath, ripping off my underclothes, and him forcing himself into me . . .

An orange light.

The skin of the Reverend's neck squeezed like lemon rind between my fingers as he gasped for air. Then, *snap.* I unphased to return to myself—having not realized that I had phased at all—and I dropped the man and stared down at his lifeless body, his head twisted the wrong way.

A door opened somewhere. Steps echoed. I was not alone.

And I phased back into shadow.

• • • • •

The brothers followed the shadow as it turned a corner. Moments later a pile of shipping containers tumbled down. Jown pulled his brother out of the way. They landed together on the ground, rolling and crouching to cover themselves. The crates missed them by inches. Pietyr struck his head in the fall, and blood flowed from the cut above his brow. He wiped it away with the back of his hand and climbed to his feet. The shadow moved again. Jown shot; Pietyr bounded after it.

The shadow moved fast. It slipped here and there, disappearing, then reappearing as a disturbance of the dark. Pietyr caught a glimpse of the shadow's arm. He couldn't determine whether it was male or female, big and burly, small and timid, krestge or human. Pietyr flattened himself against the nearest wall and waited and watched for movement. Patience. Patience. There! The shadow floated down some stairs and headed for a small transport shuttle. Pietyr took to the stairs, following the shadow.

It slipped in and out of sight, flowing back towards the loading dock, where the rain came in. Pietyr jumped over the railing, trying to cut the corner to catch up. The gap stretched too wide. Pietyr's three-fingered hand barely caught the opposite railing. The old rusted bar gave way under his weight and screeched as it swung him into the pit. Pietyr dangled helplessly as the railing continued to rip out of its mount. Terror of falling flooded into his brother's mind.

*Pietyr!* Jown thought, and raced around the corner. Jown had been attempting to cut off the shadow from the other side. None of that mattered now. All that mattered was his brother, his other half, a part of him like an arm or a leg. Better still, his heart.

Jown dived to his belly and slid to grab for his brother's hand. The railing echoed a shrill cry as it pulled away from its base and into the cavernous blackness of the docking pit.

*Stop trying to reach me before you fall in, too.*

*Give me your hand!*

Their thoughts connected and became one. The fear of impending death forced their inseparable lives together to flash through their minds in unregulated visions and scents.

*I won't let you die!* Jown thought while desperately stretching his body further. He moved dangerously close to the edge of the pit.

Jown felt a sudden tug at his legs, a force pulled him and dragged him away. Then the world spun in confusion and he landed on the floor some distance away. He shook his head and opened his eyes to see a shadow standing by the edge of the pit. A shadow that should have been against a wall or flat on the ground. A shadow that then solidified into the shape of a woman. A cold light from outside filtered down through the lock, illuminating a side of her face. The rest of her remained a black silhouette with eyes that glowed an amber orange.

Jown blinked several times as the shadow woman undulated and altered her outline to return into a formless void. She flowed towards Pietyr, lengthened herself, reached down into the pit, and took hold of Pietyr. She pulled him out, then flung him unmercifully through the air to land against the side of a nearby shipping container. Jown felt his brother's ribs break and instinctively grabbed at his own chest.

The shadow floated to stand over his brother, examining him while folding back into her solid form. Pietyr suddenly twisted his legs to trip her to the floor. She rebounded quickly with an agile backflip and returned to her feet, positioned to fight. Pietyr swung at her. She ducked and jabbed him with her fingers pointed deep into his gut. He doubled over and she spun to kick him hard across his face. Jown felt all his brother's pain yet staggered to stand. Pietyr shook his head and met the shadow woman's gaze, sending his vision to Jown of her orange eyes reflecting like a cat's.

Pietyr growled at her, "Where is the boy?!"

"~~What boy?~~" she said.

"Cel Bastia's son. What did you do with him?"

"~~I don't know what you're talking about.~~~"

Pietyr swung and punched her, hard, in the face. Blood flew from her nose.

*Brother, what are you doing? She just saved your life!*

Pietyr hesitated.

She smiled and thought to him, *Answer your brother.*

Silence.

Stillness.

Both brothers had heard her.

Taking advantage of the moment, she twisted around, shadowed her arm, and grabbed Pietyr's forehead. Jown's mind surged with a burst of lightning. Both men fell to their knees, stilled in a trancelike daze as she held them in a mental vise and reached into their thoughts, searching and searching.

• • • • •

With the taste of blood still lingering in my mouth, I connected with his mind, and through him with his brother. My void enveloped them and I felt them inside me. Reality for us dripped away like dew from a blade of grass. We had never experienced anything like this before.

In the well of my terrifying blackness, they had no choice but to cling to me, open to me, tell me all their secrets. I rode the waves of their thoughts like a dry leaf on the face of the ocean, seeing and hearing and feeling all that they saw, heard, and felt. Their minds so symmetric yet so different. Their silent conversations and constant exchange of sensations enticed me. Information swam between the two like a tiny version of the Lattice. The one called Pietyr was all images and sounds and tides of emotion. And the one called Jown was all tastes and smells and tactile feelings.

Our three minds embraced and flew upward and swirled about each other, and we were one. I searched their memories. I saw them as children, boys really. So scared but always together, exchanging thoughts. Being chased by those who didn't understand them. Their differences frightening the unenlightened ones. Then I saw the truth of who they were—what they were. It was so plain I should have known from the start. And the poor things didn't know it themselves. I opened myself to them and let them see the truth in a stream of images.

*We don't understand.*

*The children are like you, and you are like me.*

*Children . . . like the ones in the chambers . . . ,* they thought.

*Yes.*

Oceans of thoughts ebbed and flowed between them as they absorbed the information I divulged. Then their eyes flickered red. I was losing control. I had opened more of myself than I had intended, revealing thoughts and feelings that should have remained mine, and mine alone. Their thoughts, my thoughts, our thoughts, oozed black and slick and slippery like oil spreading everywhere.

*Are you the one responsible for the missing children?*

*No.*

*So why did you kill that man?*

*I didn't intend to. It just happened.*

*Where is the boy?*

Their minds sent me an image, a boy's image, a boy's scent. I knew him. I remembered him.

*I know where he is . . .*

"Stefonie?" Freddie said.

Someone suddenly appeared from around the corner. I recognized him as the pilot from the shuttle, the man I had decided not to kill, the man I had pulled from the fire. The interruption broke my bond with the twins. I flattened back into shadow, formless like a black streak of inverted light, and slipped away. I flowed towards my small transport and went inside. Moments later I started the engines and launched through the lock doors to escape.

## DUSK, 7 YEARS AGO . . .

The house felt calm and peaceful. She liked this time of the day, when everyone still slept and she, the first to wake, could be alone to absorb herself in the quiet. Though within moments, memories of all she had tried to forget flooded in. Nothing was the way it was supposed to be. This was not her home. This was not her bed. Not even the sheets she lay on belonged to her. She lived in another's home and cared for another's child, and her own child was long-gone-to-who-knows-where. Doso sat up, rubbed her eyes and forehead, took a deep breath, and pushed her feet into slippers. She needed to begin her day. The baby would wake soon for his breakfast.

In the bathroom mirror, her reflection had aged so that she hardly recognized herself. Her skin had hardened as the freshness of her younger self slipped away. She side-eyed the biomask that hung on a hook next to the mirror as she cleaned her teeth. Her job required her to wear it, but the slimy thing made her skin crawl. For now, it could hang there. She could get away without it a few more hours.

The baby lay awake in his crib playing with his toes. He made a happy *thurrrrgggulle* sound at Doso when she appeared. Aside from an occasional gurgle or coo, he mostly uttered no sounds at all. The child had no need to since he could always reach out with his thoughts to find answers to any question that came to him. Doso felt the child searching her mind, probing and learning. No knowledge would be denied him, not even her intimate private thoughts. She wondered how much he understood. He was so much like her own child. Even his eye color changed as Cora's had, and now, as he turned, a shadow writhed across his skin like a ghostly centipede.

Doso remembered how it had soothed Cora as a baby when she touched her on those dark patches. She caressed the child where the shadow crawled. It felt cool like onyx. Her fingers disappeared then reappeared as she moved her hand over the black. In some areas she could even see the front and back parts of her hand at the same time, and the child giggled, as if her touching him there tickled.

When it came to the strangeness in her own child, Doso found no fault in herself. After all, she'd had no idea what would happen when those men messed with Cora. But these people had no excuse. They must've done this to their child on purpose. *No one should ever exist like this,* Doso thought. She cursed his parents' decision to conceive such a child, condemning him to be a freak for the rest of his life.

She bathed the baby and dressed him. The child's mother would never do this herself because she was afraid of him. Doso could tell by the way the woman never held the child and found quick excuses not to touch him. Her sidelong glances every time the child came near, and her many reasons to avoid moments alone with him, made it clear that the baby she had carried in her own womb terrified her. Neira maintained a volunteer position that kept her away from the home for hours and hours. Doso believed the woman had no need to work as much as she did, and that she wanted to be away from her child as much as possible.

But to Doso the child was a salvation. A wash of love flowed through her at the very sight of him. She reached down and picked him up and held the baby close to her bosom. He snuggled to her like he belonged there, and all the hardness of her life seemed to evaporate. This child was hers. There was no denying it. And she would do everything she could to care for him and protect him.

Doso carried the baby into the kitchen and placed him in his high chair. He quietly examined his spoon with great interest while she prepared the kremer mush for his breakfast. His parents preferred that he eat this concoction. They thought it provided the nutrients a growing child needed. Doso never felt it was enough. In a box on the windowsill where she grew herbs and roots that scented the room and spiced their food, she also grew some special seedlings. She carefully plucked a leaf of one and ground it into the bowl of mush to give the baby an extra fighting chance to survive to adulthood.

The child ate greedily. Sometimes, to tease him Doso would sample a taste, placing the spoon in her mouth, pretending to love it. He would reach out when she did that, with a silent cry. She would laugh, then scoop a spoonful and gently place it into his hungry mouth.

"Good morning, Doso," Neira said as she entered.

"Good morning, ma'am."

"Why aren't you wearing your mask? Cel will be up soon."

"Yes, ma'am. Will you finish feeding the baby?" Doso said, knowing this would buy her more time without the biomask.

"No, that's okay," Neira said. "You can do that. But please hurry up and cover your face before Cel comes down."

"Yes, ma'am," Doso said as she wiped the baby's chin, then spooned some more mush into his happy, mysteriously silent mouth.

Cel hovered into the kitchen. Xe had not received xyrs morning's escoala treatment yet, so xe remained a formless walking shadow.

"~~Go-od~~morning,~~~~~Do-so," Cel said in xyrs best human speech.

"Good morning, sir."

"Doso, please put on the mask like I asked you," Neira said.

"Yes, ma'am," Doso said. She picked up the child's empty plate and placed it into the cleaning appliance.

Cel approached Neira and surrounded her like a gas. Clearly they enjoyed a healthy love life. Doso pretended not to notice. Neira giggled and handed xem a glass of a green fluid that xe began absorbing. Neira didn't wear a mask. She didn't have to. The operation she underwent as part of her commitment ceremony to Cel ensured her perceptions of the krestge permanent and their union complete.

Doso stared long and hard at the mask. Her habit before she put it on was to think to herself for a few moments about how her life had taken her to this place. The thing filled her with unease. It seemed to breathe and vibrate and hum on its own. She picked it up, closed her eyes, and slipped it over her face. It cleaved to her as if hungry, and it sucked itself into every pore and orifice. The mask acted as both a receiver and a filter, and allowed her to perceive everything around her with a clearer sight than with her own eyes. The water moving in the pipes behind the wall, the flow of current into electrical devices, the movement of the Lattice in the air were all distinguishable and calculable. It was inhuman. When Doso returned to the kitchen, she could see all sides of Cel, and somehow this being of infinite complexity made sense. Without eyes and ears, she could see xem and understand xyrs speech that existed on multiple dimensions without overloading her mind.

Doso poured another cup of fluid for Cel. Xe accepted it with thanks and absorbed the vapor into xyrs being. Neira turned on a connection to the Lattice, allowing its news stream to flow into the minds of everyone in the room. Another raid in the Outlands. More villagers killed. More children captured. And Okoni had taken responsibility for the atrocities. Then the names and ages of the dead floated by.

Doso, so caught up in the stories from the Lattice stream, didn't notice Neira approach, her eyes round with sympathy. Neira hugged her shoulder and sniffed back dry tears. In moments like these, Doso didn't know what to think. She didn't hate Neira. But there was something about her that she didn't like. Something Doso couldn't quite put a finger on. And it wasn't simply her choice of husband. In truth, between the two, she liked Cel better. Xe had been nothing but kind. This family had been good to her. They had given her this job and even put in her paperwork to receive her permanent residency card. Most importantly, Cel had used xyrs substantial influence with the city authorities to push through her petition to find her daughter's whereabouts in Night.

Then there would be these moments—these strange off-putting personal moments—when Neira displayed feelings that didn't seem quite real, as if a distance—almost a chasm—existed between the emotion and what the woman actually felt. Maybe these impressions existed only in Doso's mind. But Doso would rather have been alone in her room than with this imitation of grief. Then there was how Neira treated the child. Doso loved the boy, regardless of his deformities. But Neira—his own mother—kept her distance from him. In the end this was the reason why Doso didn't like the woman, and one day the child would understand this as well—on the day he searched Neira's mind and learned how much she wished he didn't exist.

Together we watch the day of their arrival and feel the shock of seeing their silver hulls gleam against the glow of the nearby sun, then hover above us like a menacing message. Those old enough to remember what happened on Earth put their hands across their mouths in silent horror. Those too young huddle close to their elders in frozen fear. They have come. And our EDS is only partially functional. All we can do is helplessly wait for the attack that is sure to come . . . But instead, they do something unexpected. They send a polite request for trade. No mention of the past. No discussion of the deaths of millions. Only a desire for commerce, as if the near annihilation of the human race had never happened . . .

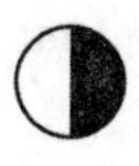

## DUSK, A WEEK AGO . . .

Akev found the girl interesting—for a human. Her little-girl-in-a-woman's-body innocence at first made her a little annoying. Yet since the night of xyrs poetry reading, thoughts of her had constantly flowed through xyrs mind. Akev had noticed how intensely she absorbed the vectors of xyrs poem, like no other human xe had ever met. It impressed xem. It touched xem. Krestge didn't see humans as humans saw themselves. This could be a wonderful thing, as Akev had begun to understand. Stefonie had an attractive inner glow, an energy that produced an internal aura. Akev wanted to know this person who had produced such a beautiful light.

Her friend had confirmed what Akev had suspected. This was Stefonie's first time in a city. Cynthia had said that Stefonie was a strong, brave person and that they shared many things in common, and she'd eagerly assisted in setting up this date between them. Akev had been with people outside of xyrs race in the past, but always with a human who had already experienced a krestge relationship. Dating a human familiarized with xyr kind felt simpler, safer. It meant skipping all the uncomfortable bits. With someone who had never spent intimate time with a krestge before, even the small talk—the getting-to-know-you parts—could be awkward, with too many silly questions about how xe ate and how xe slept and where xe lived and how xe walked, etc. etc. Akev decided if it felt too weird, xe would simply end the date early by politely making up some excuse. The long wait for her arrival suggested that she was probably not coming anyway and this whole idea had been a mistake. Stefonie then emerged from the TTS station, radiating more beautifully than she had the night of the poetry reading.

Akev decided then and there that if this was a mistake, it was one worthy of making.

"Hello," she said with a slight tilt of the head.

"~~Hello~~" Akev responded.

Akev noticed her examining xem, maybe studying the appearance of xyrs shell. The human xe had paid for the escoala session worked all morning to smooth the planes of xyrs form and harden xyrs gaseous edges. The girl had been diligent with her puffs to make Akev's shell appear as male as possible, and xe had been pleased with the results. Akev reminded xemself that the next time xe used that escoala smoker, the tip should be higher. It only occurred to Akev now that xe had not asked Stefonie's friend about her sexual preference. For a moment, xe felt panic. Akev calmed xemself and decided to push those thoughts to the back of xyrs mind. It was too late to do anything about xyrs gender expression now, and much too early for it to matter.

"~~Have you~~~eaten?~~Perhaps we~~~can have some~~ lunch?"

Stefonie smiled and nodded without showing her teeth. Akev liked this, as xe found the human habit of displaying part of their skull a bit disturbing.

"~~~There~~is a place~~~nearby with~~~outdoor seating.~~~"

"Let's go then," she said, and allowed Akev to lead the way.

Akev planned to stay in areas of the city where they could walk together relatively unbothered. Xe knew all the restaurants where a mixed couple could go without having problems. Akev wanted to be careful to make sure this date went well. Stefonie had already proven herself worthy of that effort by simply showing up. Not many—human or krestge—would be brave enough to take a chance on someone so alien from themselves. Even in these "safe" areas, they still made an unusual sight. If she wore a biomask, people would assume Stefonie was xyrs servant. Without one, they might take her for xyrs escoala smoker and/

or prostitute. Even though Stefonie appeared to be none of those things, the chance of mistreatment lingered.

At the café, the waiter showed them to a table corralled in an area on the sidewalk. A couytal provided for Akev floated near the table. Akev landed to rest on it not too close and yet not too far from Stefonie's seat. The menus appeared through the table glass, human language for her and vectors for Akev. Humans passed by, moving to and fro. The colors of them amazed Akev. Humans seemed to have an insatiable need for pigment on their clothing and on their skin. They even coated their dwellings in vibrant hues. Akev found humanity endlessly fascinating, including the woman before xem. Her inner glow still radiated, and Akev wondered what that really meant.

After they selected appetizers, an awkward silence followed. Akev's thoughts ran in a ramble and words escaped xem. Stefonie interrupted xyrs struggle to think of something to say by asking, "What do you eat?"

Akev felt a bit disappointed that she had asked such a pedestrian question and answered with xyrs typical response.

"~~~~I don't eat~~per se. I absorb~~energy~~~preferably~~-substances in their~~gaseous form.~~~This restaurant~~makes a~~nice presentation.~~~"

"Oh."

Akev watched for her reaction to the answer. Would she probe more, delving into unseemly areas of xyrs existence? Would she become disgusted with some aspect of xyrs life and a chill mark the end of this endeavor? To xyrs pleasure, she simply returned to reading her menu.

Before another awkward silence could commence, the waiter returned and placed a small plate of kremer flakes in front of Stefonie and a tube of fluorescent blue gas before Akev.

"That's pretty," Stefonie said.

"~~Yes~~" Akev replied.

Akev noticed Stefonie staring again, almost probing. Xe felt unsettled for a moment. Then the moment passed.

"You~~are from~~~the Outlands of~~Dawn~~" Akev asked, as more of a statement than a question.

"There, and other places," she said. "Is it that easy to tell?"

"~~Only~~~when you speak.~~You have a slight~~~ accent.~~"

"Oh, I didn't realize."

"It~~~has a~~pleasant~~~resonance."

"Thank you." She smiled again, widening her lips, and still not showing the slightest hint of her teeth.

"~~~So~~how long have~~~you been~~in Oros?~~"

"A few weeks."

Akev shimmered and moved the shell of xyrs arm to pass over the tube before xem, absorbing some of the blue gas. She nibbled on the corner of a kremer flake, then sipped some water.

They made their entrée selections from the menu in the glass, telling the waiter their preferences for their meal's preparation. With their order complete, the waiter let the floating images of the prepared dishes fold back into the table.

"Where are you from?" she asked. The question, so poignantly put, seemed to demand an answer. Akev sat shocked and needed a moment's pause. Krestge were sensitive about their origins and most humans knew to not ask about them. Such was the power dynamic between their peoples. It was like asking a human woman her age or if she wore her true eye color. After some consideration, Akev thought this might be an attempt at forming some kind of intimacy, so xe decided to answer.

"~~I am~~~we are~~~from an area~~~that is difficult~~~~~~to describe~~in human terms.~~~~~~We do not live~~on a planet ~~such as you do.~~~Though, there are~~tales~~that~~~once we did.~~We exist in a~~~void~~~a gravity well~~where time and space~~~have no meaning.~~"

Stefonie nodded that she understood, though Akev could not

see how, and she remained lost in thought for a few moments, then bit into her kremer flake.

"How long have you lived in this city?" Stefonie asked.

"~~A number~~of years.~~Before that~~~I was~~stationed on Earth.~~~"

"Really?"

"~~Yes~~~I lived there~~for quite a long time.~~~It's a beautiful ~~planet."

"I wouldn't know."

Silence.

Akev cursed himself for bringing up Earth. Xe knew full well that this remained a sore subject for many humans because of the violent history of xyrs ancestors.

"~~~~I'm sorry.~~That was~~indelicate of me.~~~~"

"No need to apologize," she said.

Silence.

"I was born on Earth," she said.

"~~~Really?~~~"

"Many from the Outlands of Dawn were."

"~~Yes~~~I suppose this~~would be~~because~~~you were~~ the~~last to arrive~~~on Eleusis.~~~"

"I don't remember a thing about it. I might as well have been born on this world. I've always wondered what Earth looked like, though."

"~~Have you~~~ever been to~~the Arboretum?~~~"

"No," she said.

"~~~You~~must see~~~it.~~~They have done~~a wonderful job~~~re-creating~~the environment~~of Earth.~~~Perhaps~~ after lunch~~we could go?~~"

Stefonie shifted her eyes down and tapped her fingernails together, and for a second Akev thought xe may have misstepped again. Then, with a slight twist at the ends of her lips, she said, "I would like that very much."

• • • • •

As they sped through the underground to escape the city limits, the lights dimmed and the windows opened to a view of the outside. The city diminished behind them as the TTS linked cars flew over the open Dusk landscape. The enclosed dome of the Arboretum in the distance grew larger and larger as they approached. Empty seats and *couytals* abounded, but none of them together, so Akev and Stefonie stood near each other—one hovering in place, the other holding on to a pole.

Curious humans tried not to stare. Other krestge on the train sent unfriendly vibrations towards Akev, an impolite way of telling xem that *this* was a line xe should not cross. Stefonie seemed indifferent to it all and gazed out the window as the miles whipped by, quietly humming to herself.

They moved together towards the Arboretum's gate, maintaining a delicate distance. Akev did xyrs best to match Stefonie's casual pace, using xyrs shell to mimic walking legs. Occasionally, the many sides of Akev would glance in her direction, trying to assess how well she enjoyed xyrs company. Stefonie seemed nice, but it felt as if she was being careful to hide her true self. Their conversation at the café had been slow and polite with a number of strange, tense moments, the commonality her friend had suggested that they shared had yet to make its appearance.

In all the years Akev had studied human expressions, xe still found the countless subtleties of their body language mysterious and confusing. For all xe knew, Stefonie might have been having the time of her life. Yet, Akev couldn't shake the nagging feeling that she had her mind elsewhere. But the date was young, and they had made it to the Arboretum without incident. Perhaps the beauty of this place would add some light to the wallowing afternoon.

The Arboretum's gate, made of twisted black metal, was carefully welded into the forms of tall tree trunks with winding branches. Near the entrance stood a stone pillar. The plaque on it read:

THIS ARBORETUM WAS MADE POSSIBLE BY THE SEEDS BROUGHT TO THIS WORLD IN THE SHIPS THAT CARRIED EARTH'S LAST HUMAN INHABITANTS AND PLANTED WITH THE ASSISTANCE AND CARE OF OUR KRESTGE FRIENDS.

The couple admired it for a while before they passed through the entrance to find a different world on the other side. All about them blossomed flowering plants and trees that scented the air with an overwhelming sweetness. White and pink petals drifted down like snowflakes and scattered across the grass. A projected sun hung in the artificial horizon, while invisible undulating panels mimicking the sky caused a slight breeze to blow. Adding to the magic of the scenery, faintly in the imitation daylight sky hovered a replica of Earth's waning moon.

Stefonie sneezed several times and said, "It's so bright in here."

"~~So it is~~~to your eyes~~" Akev said. "On Earth~~this is considered~~~quite normal light~~for this time of day."

"Excuse me a moment," she said, and went to the visitors' center to receive an allergenic, as the shot had come to be commonly called, and a biodisposable cloth to dab her eyes.

The Arboretum was large enough that as they walked its winding paths, they saw very few other visitors. It felt as if they existed in a private garden of their own. They made a little game of finding the small signs next to the flora that interested them, and pronounced aloud their Latin and common names. Around a bend in the path and behind some trees hid a lovely pond where a variety of winged animals—the likes of which Stefonie had never seen outside of a history lesson—sunned themselves and napped. Stefonie left Akev on the path and went to touch the bark of a tree, almost caressing it. When she returned, she sat down on a bench. Akev floated nearby. Xe noted that she discreetly wiped away the moisture that fell on her cheek.

"Is this truly how Earth is? Was?" she asked.

"~~~In the springtime~~in some places~~~yes~~this is~~very much as it appeared~~~~the last time I saw it.~~~

"When this arboretum~~was first proposed~~~there were~~ many krestge~~that opposed its construction.~~~~My parents among them.~~They felt that~~it was~~too close to~~~an apology.~~We argued~~~many times over . . ."

Akev made a sound akin to a grunt.

"Over what?"

"~~~~~~Over~~our~~~past~~treatment~~of~~humans.~~~ And humans in general.~~~~"

"I don't understand."

"My parents~~and others like them~~~felt that~~~there was no need~~~for an apology.~~~~I'm afraid~~~that some of us~~still~~~~feel no regret~~~for what our~~~~ancestors~~~ have done~~~"

Stefonie smoldered, her clenched jaw clearly visible.

"Why did your people follow us here to Eleusis?"

Akev paused, making sure xe carefully phrased what xe said next.

"~~I cannot speak~~~for all~~of my people,~~~only for~~ myself. ~~~I came~~because I wanted~~~to know~~humans.~~~I wanted to~~~understand~~you.~~~"

"And do you?"

"~~~Not in the least.~~~~Though,~~I keep~~trying.~~~"

A fragrant wind drifted by, cooling and seeping through Akev. Xyrs shell had fallen away little by little in places as the day progressed, so that visible cracks opened here and there. Xyrs edges became less distinct, and the panes of xyrs form shifted more and more into shadow.

"I'm sorry," Stefonie said. "I didn't mean to sound so cross."

"~~~There is no need~~~to apologize.~~I understand. ~~~~These are~~delicate~~~matters.~~"

Akev vibrated in sympathy. Stefonie seemed to understand what xe said. She wasn't supposed to, and yet somehow she did.

Words formed from the clouds in the sky, saying the Arboretum would close soon and that all patrons should now begin making their way to the exits.

"How about we continue talking at your place?" she said softly. Akev had not considered the possibility of her coming home with xem today. The idea was intriguing.

"~~I would like~~~that very much.~~~I can~~prepare~~a meal~~for you."

"*You* can cook human food?"

"~~I make~~a very good~~takeout.~~"

Stefonie laughed with her mouth open, showing the whiteness of her teeth. This didn't disturb Akev though, quite the opposite. It warmed xem from within. At last, Akev understood the pleasure of a human's smile.

• • • • •

Akev's large apartment had chairs and tables and other furnishings that belonged in a human home. Stefonie walked around examining the art on display, lightly touching delicate figurines of porcelain and sculptures of stone.

"~~I don't need so much~~~space~~but I like~~~company.~~I hold~~~many meetings~~with humans~~~here,~~poetry workshops~~~and readings.~~~"

"I see," Stefonie said.

On a shelf, sandwiched between two carved wooden sculptures, were seven old-world books made with actual paper pages and cardboard covers.

"I've only seen these in pictures. They must've cost a fortune."

"I love~~your ancient way~~~~of reading.~~I find~~it~~~intriguing."

"May I?" she asked, pointing to one of the books.

"~~~Please.~~"

Stefonie removed a book from the shelf and opened it. The sweet scent of old paper filled her nose as she gently turned the pages and leafed through it, then read aloud—

> "I said you. Take you, my daughter. Because I saw the tall man see you as a human child, not pieces of eight . . ."

"~~That is a~~genuine~~~reproduction of a copy~~~archaeologists~~found on Earth.~~"

She continued to examine the book.

"~~It must seem~~strange~~that I live~~~this way.~~"

"Kinda," she said, closing the book, and looked up with her usual closed-mouthed half smile. Then she carefully put the book back on the shelf.

"~~Can I get you~~~anything?~~I have wine.~~~It's an experimental vintage~~made from~~~actual grapes~~grown in the~~~~southern regions of~~Dawn.~~~I am told~~that it is~~~quite good.~~~"

"Do you have escoala?" Stefonie asked. Akev noticed something suggestive in the way she spoke that made xyrs panes shift in pleasure.

"Escoala," Stefonie repeated. "Do you have any?"

"~~~Yes~~~" Akev said.

"Your edges are loose. I could help you with your form . . . I can also help you with something else."

Her posture and the way she looked at xem . . . even Akev, with xyrs lackluster understanding of human body language, could read her meaning.

"~~~I thought~~~that you~~~had~~~never been with~~~a krestge~~before.~~~~"

"Well, I've smoked escoala before. I only need to blow the smoke at you, right? I want to try this. See what it's like."

"~~I~~~I~~didn't~~expect this.~~"

"You don't want to?"

"No, I do.~~I only thought~~that~~~I didn't think~~so soon~~~~"

Akev left the room and returned with a package and laid open its contents on the table, a medium-sized pouch of escoala and a small box of roll papers. Stefonie opened the pouch and took a long sniff.

"This is fresh."

"I~~bought it~~only a~~few~~days ago.~~"

She poured some into her hand, sniffed it again, then rubbed it between her palms. Akev felt an emotion xe hadn't felt in a long time. Xyrs planes moved and shifted into shadow, then shimmered in anticipation. Stefonie placed the escoala neatly onto a sheet of roll paper and carefully curled it around the dried crushed leaves. She twisted it tightly, then licked it so that it held together in a neat, tiny cylinder.

Xe desperately wanted to explore human sexuality. Rarely had xe found a willing human partner. Usually Akev had to pay for the experience, which xe was sure lacked the true intimacy. Now more than anything, xe wanted try intercourse with *this* human. In truth xe had wanted it from the moment xe saw her at the poetry reading. There was just something about her. Xe couldn't explain to xemself what it was.

Stefonie lit the escoala cigarette, inhaled, then blew. The puff of smoke orbited Akev as it pulled xem out of xyrs extradimensional plane and solidified xyrs being. Xyrs shadowy form melted into a solid form, and xe hardened. Stefonie slipped off her dress and stood before Akev naked and smiled. Akev moved nearer to her, excited and confused. Xe reached out and touched her, wrapped xemself around her, then entered her. The smoke made the intimate touch especially intoxicating. They writhed together to a rhythm of their own making. Then Stefonie shifted into shadow and became void. Akev had not known such ecstasy was possible. Inside became outside and outside became inside. She entered xem and swallowed xem whole, then grabbed xem hard. Mesmerized and terrified, Akev tried to loosen her grip, but she was too strong. Xyrs thoughts leaked into her and xe could not make her stop.

"~~What are~~you~~ doing?~~~"

She didn't answer, only entered deeper.

"~~~What~~are you~~~~~~~~~~~~~"

*There are things I need to know and you are going to tell me.*

"~~~What~~~~~~~~~~~"

*Why are you here?*

"~~~I~~~don't~~~understand~~~~~~~~~~~~~"

*Why are your people here?*

Stefonie squeezed, inflicting what in human terms could only be described as pain.

*You are going to tell me the truth.*

"~~I've~~told you~~before~~~we wanted~~~to know humanity.~~~~~~~~~"

*Why?!*

"Because~~~because~~~~"

Akev tried to hold back. Stefonie could feel the strain of xyrs efforts to hide a closely guarded secret.

*Tell me.*

Her demand echoed throughout Akev's being. If it had been possible for xem to weep, xe would have.

"To~~protect~~you.~~~~~~~~~~"

*From what?*

She squeezed harder.

"From us~~from the other krestge.~~~Our presence here~~~ prevents the others~~from harming you~~~again.~~Krestge~~ don't kill krestge.~~Because~~we are here~~they do not come.

~~~~We were~~afraid~~if humans~~~knew this truth~~it would ~~break the~~peace.~~~~~~~~~~~~~~"

Stefonie reached deeper and saw that the krestge now living on Eleusis had indeed volunteered to use their very bodies to protect humankind. And they were doing so because they believed it to be the right thing to do.

*What do you see when you look into the sky?*

"~~~~What?~~~~~"

*You don't see anything, do you?*

"~~~I don't~~~understand~~~~~What you are~~~talking~~ about.~~~~~~~~~~~"

*You really don't see anything, do you? You really don't know a damned thing . . .*

Then she reached into xyrs mind and turned off xyrs consciousness.
~~~~

## DUSK, 15 DAYS AGO . . .

The rain turned to light drizzle. The ground felt slippery beneath their feet, and a cold westerly wind chilled exposed skin. Freddie and Jown helped Pietyr into the zepher and placed him gently into the passenger side. He sank heavily into the seat while holding his chest, wincing with each movement. He bowed his head as if in prayer and moaned in pain. After making sure his brother sat steadily, Jown went into the back compartment of the zepher to search for a med kit. The sounds of his thrashing echoed into the dark, gloomy night. He returned with a medical wand and waved it over his brother's chest. It glowed red in two areas.

*You have two broken ribs,* Jown thought to his brother.

*I feel as much.*

Jown pulled out a bone fuser from the med kit, then wrapped it carefully over his brother's chest. He fastened it firmly in place. The cloth warmed as it worked on the injured areas, sealing the breaks in his ribs.

*This is gonna ache for a while,* Jown thought to his brother.

*Yes, it will.*

Freddie rubbed at his temple as if experiencing a very bad headache and said, "What just happened?"

"We are not sure," Jown said.

"We could hear her—"

"—in our minds."

"I didn't know anyone could do that," Freddie said.

"We didn't know either," the twins responded in unison.

"What did she say?"

"There were no words—" Pietyr said.

"—more like thoughts and images," Jown completed.

"You called her by name," Jown said.

"How do you know her?" the twins said together.

"She's the girl from my last job. The one I picked up in Night," Freddie said.

"Okoni," Pietyr growled.

"We could see that she is planning to do something," Jown said.

"Like what?" Freddie said.

"We couldn't see exactly," they answered together.

As questions and more questions enveloped Freddie's mind, he turned to the twins, intending on suggesting that it was time to leave. Instead he stilled, and a cold chill crept up his arms. The men he had called his closest friends, whom he had known for most of his adult life, now looked at him with inhuman eyes that flashed scarlet. He had to blink twice and stare hard to make sure his sight was not deceiving him.

"Give me a minute," Freddie said, and walked away from the zepher.

He needed to think. He needed to understand what the hell was going on. He looked to a sky clearing of rain where gray clouds drifted by that revealed patches of blue and the orange-pink of the sun. Since Suez had introduced him to the twins all those years ago, he had seen them do many things. Like the time they'd broken a man's arm in three places without either of them displaying even a twinge of remorse. And the times he'd seen them make sure an orphaned kid had a hot meal and a warm bed—sometimes in a shelter, sometimes in their own home. They were strange, no doubt, but they'd always had his back. Through thick and thin, they'd never failed him. But that girl had triggered something in them. Something that was already there.

He secured a bioconnection by tapping the metal tab attached to his cheek.

"Eben, it's me," he said. "I need you to do something for me . . . I can't tell you over the Lattice. I'll pick you up in a bit . . . No, not at the twins' apartment, your house . . . Don't worry about how

I know where you live, just be ready when I get there . . . Look, I can't tell you now . . . It's about the twins . . . I'll tell you when I pick you up."

Freddie wiped his eyes and marched back to the zepher without looking at the twins.

"The cops will be here any minute. I think we need to get the hell outta here and go someplace where we can figure all this out."

The twins said in unison, "Agreed."

"Get in. I'm driving. We're going to one of my safe houses."

• • • • •

The round-faced boy with large teal—not blue, teal—eyes waited patiently, leaning against the building he had been told was his home. He melted into the background as if by practice, becoming one with the material that formed the wall. No one who passed noticed him. This had never been a home to him. It had only been a place where he stayed. A place where the city had put him because he had no real parents. A place where the city awarded the shares for his care every month. A place where he never received the care the city paid for.

Upstairs, the people who collected the community service shares for his upkeep wouldn't care about his late-night departure. They honestly didn't give a damn where he went as long as he could be found in reasonable shape for the occasional inspections by the city. The reality of his neglect was as mundane as it was dangerous. In this place where very bad things could happen to a small kid, he waited outside alone. He could do this without fear because of the unsaid words floating through the neighborhood streets that whispered a warning that Eben should remain untouched or face the wrath of the two look-alike men with green eyes who could beat you ten ways to Sunday. So that even while alone, he remained under their protection. The twins did that for him, and he loved them for it.

The zepher hushed around the corner, then its door swung

open. Freddie leaned out, ushering Eben to come inside. Eben felt suddenly conspicuous. People turned to look, and there was a menace to their attention. They could have been jealous of him, or fearful for him. Either way, they would be right to feel so. Eben climbed inside and shut the door, then the zepher sped away.

"Sorry to get you out of bed, but I need you to look up something."

"What's wrong with the twins? You said they were in trouble."

"We need to find out more about them."

"We know about them."

"No, we don't. They don't even know about themselves."

"What?" Eben sneered. "This some kinda joke?"

"I wish it was," Freddie said. "I think they're in trouble and I have to know more about them so I can help them. I know you're only a kid, and I hate to lay this on you, but you're also the only one I know who can access the Lattice without a biosignature."

Eben felt a chill. He rubbed his arm, then stared out his window at the sleeping city speeding by.

"I need you to find anything and everything about the twins' origins," Freddie said. "Who were their parents? Where were they born and when? And this is very important—I need you to do that without leaving a trail of your search. Can you do that?"

Eben thought of the twins' strangeness. He never really wanted to think about it, but he had to admit to himself that normal people didn't telepathically talk to each other. Normal people didn't split their sentences in half to complete a thought. And nobody had eyes like them. He'd seen all kinds of colors, but never ever the kind of glint and glow that they had.

"Okay," Eben said, "I'll help."

• • • • •

The spacious loft located on the far edge of the Quarters was one of the many safe houses Freddie kept because he didn't like to stay in any one place for too long. Pietyr sat down, his face an amalgamation of pain and discomfort. An expression that turned to fury when Eben walked through the door.

"Hey, guys," Eben said, and yawned.

"What is he—"

"—doing here?" Pietyr completed, nearly standing to his feet. The pain forced him to remain seated.

"I brought him here because we need him," Freddie said. "And because I think he's safer here."

"We don't want—"

"—him involved," Jown said.

"Knowing what we know, would you prefer him out there?"

And Eben, with his eyes of teal—not blue, but teal—suddenly seemed more vulnerable than the twins had ever realized. Now they knew it was not random perverts in search of a child who had tried to kidnap him before. Those people wanted Eben for something specific, and they had no idea what that was.

"Like it or not, he's involved," Freddie said.

"He's right," Pietyr said. "Eben is better off here with us."

The twins exchanged some more silent thoughts and Jown relented.

"Good," Freddie said, and pulled out a chair before a table, gesturing for Eben to make himself comfortable.

"Hey, what's up with their eyes?" Eben whispered.

"We'll talk about it later. Just get to work."

Eben sat down and slipped on a biomask that he pulled out of his pocket. It formed a white gloss over his face as it accessed his frontal lobe, and he began fingering in the air.

Eben established an anonymous channel into the Lattice. The system, unable to identify him, spun a public join—a join without an authorized signature—to the channel into the Lattice. He began to navigate, journeying through the Lattice as if wading through a waking dream, into the trace memories of those who had any connection with the twins. He downloaded all those traces and stored them into a repository.

To break through the barrier to the twins' past, Eben floated past hidden trace repositories located in their memory downloads. He bypassed the security protocols and the many unusual barriers to the data. The Lattice storage units behind locked, encoded barriers opened to him as if they weren't even there. Something about his mind allowed him to do such things. He even began to see the patterns in the traces. His mind swam through the eddies and currents of the Lattice, and he accessed a data stream that identified the twins. Then he floated through it.

There was nothing inside, though. Not even where they were born. Everything about any citizen was kept in these types of repositories. Eben had been in repositories like these before and found out all kinds of things about people. But for the twins, they were blank.

He continued searching. He tried to access their parents' data. This took a long time because of a lack of traces in their identity repositories.

Eben grew tired and hungry after a while, and took off his bio-mask and asked for something to eat. Freddie patted him on the back and left him alone with the twins sleeping on the couch to pick up some wanaga burgers from the restaurant up the street.

In an uncomfortable silence peppered with the occasional snores of the sleeping men who had once saved his life, Eben waited. He felt like a creep poking into their lives without telling them and wondered if he should really be doing this. He also wondered, how the only friends he'd ever known possessed no trace data and no memories from anyone. They seemed to have come out of nowhere. Eben understood everything through the Lattice—and everything that was right and true to him had a trace. That knowledge and his ability to manipulate Lattice data helped him feel secure in a world where nothing else felt real. And people with no trace data made no sense.

Freddie returned with wanaga burgers and kremer fries. They ate together, sipping occasionally at the drinks that came with them.

Eben looked up from his burger once in a while and wondered if Freddie could be trusted. The twins had described him as an accomplished liar on numerous occasions. They had also said as many times that they trusted him because he never lied to *them*. Eben decided that later he would find out more about Freddie, as well.

After eating and resting a bit, Eben returned to work with renewed energy. An idea came to him to approach the problem of identifying the twins through the more accessible memories of their mother, rather than the sketchy memories of their father, who would appear and disappear, fading in and out of focus almost as if he'd never existed.

Eben found heavily encrypted repositories under the name //CADUCEUS. After some time and effort, he uncovered their mother's impregnation date. She, like most humans, had worn a mask to communicate with the krestge. Her thoughts, her emotions, her impressions while wearing the mask had been traced and stored. Her most intimate thoughts and the secret of the twins' origins opened for Eben as they had never done for anyone.

"Oh, man . . ." Eben said, taking off his biomask and feeling squeamish. Freddie, who had drifted off to sleep in his chair, suddenly jerked awake.

"You got something," Freddie said, rubbing his eyes.

"Yeah, and I think the brothers should see it, too."

Freddie reached to put on his biomask, then stopped midmotion and asked, "The connection is secure, right? No one will be able to identify me?" Eben cynically smirked, insulted that he would even ask. So Freddie placed the biomask over his face and the information flowed.

"Oh, man . . ."

• • • • •

Jown connected to the trace, and through him so did Pietyr. They could see their mother as a young person, an odd sensation, and a bit disturbing. Her thoughts, her exact feelings, seeped into their minds as if they belonged to them. Even with the risky conception, their mother remained clear that she wanted to have a baby. She wanted to have a child with the one she loved, who happened to be a krestge. By becoming part of an interspecies study, she had a chance to create a new life, a new species, a new future.

Her memory repositories indicated that the series of biosynthetic chemical agents introduced into her system that allowed for the conception of her mixed-species child also contained programmable self-replicating nanoids designed to propagate into the growing fetus. The nanoids were to help form a bioconnection to the Lattice as well as help to make the child develop certain properties possessed by krestge, such as their ability to cross dimensional lines. In this experiment in human hybridization, the hope was that the resulting child would have control over this trait and would be able to flow across dimensional lines at will.

Identical twins were an unforeseen outcome. And the nanoids instead mutated in their systems and formed a kind of communication link between the children. Immediately after their birth, the twins also began communicating with the minds of everyone around them—their mother, the doctor, the nurses, their father. They passed images and scents and injected questions and impressions. Their krestge father became unnerved after weeks of these invasive mind conversations and eventually left, never to be heard from again. The twins, given their inability to cross dimensional lines, were failed out of the program, released back into the general public with their mother, and allowed to go their own way.

From here their mother's impressions became more painful. Every one of her friends shied away. She found herself alone with no one but her mixed-species sons. She moved to an area predominantly inhabited by krestge, far away from the prying stares of judgmental humans. She had hoped that her boys could grow up around others of their race and experience the culture of their father's people. But they weren't fully krestge and they weren't fully human, from two worlds and a part of none. Eventually she moved to the Bottoms, where she did her best to hide her sons' krestge background from them and from the people around them.

Jown removed his mask. Pietyr disconnected from his brother.

The brothers would never share with each other what they individually thought in the following silent moments. Their eyes still blinking a scarlet red.

• • • • •

Freddie waved his hand over the table, initiating his bioconnector to establish a hyperscreen. It hummed softly and flickered in the air, waiting for input. He picked up Pietyr's discarded ruined shirt, scraped some dried blood off the sleeve, and let it land on the table.

Freddie said to Eben, "I need you to access all the data on the girl this blood belongs to."

"Yes, we would like to know more about this girl as well," Jown said for himself and his brother.

Eben went to work instructing the system to separate out the blood of the twins and to isolate a sample of the remaining foreign material. The Lattice quickly identified Stefonie and her image appeared, hovering within the hyperscreen over the table, her amber eyes wide and inquisitive.

"The Lattice has traces of her presence in the city as of a few weeks ago," Eben said. "Let me look back a bit more . . ."

Eben found some markers and followed them through the Lattice. His thoughts swam into the repositories as they opened and all the information within them flowed into his mind. Bursts of images appeared over the table as Eben's mind went deeper and deeper into the murky depths of the data. Then the information appeared . . .

**The biological sample provided matches that of a child reported missing from the Outlands approximately ten years ago . . .**

Stefonie's image over the table age-regressed by years, blurred in the quickness of its changes. The image then stilled to that of a little girl with a soft, puffy body and the same wide, inquisitive eyes the color of amber.

Report initiated by familial relation: Mother

The image of her mother appeared over the table alongside Stefonie's with a striking resemblance.

"Isn't that the Bastias' nanny? Doso?" Pietyr said.

"Yes, I do believe it is," Jown said.

"Perhaps we should have a talk—"

"—with this Doso woman again."

"Wait . . . There's more," Eben said. "Here ya go . . ."

: Current location—UNKNOWN

: Current status—UNKNOWN

: Biological scans—CLASSIFIED

***QUERY ACCESS TO ALL FURTHER DATA DENIED***

The biomask Eben wore turned pink. He began to twitch and seize, then fell to the floor.

"Shit!" Freddie exclaimed, and struggled to hold Eben in place. "Get it off him!"

"Hold him still!" Jown said as he attempted to take the biomask off. The three men struggled with Eben as he twisted and shook violently. At last, by pressing the pressure points at the sides of the boy's head, the thing released and slithered off the child's face. White foam oozed from the side of his mouth, and his irises had turned amber.

"I can see her," Eben whispered.

"See who?" Freddie replied.

"I don't think she sees me . . ."

"Who?" Freddie said again.

Eben put up his hands as if the wind flowed through his fingers and said, "So beautiful . . ."

## DUSK, 6 MONTHS AGO . . .

The boy came home, slamming the door behind him, and ran up the stairs to his room, not saying a word to Doso. She usually waited for him outside after school, and he would chat the entire way home about whatever had gone on during his day. Yet with school not due out for hours, he had come home—alone. Something was obviously wrong. Doso stopped chopping the vegetables she had been preparing for the family's dinner and wiped her hands.

As Doso ascended the stairs, she could hear the boy banging around in his room. He didn't answer the first time she gently knocked. So she knocked again.

"Leave me alone!" he screamed.

"What did you say?" Her voice calm, but held the tone of *Remember yourself, child.*

"Please," he added quickly.

"What happened at school today?"

"I don't wanna talk about it."

"I'm not leaving until you tell me."

She waited, and knew that he knew that she still stood there. Moments later, the door cracked open and Doso walked in. He sat on the edge of his bed and she joined him there.

The boy understood that Doso would not force him to talk. She had watched him grow from a little baby, quiet and cooing, to a toddler learning to walk, to a child, feisty and strange. She was always there, always loving, always a steadily persistent presence. Now that he went out on his own and had his own interests and friends, he almost believed that he didn't need Doso anymore. But in truth, he needed her more than he needed his own mother.

He took a deep breath and said, "My eyes are changing color again."

He turned to show her his irises. They had become a shade of amber with a slight but noticeable glow.

"How long have they been like this?"

"Since this morning at school. Some kids saw. I got scared, so I came home."

The dark shadows that used to slither across his body had long since disappeared, only to be replaced with other indications of strangeness, so very much like the child Doso had lost long ago.

"Get your coat," she said.

"Why?"

"Because we're going out."

This was the boldest thing she could think to do—and the riskiest. The only thing she knew that could possibly help him was her faith. Nafaka was powerful, and she'd seen it do miraculous things. Cora didn't believe. That's why she never got better. She never tried hard enough, believed hard enough. But this boy could be saved. She had wanted to do this since the first moment she'd picked this boy up as a baby and seen those dark void marks wiggling across his body. She had kept silent and tried hard to simply mind her own business and do this job without care, without concern, without investment. In time, she had grown to love this child. And now he clearly was in trouble.

Cora had been like this. In the Outlands, she would be all right as long as no one talked about her to the authorities. And no one in the village would. She could have lived her life peacefully among her people, away from those who would want to investigate and test and god-knows-what. But this child was in the city. There were many who wanted children like him. If someone were to turn him in, they'd take him away for sure.

So the woman from the Outlands and the child of privilege hurried out into the cool, damp air. They took the TTS to the Bottoms and walked the rest of the way to the place she attended every Thursday night. In the Outlands they worshipped in a cave, which was more proper. Here, the believers in Nafaka met in a converted storefront. On the nights of worship, it became an abode for the holiest of holy. Her sanctuary. Her secret tabernacle. Her place of solace in a world that had taken everything that mattered from her. In this storefront church she let the spirits ride her back, and she shouted out her pain and released her burdens. For a few hours a week, Doso was greater than who she appeared to be. She became Maumon, a mother of the temple and a powerful Nafaka priestess.

Her faith had to be shared with the boy. It was his only chance. Doso had panic-called her temple sisters and explained to them the boy's condition. They could see from the child's eyes that his situation was indeed dire.

They took off their coats, wet from the dreary weather, and gathered in a circle, placing the bewildered boy in the center. Doso picked up a bowl and poured some honey kept on the table and prepared a thick liquor. She drank from the bowl, then handed it to the boy. Trusting her, he drank until his head drunkenly wobbled.

Doso sang out, *"Ala a obba waaaa . . ."*

*"A obba waa,"* the sisters responded, and began to sway and clap.

Doso sang out again, *"Ala a obbo (click) eeeee . . ."*

*"A obba eeee,"* the sisters responded.

They spun the boy around and around and flicked water at him. Someone began to bang on the drums, *on-gonga-kee . . . on-gonga-kee . . . on-gonga-kee . . .*

*"Insah a olo aaaaa . . ."*

*"A ongo* (click) *eeeee . . ."*

*"Eeee olo* (click) *aaaa . . ."*

"Oi!" Doso screamed.

"Oi! Oi!" the sisters replied.

*"Ala o obba waaaa . . ."*

The sisters sang, *"A obba waa . . ."*

*"Ala o obba yooo . . ."*

The sisters sang, *"A obba yooo . . ."*

*"Tah!"*

And the boy fell to the floor and began to shake. His body writhed and twisted and turned, and his eyes turned back into his head so that only the whites showed. And then dawnflies surrounded him . . . They surrounded me.

I am here then and now. This is not now and yet it is. The boy jumped out of his body and became an electrical charge, a floating dot of light, and joined with the other dots who had appeared hovering near the ceiling. Then I floated down and entered the boy's body, and sat up and spoke.

: **Hello Deidra**

• • • • •

The service lasted for a few hours, then the sisters went home, leaving Doso alone with me. They wished her well while avoiding glances at the child, who still appeared spirit-drunk. Doso walked into a nearby park, empty because of the hour, with me inhabiting the body of the boy-child she loved. I hopped onto a swing, moving his legs slightly to oscillate back and forth. Doso sat in the swing next to me and held on to the chains, dragging her feet a little along the pebbled ground.

: **I've looked in on you every so often**

"Yes?"

: **Yes**

: **I wanted to make sure you were all right**

"It's not me that has the problem. It's that boy you're inside of."

Cate stopped swinging the boy's feet and did a check on the body she inhabited.

: **This body has been genetically altered**

"And his stepfather at home is a krestge."

Cate did a trace check on that information.

: **Oh, I see**

"The boy cannot live in that house like this. Maybe you can fix him?"

: There is nothing wrong with this body that needs fixing

: This body is developing within its design parameters

"Maybe slow down the progress of his change then."

: I don't believe I can

"For everyone in his family's sake, please try."

: This is how his body works

: Nothing I do will change that

Doso turned away for a moment, accepting the information like a blow.

: One more thing

"Yes?" she said while wiping at the skin beneath her eyes.

: I found your daughter

Silence.

Doso—Deidra—Maumon—for a moment her heart stopped. Then it raced so fast the blood rushed to her head so that she couldn't see.

"Where is she?" she begged.

: She is in Night with Okoni

"We knew that."

: But now I know of someone through whom you may be able to contact Okoni

"Who?"

: His name is Raul Rodolfo Suez

"I've heard of him. I think a lot of the escoala from our farms back home ends up with him."

Cate pulled a slate out from the boy's pocket and displayed an image of a man with a large white beard. Doso stood. Her whole demeanor changed from that of an old woman to a very angry woman.

She pointed at the image. "*That's* Suez?"

: Yes

: Do you know this man?

As Doso stared at the image, a flash of heat ran across her face and body. Her heart pumped hard enough so that she could feel it in her ears. She shut her eyes, tilted her head, and exhaled to force herself to cool. "Yes, I know him," she said. "That's Cora's father."

• • • • •

A drizzle began while they sat in the park. The heaviest part of the downpour caught them as they made their way to the TTS station. They spent their time in the tube wet and solemn. Cate had left the boy exhausted, and he rested his head against Doso's shoulder all the way home. They arrived to find the house dark and Neira sitting in the living room waiting for them.

"Where have you been?" she said as they entered.

Doso cursed herself for not thinking to call or leave a note or something.

"I had some errands to run," Doso said.

"This late?" Neira said.

"Don't be mad at Doso, Mom. She was trying to help me."

"Help you with what?" Neira's red-rimmed eyes narrowed. "Where did you take my son? Did you take him to that church of yours?"

The very air they breathed became thick and syrupy. There was no escaping the awfulness about to occur.

"Wait," Doso said with authority, and bent down to take off the child's wet coat. She left the boy and mother alone while she placed the wet things on the hook in the mudroom. Then she placed the boy's little hand in hers and went up the stairs with him and put him to bed.

When Doso descended the stairs, she faced the mother of the child she loved in full righteous fury about the well-meaning wrong Doso had just done.

"You took *my son* to that crazy church of yours! How could you do that? It's one thing for you to believe in that mumbo jumbo, but you will not indoctrinate my son!"

"The boy needs protection," Doso said.

"If my child needs protection, he'll get it from my own church, thank you. We are good, decent Builderists in this house. You had no right to take him there!"

"Somebody had to do something. You *know* what he is. Pretending that everything is okay will not help that boy."

"I think it's time for you to leave us," Neira said. "Pack your things and go."

Doso heard the words but not their meaning. She had been a loyal, faithful caretaker to an unloved child for years, and now she was to be tossed away like so much trash. Her gray head straightened. Her bent body straightened. Her stance straightened. She was Doso no more. She became again Maumon Deidra, Keeper of the Seed.

"I know you never filed for my residency card," she said. "You never had any intention. You've been lying to me for years. I found the application in one of your drawers when I was cleaning years ago. You kept me here working for almost nothing while you ran off to your *volunteer work*. All because you're afraid of your own child. I stayed because I love that boy, and he needs help. I'm telling you he needs not to be in *this house*."

## NIGHT, 8 YEARS AGO . . .

Cora was numb, skin and bone, huffing and puffing clouds of mist in this place where the shadows dwelled and the wind moaned pleas to be set free to warmer climates. The texture of this land of ice stood hard against the austere sky. The three stars sparkled a cold, blue-tinted white, and mountainous glaciers that had broken their way across the outer crust, etched deep valleys of frozen water that smoothed and wound over the vista. Particles of frozen water fluttered about as if from a scene in a souvenir snow globe, to finally come to rest and split the light so that a sea of tiny rainbows glittered all across the alabaster landscape. Surely if an afterworld existed for the torment of sinful souls, then this was the frozen version of it.

They passed one of the many cracks that crisscrossed the region. Beyond it lay a very familiar sight edging its way out of the snow, the remains of forgotten transport ships jutting upward like giant metallic headstones in an icy graveyard. Some of the first arrivals had had the misfortune of having their transports land here. They'd had to walk to the habitable ring to Dusk through these wintery ridges. Tales to terrify children often famously featured the long echoing screams of those who fell into the crevasses of this place as they sank deeper and deeper into the infinite depths, into the heart of the world.

In this seemingly endless journey, Cora struggled along in a cold so deep it burned. The children were being marched to join the main body of Okoni's army. There they would train together on how to fight to rid the world of the great evil of the krestge. Cora wondered how this supposed battle would take place. She had never seen a krestge in her life, but from what she had been told, they were a people of multiple dimensions whom you could neither really see nor touch. Cora looked around at all the starved, exhausted children alongside her and thought, *How could this group possibly fight such beings?*

Snowflakes touched the tip of her nose and melted on her cheeks. They drifted into her eyes and collected on her shoulders. Before long a full blizzard blinded everyone except Cora, whose eyes could see everything. The wind blasted thick white in every direction. She bowed her head against the storm.

The Commander's voice echoed for them to stand firm, and the army stopped in its tracks. Cora screamed out her number in turn like all the rest during the count, assuring them that she had not wandered off. Something about hearing her own voice say that number instilled in her mind the idea of escape. She found herself imagining finding shelter in the remains of one of the ships that lay over the ridge—of how she could hide there, of how no one else could see that far, of how, if she planned it right, no one would notice her slipping away.

When the march began to move again, Cora drifted ever so slightly further and further to the back. The provisions she carried weighed heavily on her, yet she trudged on, quietly moving at an uneven pace, lifting her legs high even as many passed her. Before long, her slowed pace put her at the very end of the pack. A boy next to her glanced over. For a moment she thought he knew what she was doing. Yet his inset eyes showed little emotion. The larger soldiers, who struggled themselves, didn't seem to notice or care that one small snow-covered person had slipped past them. Then she was far behind them. Then she was all alone. Then she turned and ran.

She ran hard and long into the nothingness of the snow. She ran without looking. She ran without caring. Her legs felt like they would snap in two beneath her, but she kept running until no one was around as far as her eyes could see.

• • • • •

The transport wreckage where she intended to hide lay further away than her sight had led her to believe. She'd been walking and walking, and it seemed no closer than it had hours before. It had never occurred to her until now that the loose security among the march was because no one thought anyone foolish enough to run out into this wasteland alone during a storm. *I'm gonna die out here,* she thought as the wind covered the sounds of her steps.

As the hours set in and the high from her last intake of escoala wore off, she felt the emptiness of her belly. She ate so long ago, and the thought of food made her feel hungrier. She tried hard to think of something else, like the religious ceremonies of her mother's church. All the endless singing and chanting and praying for deliverance from sorrows. Her mother's secretive cult of Nafaka met in the caves far outside her village. So while most of the other girls attended the stoic Church of Sts. Adrian & Antoine and could wear pretty dresses that showed off their knees, she had to wear those damn gonars. She'd also have to stand in that dry cave while their prayers went on and on. Very few, if any, received an answer. Yet still her mother remained faithful and demanded that Cora follow the religion as well, even as so many others had fallen away from its practice.

Sometimes Cora wondered how much her mother really believed, or did she simply not know what else to do with herself. The funny thing, Cora on some level wanted to believe that there was a force or personality greater than herself in charge somewhere up there. Someone all-seeing and all-knowing who had a plan that included her in some way. But right now, in the freezing cold, after all she'd seen and been through, having faith seemed like a load of foolishness. She laughed at the stupidity of it all, and her voice rang high off the glaciers.

If a god existed, how could she be made to suffer so much? This quiet, suffocating suffering. This collapsing wall of no escape. And now she would die out here. Before she reached the wreckage, she would freeze to death, forgotten and alone. She only wanted to understand why all of this had to happen. Why did she have to perish like this? She had tried many times to phaseshift during her time with the soldiers. She had tried so hard to make the sickly feeling of losing herself into the void. It simply would not come, no matter how deeply she focused. Her shifts into phase seemed to happen completely randomly. If only she could control her phasing, she could have saved so many. She could have saved Jessem.

*Why did Jessem have to die like that?*

"You tell me why!" she shouted to the heavens, feeling the warmth of water flowing down her cheek.

Only the empty whistle of the wind replied.

Nothing made sense, not that anything ever did.

Cora began to sing. She sang an old song her mother had taught her for when she worked in the fields. A song that asked for deliverance from a world of sorrow. It was the closest thing to a prayer that Cora would allow herself to make.

Her numb legs moved robotically towards the wreckage. She was falling asleep on her feet. The wind had died down, so that in the silence the crunch of her feet sounded loudly. Her senses had ceased to function, even her sight began to fail her. In her dreamy, exhausted mind, she thought she could feel the ground sway from the undertide of the great ocean that lay beneath the surface of the ice.

She touched the metallic hull that now loomed large before her. It felt warm, as if something lived inside. Kneeling before it, she searched for a way to enter, then pounded on it hard. An empty *klang* echoed back. She concentrated hard and forced herself to see through the metal to deep inside, down into the shadowy depths of the ruined ship. Below swirled water with creatures both great and small. Images filled her mind of the undulating things with their nether parts slowing, swimming in rhythm with a current, ballooning open and close like a dress in the wind. The many colors of them swam, laid eggs, lived, and died in the waters. And now they rose, humming like a horde of bees, coming to answer her call.

They banged at the hull, dangerously close to her face, denting the metal. She jumped backward, finding strength in legs that only moments before had refused to move. Stepping high and fast through the deep snowpack, she tripped over her own feet in her haste and fell forward to roll and roll and roll, then stopped.

A slight wind passed to part the fog, exposing the edge of a ravine and a precipice that overlooked the vastness below. Recently fallen chunks of ice from the shelf lay on the still water of the frozen stream at the very bottom. She stayed there motionless and quiet, surrounded by a mist that lingered as if suspended by some ethereal glue. And on the other side of the chasm, she stared in disbelief at the sight of a settlement of houses, and the naturally formed ice bridge that led there.

• • • • •

Through the snow piled high on unused paths, she trudged. From one house to the next, through frosted windows, she saw tables with half-eaten meals covered with ice, knocked-over chairs, and broken-down doors. The people who had lived here had left in a hurry, abandoning their homes to the cold. This place must have been nice once. A community. In any case, these people had been gone a long time.

A building in the center of town stood more intact than the rest. As she approached, an elegantly carved star made of a plus sign with a large X through it could be seen etched into the door beam, the symbol of Builderism and the Church of Sts. Adrian & Antoine.

"Hello!" Cora called out, only to hear her voice return.

Cora didn't feel comfortable entering, so she moved on.

She pushed open the door of a cottage that still seemed

in relatively good shape. Its frozen hinges creaked loudly. In the main room lay a cold fireplace, a table, some chairs, and a storage box for food, emptied of its contents. She broke up a small wooden chair, tossed the pieces into the fireplace, and attempted to light them. It smoldered a little, sending a thin line of smoke to drift upward. In the gear she'd been carrying she found some papers that she crumpled up and tossed over the frozen wood and set aflame. That helped to warm the wood enough to become a fire. She also unearthed some food packs, a few precious protein bars and some containers of nutrient gelatin that she ate greedily.

In the bedroom she found some blankets made of a rough material. She wrapped herself in the frozen cloth and sat near the fire and lay down to rest. So very tired. Her head feverish and sweaty. She drifted off into waking dreams of the muted light through her chamber door window. So small, so young. Her eyes wide open in complete blackness, unable to move or breathe or scream. Aged by years, and her body was not her body. It belonged to someone else. Her, but not her. The door opened, sending her sliding out covered in the suspension fluid onto a cold, hard floor. She shivered for the cold and felt hot and coated in wet, her body fixed in place as if glued by adhesive. The fluid packed into every orifice: her mouth, nose, down her throat, even into her anus. Involuntarily, fluid came spilling out from deep within her lungs. She coughed to choking as the clear mucuslike ooze flowed out of her mouth to surround her face with its soft warmth.

Awake and in the cabin, asleep and in the transport, which was which? A pinhole opened near her nose—a bubble in the fluid that had popped, making a tiny space where cool air could sneak in. How sweet the feel of the wind of life passing through her lungs and into her body.

She remembered things she had not actually experienced, but had heard repeated over and over during the long journey to this world. They'd tried to program her, told her about god and faith and spiritual things. Told her to pray for their love and acceptance. The men who must be obeyed, for they spoke for god. She wondered how anyone could speak for god. Couldn't god speak for herself?

Her mother stood in the doorway looking into the distance. Not at her. Never at her. Cora wanted to call out, but no sound came out of her mouth. A man handed her mother something—a paper—and they spoke. The procedure, they said, had been done. The informational scans due at the end of every calendar month. She must perform the scans on her daughter herself. Watch for abnormalities and report them immediately. Cora wasn't supposed to know this. She wasn't supposed to understand. She wasn't supposed to remember. But she knew and she remembered. It lay always, always in the back of her mind, even as she tried so hard to forget.

Cora prayed then. Not a chanting prayer or a memorized one. A prayer from her heart. She prayed that she would wake up soon and not be here. As she drifted off into a fevered sleep, she whispered, "I'm so mad at you. But I'm scared and I'm tired and I would do anything if you would please help me."

• • • • •

"Search every one of these cottages and bring anyone you find to me! I told these people if they didn't get out of my territory there would be hell to pay."

"We have found no one yet, sir."

"Keep looking. That smoke had to come from somewhere."

"Yes, sir."

"Over here!" one of the soldiers called. The rest of the troop came running. Their leader went into the cabin first.

"From her clothes she must be from one of our regiments, sir. She must have gotten separated and wandered here."

He stared down at the girl, feverish and shivering. Her eyes opened, and she didn't speak, as if she could not comprehend the people surrounding her.

"Look at her eyes," he whispered. "Could it be?" Their leader reached down to where she lay and touched her flawless brown complexion. To him she was the answer to the sincerest yearnings of his heart. The sign of his work, planned so long ago, had finally come to pass. So many years he had waited and had begun to lose hope. Then here she was like out of a dream, with her eyes—her precious, precious eyes—with irises the color of amber.

He wrapped her in his coat and ordered his men to bring heating blankets. He lifted her head gently, and he knew that he could love her—that he would love her.

"Don't worry," Okoni said. "I have you. I will take good care of you now."

## DUSK, 3 WEEKS AGO . . .

Freddie unconsciously nodded to the light background music as the numbers changed and they traveled up to the topmost floors of the tallest building in the city. The twins, ignoring him, faced forward in a trancelike silent conversation, mindspeaking with flashes of scarlet in their eyes. Higher and higher they went, then suddenly the coverings of the walls fell away. In the now-transparent elevator, they continued upward in a tube of glass that made it seem as though they were ascending into heaven.

The world spread wide below them. The streets, the buildings, the people diminished towards the outer edges of the curved horizon. The closer, innermost buildings rose up by levels, gradually sloping as if on the side of a mountain. The terraces of the wealthy with their large, elaborate homes passed by like moving steps, and Jown and Pietyr exchanged thoughts about the house and the family of the boy for whom they searched.

The elevator finally slowed to a stop, and the doors opened to a long, wide hallway. An orange light flooded in through the large panes of glass that lined the wall. On the polished stone floor lay a plush red carpet that led down the hall. Freddie and the twins followed the path to an open heavy door, to find inside their employer, Mr. Raul Rodolfo Suez, the richest, most powerful man in Oros. He sat in a chair surrounded by piles and piles of books and was completely engrossed in reading while stroking his bountiful white beard. After a while, he pulled his eyes away from his book and acknowledged his visitors.

"Humph. What do you boys want?"

"I don't want anything," Freddie said defensively. "It's these two."

"So what is it?" Suez said, seeming disinterested.

"That job you sent us on—" Pietyr said.

"Yes, the missing Bastia boy," Suez interrupted. "So, have you found him?"

"That's what we came to talk to you about," Jown said.

"We found something—" Pietyr said.

"—and we want to know what you knew about it," Jown completed.

Suez stroked his beard some more, which made him look forever like a devilish brown Santa Claus. "I haven't seen you two for weeks, and when you do find your way up here it's to ask *me* for something."

"We apologize for being unavailable—" Pietyr said.

"—but this is a matter we feel—" Jown interrupted.

"—we must bring to your attention," Pietyr completed.

"Having a conversation with you two is quite an experience, you know that?" Suez said, and stood, casually put his book down on a table, and walked a few steps, wobbling slightly, as if his left leg pained him. "So what do you wanna know?"

"We want to know what you know—" Jown said.

"—about the trafficking of children," Pietyr completed.

Mr. Suez scrunched his nose as if the men had made a terrible smell.

"You boys are in way over your head. Just find that Bastia boy and let it end there."

"Then you do know something—" Pietyr said.

"—about the missing children?" Jown completed.

Suez opened his mouth as if to say something, thought better of it, grimaced, and waved the men off as if batting away a fly. He then limped towards the wall-sized window on the far side of the room. There the vista of the city's thousands of roofs woven in a loosely arrayed tapestry cast a majestic view. The peaks of the mountains beyond caressed behind thick, dark clouds, were outlined in a palette of tangerine pink. And even against that setting, Suez made an imposing shadow.

Suez stood there remembering how *she* had entered the lobby of this very building—a ghost out of time on his security feed—and demanded that he answer a similar question. Deidra, his long-ago wife, dressed as if she was some kind of domestic servant, had yelled loudly enough for her voice to echo off the floors and walls of polished stone. She had stomped through those doors and walked right up to him—the most powerful man in the city—and slapped him across the face.

"You've been here all this time?" she had said.

Not a question, an answer.

"Hello, Deidra," he said in response.

"How the hell did you get here?"

"I arranged for myself and certain few other people a small private transport."

"But not for your wife and daughter?"

"I told you that I couldn't leave Earth. Not then. There was work I had to do—"

"You are a bastard." And she hit him again.

"I did what I thought was right."

"Really? And what about after you got here? You could've tried to find us."

"I thought that maybe you might not want to see me."

"Well, you were damned right about that, I don't want to see you. But our daughter—*your daughter*—you could've cared about her. And now she's missing. And I tell you what, you're gonna find her. Okoni's men took her and you're gonna make him give her back."

"And how am I supposed to do that?"

"I don't know and I don't care."

"Deidra—"

"If I had known that all this time my escoala was being sent to you, I would've never grown that damned weed . . . So there, that's where you live. You don't care about me. You don't care about your daughter. But I know what you *do* care about. I'll make sure that all the farmers stop growing escoala. I'll make sure that you won't get one ounce of it until I get my daughter back."

"Deidra, be reasonable—"

"You're lucky I don't cut off your balls with my bare hands."

As she left she called back, "Not one leaf, not one twig, until I get my girl back!"

She had been true to her word. The escoala had stopped coming in and his supply had become dangerously low. At the end of his reverie Suez dreamily said, "Do you know that this city runs on escoala? It used to be an esoteric thing from the Outlands and now it's everywhere. Of course it's illegal. You know why? Because it's made from kremer seed. Could you imagine how the people would react if they knew that the seed that we need for food and for the atmosphere was being used for the recreational pleasure of the krestge?"

The twins passed a thought between them. Their eyes flashed scarlet.

Freddie sat down and wondered where Suez was going with all this.

"There is a balance in commerce," Suez continued. "When a customer requires something, a smart businessman tries to supply it. The better the businessman is at supplying the product, the more successful he is."

"We are unsure what this has—" Pietyr began.

"—to do with the missing children," Jown completed.

"Gentlemen, you continue to ask all the wrong questions." Suez sighed deeply. "Children go missing every day. I even hear that Okoni has an army of them."

"The rebels only exist—" Pietyr said.

"—in the Outlands," Jown completed.

"You think so?" Mr. Suez said, laughing lightly so that his shoulders shook.

"Still, what does any of this have to do with the missing boy?" Freddie interrupted.

Suez left his window. He waddled back so quickly it seemed almost comical until they could see the expression on his face.

"You." Suez pointed to Freddie, his voice repeating off the ceiling, "you do that little job I gave you?"

"Sure." Freddie nervously straightened.

"Any problems?"

"Nothing I couldn't handle."

"Yes, I can see that."

Freddie smiled and blushed a bit, scratching at the fading bruise still left on his chin.

"So where's the girl?" Suez demanded—not being able to say the words *my daughter*.

"Well . . . um . . . it's like this . . ."

"Yeah, yeah. You lost her, didn't you?"

"No, not exactly. I got her here . . ."

"Then where is she?"

"I dunno. She didn't go where she was supposed to go."

"Well, you better find her, and fast. You hear me?"

"We did find her, but then we lost her again."

Suez made a sound of disgust.

Freddie quickly added, "We ran into her at a warehouse when we were looking for the Bastia kid. That's where we found some other kids frozen for shipment in a crate . . ."

"Yeah?"

"Yeah, that girl is freakishly strong. She attacked the twins. Damn near killed them, too . . . She was kinda like . . . kinda like . . ."

"Kinda like what?"

Freddie held his breath a bit as he carefully chose his words. "She looked kinda like a krestge."

Suez squinted at Freddie, his interest finally piqued.

"We think the missing boy and this girl—"

"—are connected in some—" Pietyr said.

Suez held up his hand for them to stop speaking and stroked at his beard, lost in thought.

"What were her eyes like?" Suez said.

"Her eyes?" Freddie stammered. "Well, um, they were a little spooky. They glowed, and I think they were a bit orange-ish."

"Hmm," Suez said thoughtfully. "Like amber?"

"I guess so," he said, then added shyly, "And she did something to the twins." He pointed to his own eyes.

"Yeah?" Suez wandered closer to the twins. "Look at me, you two."

He placed his hands on the sides of Pietyr's head and stared directly into his eyes. Then he did the same for Jown.

"Well, I'll be . . ." Suez said. "You both have a headache?"

"Yes," they said in unison.

"What has—" Jown said.

"—happened to us?" Pietyr completed.

"The girl," Suez said, clicking his tongue in astonishment. "That Okoni is one stubborn son-of-a-bitch . . . I never thought he could do it. But damn, he quite possibly has the correct genome in that girl . . . Damn."

"What does—"

"—that mean?"

"Yeah, what does that mean?" Freddie said, visibly shaken.

"It means forget about the Bastia boy for the moment and find this girl, whatever it takes," Suez said, emphasizing every word. "Okoni has probably talked her into doing something very, very foolish that could mean the end of all of us. You need to find her and stop her.

"Connect me to Cel Bastia," Suez called to the Lattice.

: Cel Bastia is no longer in Oros

"Then where the hell is xe?"

A hyperscreen opened and hovered in the air, displaying a map of Eleusis. A red pathway appeared, zipping across the globe to a location in Dawn.

"Dammit to hell. Is that Deidra's place?"

: Affirmative

He banged on the table, then turned to Freddie.

"I need you and your staff there to deliver a message to Bastia," Suez said. "You need to tell xem to take you to the EDS facility. Cel is one of the few who has the security clearance to gain access. The girl has a head start, but you're faster. This is really, really important, you understand? No joke. You find this girl and stop her before she does something stupid. No delays, no mistakes."

Freddie took in the information, and from the corner of his eye he glanced nervously at the twins.

Suez continued, "Make sure to tell Deidra that you will be bringing her daughter home, understand?"

"What about Cel Bastia's son?" Freddie asked, his throat as dry as sandpaper.

"You can finish that job after you stop the girl." Suez rubbed at his forehead, then said, "Look, Freddie, you may be my kid and I love you to bits, but just for once, do exactly what I tell you.

"And you two," Suez said to the twins. "I took you in because I always liked you and I thought you could watch over Freddie here and keep him out of trouble, which you do most of the time, but I swear to god, if you mess this thing up, there'll be hell to pay."

## NIGHT, 8 YEARS AGO . . .

I can feel the air passing with difficulty through her lungs. And I can see that he stayed with her throughout the night watching her struggle for each breath.

In her sleep she tossed and turned in a delirious sweat as though battling with an invisible foe. He held her hand like a delicate flower, precious and easily crushed. He noticed what he believed at first to be a birthmark on her neck, only to realize upon closer inspection that it was a bruise. He found other marks such as this on her wrists and arms, on her shoulders, and seemingly more extending down her back. He had her examined by the women and they reported that she had several scars and bruises throughout her body, and that she had been sexually violated repeatedly over a long period of time. He would most certainly find out by whom later. But for now, she must heal. She must get well.

• • • • •

Cora woke to find herself lying in a comfortable bed surrounded by the warmth of thick blankets and a bold fire blazing in a metal fireplace in the center of the room. A woman facing away from her tended to something near the window, making only the slightest sound as she moved. The rustle of sheets caused the woman to turn and notice Cora sitting up. She grimly smiled and bent down to gently stroke Cora's forehead and cheeks, feeling her temperature. Her cool hands smelled of soap. Cora allowed this stranger to touch her. None of the words forming in her throat reached her lips.

"It looks like you had a rough time of it out there, eh?" the woman said. "Someone made good use of you, eh? Your body scarred all over. A woman's life is not easy. Never mind, that part of your life is over now."

The woman stared into Cora's eyes, not connecting but examining.

"You are a very lucky girl. Okoni himself found you, and he likes you. He likes your eyes. They are pretty," she said. "Okoni has been with you every night since you've been here. He watches over you and only leaves to attend his important business."

Cora rubbed the top of her head, feeling the neat rows of starter dreads.

"We did that for you while you were sleeping," the woman smiled and said. "In a few years, with care, you'll have beautiful locs, eh? Better than the mess you had, eh?"

The woman neatly folded some towels and placed them carefully on a shelf nearby, then picked up a pan and walked towards the door. She turned to Cora. Her expression read something like sympathy, maybe more like pity.

"Let me give you some advice, eh. Be nice to Okoni. Give him what he wants. He is not a man to play with. If you thought life was bad out there, disappoint Okoni and you'll find out that it can get much worse."

• • • • •

Over the next few days Cora woke and drifted off, woke and drifted, woke and drifted, then woke again to find that she still remained in this cozy room in this unknown place, under clean sheets, and surrounded by the warmth of a fire. Only women had come in to see to her since she woke. They brought her meals, left clean sheets and towels and picked up the used ones, and straightened up the room. They seldom spoke, and exited as quietly as they'd entered. She actually felt glad for the loneliness, and for the sleep. Maybe it had all been a fever dream? Maybe she still lived in Dawn with her mother and the fields of kremer? Maybe the army and the killings and the rapings never happened? This peaceful respite seemed too good to be true. In Cora's experience, nothing good came without a price. And she anxiously waited for what she would have to pay for the small luxury of rest.

• • • • •

After about a week Okoni himself entered her room carrying a tray of food. She knew him without him saying a word. He was tall, but not as tall as Cora had imagined, and old, yet she couldn't quite guess his age. He stood silently before her. His glare penetrated with intensity, as if he were in deep concentration.

"Hello," he said.

"Hello," she replied.

He carefully placed the tray on a table and pulled a chair close to her bed and sat down. He seemed shy and at a loss for words.

"They tell me you are feeling better," he said at last.

"Yes, much better, thank you."

Silence.

"Has everything been all right here? Are all your needs being met?"

"Yes, I'm fine."

Cora thumbed at the edge of her blanket as a thick quiet rained down again.

"Perhaps I should leave you to eat your meal."

"No," Cora found herself saying. "Please stay."

His rich, dark skin smoothed with delight. He smiled widely, showing all his strong white teeth. He stood to carefully place the tray on her lap.

She pinched a small amount of the crust from one of the three kremer rolls, still warm out of the oven, and placed it delicately in her mouth.

"Is it good?" he asked.

After her swallow she replied, "Yes, quite good."

He continued his contemplation of her as she nibbled at this and that. In truth, she ate very little, mostly pushed food around on her plate, afraid to take larger bites in front of the man who had killed thousands. The sound of her swallows and the cracks and pops of the wood burning in the fireplace nearby filled the emptiness. She sipped some water and put down the glass as if the slightest quiver of her hand could cause it to explode on contact. Occasionally she glanced up to find Okoni's eyes resting hotly upon her. She curled the ends of her lips into what she hoped appeared like a smile.

"You look tired. We can speak again tomorrow."

She agreed, because this encounter had indeed drained much of her short energy.

Okoni called for someone to attend to the room. A woman entered and put aside the food tray, then tucked in Cora's blankets, ensuring that they covered her warmly. Okoni stood and politely excused himself, bowing ever so slightly before he left.

And Cora thought to herself, *Strange man.*

• • • • •

Cora sat by the fireplace watching the sparks and sprites dancing in the flames. They were turning and twisting and performing pirouettes when three women came into her room unannounced. Each held a dress in her arms and draped them across the bed.

"What is this?" she asked.

"Tonight you will dine with Okoni."

Cora timidly touched a dress of an intoxicating shade of blue with golden thread woven throughout. She picked it up and held it across her body.

"Please try it on," one of the women said.

Cora cradled the dress in her hands, then slipped behind the screen in the corner. Minutes later she stepped from behind the screen wearing the dress unfastened in the back. One of the women zipped her up as she stood in front of a mirror. Cora passed her hand over the delicate fabric and thought the dress belonged on an older woman, not the girl-child of her reflection. And yet it was so pretty.

"I've never worn anything like this before," Cora said.

"We can alter it," one of the women said as she lifted the dress at the bust area, then tugged at the waist.

"You will look beautiful," said another.

Cora wondered who had worn the dress before and what had become of her. She forced herself to grin, which made her appear even more childlike in the mirror. She thought about the moment when these niceties would end and when Okoni would do to her what clearly lay on his mind. She wouldn't be able to stop him any more than she could stop the Commander. She had no way out. She intended to survive, though, even if it meant smiling through every disgusting thing that happened next.

• • • • •

High above the encampment on a balcony kept warm behind a transparent field enclosure, Cora and Okoni stood together. Above them, a night sky filled with an abundance of stars opened like a doorway to the many dimensions. The void folding and unfolding in mysterious harmony with the sounds of the shifting snow of the distant dunes. Okoni positioned himself to be near to her, yet not too close. He treated her like a fragile object, as if the slightest touch could snap her into a million pieces. She did appear frail in the dress that slinked over her almost skeletal body, her thin frame the result of weeks of starvation.

"I know more about you than you realize," he said at last. He declared this not as a tease, but more like a man with the secrets of an all-seeing god.

She tilted her head and crinkled her nose.

He laughed a little then, and said, "Tell me, how many times have you shadowed?"

Cora's stomach dissolved into water.

"Don't be shocked," he laughed again. "I am Aidoneus Okoni . . . Dr. Aidoneus Okoni. You see, there, already I've told you something that no one else here knows."

He cleared his throat.

"I," Okoni said, and placed his open palm to his chest, "was one of your original designers."

"What do you mean?" Cora asked, or maybe demanded. This was not about fear anymore.

"I am many men. One of them is the leader of this rebellion. Another is a researcher, a scientist, or at least I used to be a long time ago. On our homeworld, a team of us attempted to design a defense system against the alien. A machine was to work in concert with a human of a certain genome—a program that those fools in the capital abandoned. They forget too easily what those things did to us. But I will never forget."

"I don't understand," Cora said. A rising tide of anger welled from an unknown source deep within her as she struggled to remain calm.

"Think of what we faced: our world ravaged by an alien race that we could barely see or touch. Then our research team discovered a weakness in the alien. They are more like us than you would believe, and we calculated that with certain mutations to the human genome, we could create soldiers to defend us against them . . . We tried so many permutations. We made so many mistakes . . . We programmed in a telltale sign for when the correct genome was present—a certain eye color. It never manifested itself in any of our test subjects. I had almost given up. But here you are, delivered to me as if by providence."

Cora didn't know what to say. She simply stood firm, trying to take in all this information.

"You must understand how much you mean to me, how much I need you to trust me. You are the answer to my dreams. I promise you I will teach you how to control your abilities, how to use them. Together we will do such amazing things."

Okoni called for someone to retrieve a slate. When he received it, he held it to his chest, then handed it to Cora.

"What do you see?"

Cora took the slate into her hands and touched its matte surface. She looked into it, her eyes shifted left to right until she made a connection. She saw shadows dancing over light, slipping and moving in and out of focus, and colors like the spectrum, twisting like a braid, running like a river over a desert, sliding across chasms of ice and snow, rising over mountains, channeling through valleys, invisible to the naked human eye, soundless to the ear, and as real as the wind, rolling, rolling, forever rolling. And it was beautiful. This was her gift. This was her curse. She received the data and released the connection.

"I see a map," she said, handing the slate back to Okoni.

"Excellent," he said, and touched her on the arm.

They shared eye contact for a moment. She pulled away and wrapped herself in her shawl to cover her bare shoulders in a vain attempt to conceal her fading bruises and scars.

"We don't have much healing plaster here," he said with genuine sincerity, then added, "Who did this to you?"

His palpable anger made her cower. He spoke again more softly. "Your clothing and gear when we found you tells me that you were with my army. So, tell me, who hurt you?"

Cora's hands shook uncontrollably. She couldn't will them to stop. She grabbed the ends of her shawl and tried to hide jittery fingers within. She thought for a long moment of what she should say. Her eyes moved from Okoni to the floor, then back again. Inside she felt that she could tell Okoni, that he actually cared about her, that he would in fact protect her. Maybe this could be a test to see if it was true. She leaned in close, and he bent down so she could whisper in his ear. Then she said the two words that frightened her most in all the world: "The Commander."

He whispered in return, "We have many commanders. Would you remember his face?"

Outwardly she nodded. Inside she screamed, *I will never forget that face!*

"So tell me," he said, "what does he look like?"

She pointed to the area underneath her eye and said, "He has a mark here."

"Ah," Okoni said in recognition. Thinking for a long moment, he moved away while a storm inside him brewed. He paced about and mumbled to himself.

Then he shouted to no one, "He took from me! That traitor took from *me*!"

Cora backed up and edged against the wall. Okoni seemed to have forgotten her while he railed and shouted. Tiny pockets of foam formed at the corners of his mouth.

In a moment of lull, Cora said only just above a whisper, "I would like to go back to my room now."

Her trembling voice pulled Okoni back. He softened and approached her gently. "I apologize for losing my temper," he said. "It makes me so angry to think of someone harming you. Forgive me."

He held her in his arms and she stayed there, too scared to pull away and yet strangely comforted by the strength of his embrace.

"That creature who mishandled you will pay for his crimes. I will never allow anyone else to touch you ever again."

• • • • •

The Commander, chained by each arm to a wall of the cell, hung unconscious from a night of beatings. The guards hosed him with cold water to wake him. He coughed and gurgled as if drowning.

"You can stop that now," Okoni said to his men. The Commander, drenched with water, blood, and sweat, said to the man who had imprisoned him, "What have I done to deserve this?"

Okoni shouted, spraying spittle from his mouth that landed on the imprisoned man's forehead, "You took what was mine!"

"Never!" the Commander answered. "I've only served you! Whoever told you different is lying!"

A shadow behind the cell door slowly entered. Each of her steps echoed. Cora felt powerful, like a goddess approaching a devotee, and stared down at the creature who had raped her and beat her and haunted her every waking hour. Never had she imagined she would see such a sight—the man she had feared so much tied like an animal, and groveling.

"You?" the Commander said.

"She is mine!" Okoni shouted. "Apologize for what you did to her!"

"I beg of you—" he said. "I didn't know . . . I—"

"Apologize to her!"

"I—I'm sorry," the Commander begged.

"Do you accept his apology?" Okoni asked Cora.

She answered, "No."

"I thought not." His voice reverberated in the bloodstained cell. "Shoot him."

"I'm sorry. I'm sorry. I'm sorry. I'm sorry . . ." The Commander repeated until he was out of breath, and even a little beyond that.

"Don't," Cora interrupted.

Okoni put his hand up to still the guard.

"Please . . . I'm sorry. I'm sorry," The Commander continued to whisper, his voice hoarse, and he breathed heavily. "I'm sorry. I'm sorry. I'm sorry. I'm sorry . . ."

Cora examined the Commander as if appraising livestock. She put her finger on his face and ran it along his forehead and cheek and touched the raised mole under his eye, then pinched it between her thumb and index fingernails until it bled. She bent low, close to his cheek, as if to kiss him, and whispered, "This is for Jessem."

What she did next happened so fast it was missed by even those who were there and were closely watching. Cora grabbed a gun from a guard and pointed it at the Commander's head and pulled the trigger. Blood and brain matter splattered against the walls and on her dress and face.

A long time passed before anyone moved, or even seemed to breathe. Cora stared down at the limp, broken body of the man who would no longer be the center of her nightmares while the echo of the shot still rang in her ears.

Okoni touched her shoulder and said, “Today you are a woman . . . But you still have a child’s name. You should have the name of a queen . . . I shall name you Stefonie. Yes, a crown for my beautiful dark queen.”

## DAWN, A DAY AGO . . .

In a dimly lit house, richly scented with herbs and other growing things, sat a woman. The rosy light that shone in from behind her through an open window set her in shadow. Her name was Doso. She was also known by other, more powerful names—Deidra, Maumon Deidra, the Rebel Rouser, and the Keeper of the Seed. Around her table gathered the heads of all the large farming communities of Dawn—the men and women who represented the many who worked the fields—here to discuss the matters of the farmer's strike, the missing children, and the very low kremer yields. And shimmering nearby stood the folding darkness of Cel Bastia, Deidra's former employer and now current petitioner, who sought audience with these people who held the world at their mercy. This disparate assemblage of people now turned to face those who had recently entered and interrupted their meeting: three men and a boy, tired and dusty from the outdoors.

• • • • •

Across the lands of Dusk, then deeper and deeper into Dawn, Freddie, Jown and Pietyr, and an exhausted Eben had traveled in a rented skimmer of swift slithering legs to the Outlands. Along the distance they passed fields left fallow, the untended crops shriveled to gray, and in areas smoke rose into the air from slow-burning crops that had been purposely set aflame. They stopped their skimmer and allowed it to graze when they neared the coordinates given to them by Suez. Eben sleepily pointed to a crowd of people in the distance. They knew that this had to be the right place. The four of them, it was decided, would walk the rest of the way on foot.

They could plainly see that the crowd was protesting. Hands that normally worked the land held aloft placards painted with the words "Bring Our Children Home" or "Security for Our Families" or "Our Children or No Food." When the three men and the boy approached, all eyes fell upon them, and the people went silent. Closer and closer, the people closed in. A dark woman dressed in white said, "Maumon told us that if we stood together, the city would have to respond. And now, here you are."

• • • • •

"~~I~~~was not~~expecting~~to see~~~you~~~~here~~~" Cel's voice echoed towards Jown and Pietyr. "I~~~thought you~~ were~~~searching for~~my son?~~~"

"That is partially why we are here," the twins said together.

"We have been sent—"

"—by Suez to find you—"

"—and to speak with—"

"—Doso."

"I told you I had nothing to do with what happened to that boy," Maumon said.

"And we asked you to stay in the city," Pietyr said.

"I don't work for you." Anger rose in her voice. "And I don't work for him either," she said, looking at the dark shadow standing beside her.

Overwhelmed by the smells of the hanging plants and drying leaves covering the walls, Jown could read nothing. While Pietyr saw visions of a little girl roaming the small stone house, picking up dishes, then wandering out of her room with rolled-up bedding.

• • • • •

Outside the twins had readied themselves for action, opening their coats to allow their sonar guns to be seen. Freddie touched Jown's arm and pointed with his eyes to a terrified Eben. Pietyr and Jown exchanged a thought and covered their guns. The three men moved in to shield Eben with their bodies, then backed away.

"You don't need to be afraid of us," the woman in white had

said. "You are our guests, and we don't hurt our guests. We know that you've come to join with the others to speak to Maumon." Then she had said to the crowd, "See that they are allowed to go on their way." And the crowd did indeed part so that the three could walk unimpeded to Maumon's front door.

• • • • •

Nervously, Freddie took in all the faces staring at him, then whispered to Deidra, "Maybe we can speak in private? I have a message from Suez."

Maumon turned to the gathering inside her house. These people who had come all this way for answers—for a strategy—for a plan. Their faces said that they didn't like this. They didn't trust this. Whatever *this* was.

She said to them, "Excuse us for a few moments."

The members of the meeting reluctantly exited the house to join with the others outside only because they trusted her and believed in her. Because they believed that she would not betray them. Because she understood their pain, because it was her pain as well.

"And, um," Freddie scratched his moustache, "can we find someplace for Eben? It's been a long trip."

Eben squinted at Freddie, strongly wanting to deny his fatigue.

"Come here," she ordered Eben, and waved him towards her. "I won't bite."

He tentatively stepped forward. She tenderly cupped his chin in her hand and examined his eyes. Then she went into her cupboard and took down a jar and showed Eben its contents.

"I baked these yesterday. Sometimes the village children like to visit, and I don't mind having one on occasion myself."

She put the jar on the table.

"Go ahead and take as many as you like. Put them on this plate here."

She tried to maintain her composure as the giddy child piled cookies to the point of toppling.

"Okay, now, that's enough. Take them and come with me," Maumon said.

Eben followed her, balancing his mountain of cookies.

"You can stay in here. This is my Cora's room, so don't make a mess."

She closed the door behind the child, then returned to her seat.

"What does Suez want?" Maumon said.

"He wants you to know that we—meaning me and the twins here—are on our way to find your daughter."

"Really?" she said cynically.

"Yes," Freddie said. "Actually, I brought her across the border into Oros."

"Then where is she?" she said, gritting her teeth.

"She was supposed to come home but I guess she didn't. Suez thinks she will go to a place called the EDS," Freddie said. "And he believes that Cel knows where that is and can get us inside."

Cel's eerie form motioned, a shadow moving upon shadow yet remaining perfectly still.

"~~~~The~~facility you~~~speak of~~is in the~~~the region ~~~you call~~Day.~~~It has~~been abandoned~~~and has~~~ never~~been~~~operational~~" Cel said. "Why~~would she~~~ go~~there?~~~"

"Suez believes that Stefonie—I mean, Cora—will go there because she may know how to make it operational," Freddie said.

Cel shuddered, then became iridescent. Xe moved about xemself in an irrational pattern.

"~~How~~~would she~~~be able~~~to~~do~~that?~~~~"

"Suez says there is something about her genes. Something that was done to her that may enable her to make the facility functional."

Maumon scrunched her face and rearranged herself uncomfortably in her seat and said, "They changed her. They made her into something different . . . Cora could see things . . . Things no child should see . . ." Her eyes darted to and away from Bastia, then she said, "Her body . . . She is like your son." Maumon looked at

Cel Bastia with pity and sadness. "Your son is dangerous for you, and you are dangerous for your son."

Cel moved in and about xemself again, a shadow upon shadow, xyrs colors shifting, then fading to black.

"I'm not lying to you, Cel," Maumon said.

"~~~The truthful-ness~~~of your words~~about~~my son is~~~neither~~here nor there~~~for the moment.~~~The~~more important~~issue is~~~your daugh-ter.~~~If she~~can indeed~~~make the EDS~~~functional~~~she needs to be~~stopped~~" Cel said. "~~~It is~~~a~~most de-struc-tive~~~~weapon.~~If she~~act-i-vates~~~it,~~~she could~~restart~~the~~war."

The tension of the moment was broken by Freddie. "I think we need to leave right now. All this other stuff can be settled later."

"We should take your shuttle—" Jown said to Cel.

"—It will get us there faster," Pietyr concluded.

"And please, watch over Eben until we return," Freddie said to Maumon.

Maumon agreed and walked them to her doorway. The crowd outside moved aside upon her nod. The farmers who stood in the arid heat, the mothers who prayed daily for the safe return of their sons and daughters, the fathers who worried themselves into endless nights of no sleep and ill health, allowed these visitors to pass, so that the three determined men and the alien skirted through the gauntlet of silent protesters and entered the shuttle, which soon lifted off, spreading dust and debris in its powerful wake, and sped towards the red sun.

Maumon watched it all from her front entrance, then turned away from the questioning crowd without saying a word. This woman, this high priestess, this Rebel Rouser, this Keeper of the Seed, went back inside feeling something she couldn't quite name. Maybe it was hope. Maybe it was sorrow. She peeked into the room that hadn't been used in years to see through the crack of the door, fast asleep on the bed, a little boy with cookie crumbs on his lips.

She believed in Okoni. The brilliance of that belief shone in all colors, and she was transformed. She loved him, and he told her he loved her. But she was no fool. She knew that Okoni didn't always tell the truth. He may have believed that everything he did benefited his people, but that didn't make the things he did right. It also didn't make them all wrong . . .

## DAY, TODAY . . .

The front shielding protected her from the glare of the unwavering sun, while the engine whined a high hum and the sand scraped against the hull. In her mind, the image of arid desert formed the totality of what this uninhabited land would be. She had not been prepared for the actuality of the untold wonders far below her shuttle. The air currents, dust storms, and the shimmer from the heat were dazzling sights. Though the most striking vision was the ocean of undulating solar panels glittering in slow tidal movements as far as her eyes could see. She watched them, mesmerized by their beauty, and amazed that they absorbed enough energy to feed all the needs of the cities of Dusk. The same people who had designed all this had also designed her. This gave her some comfort in her own creation. They had understood—even as many did not—that one day humanity would need someone like her.

Last night, as she lay in her bed, she stared up at the ceiling following the lines and folds of the cracks in the peeling paint that made nonsensical patterns. After pointless hours of her mind turning and turning, a not-so-timid knock had sounded on her door. It was Cynthia, mad as hell.

Akev had not told her exactly what Stefonie had done. But it was clear that she had left xem in a terrible state.

"You can't do this to people!" Cynthia had said.

"It is not a person," Stefonie replied.

"Akev is a person, and you hurt xem! Whatever you did, you hurt xem!"

"Cynthia," she had said with pause and patience, "where are you?"

"What?"

"Where are you living?"

"What's that got to do with what we're talkin' abo—"

"This isn't the world of *your* people, is it? Don't you ever ask yourself why you are here?" Stefonie purposely paused again to let the question sink in. "You are here because those things that you call people took our world from us. We are here because they made us come here. This is not our home. They took our home from us. They took our history. My god, they even take our faces with those biomasks of theirs. I know that you don't understand. I don't expect you to. Just know that what I did, I did because I had to. I am sorry that Akev got hurt. I really am. But I had to do it."

"You're crazy, you know that? You are really, really crazy. And I don't want anything to do with you anymore."

After Cynthia left, Stefonie remained in the quiet on the edge of her bed for a long time, staring through her filthy window. There she saw what she had always seen—the future, past, and present laid bare, swirling together beyond the wispy slow-moving clouds and the pale pink-gray-blue of the sky. Stefonie of all people understood the deep shame of being made a victim. Thoughts of what she had done to Akev haunted her, and she found herself searching for her secret stash of escoala.

After a few puffs, she drifted into the ease of thinking about the carefree life Cynthia had shown her, an existence of friends, poetry, and music. If only she could have that life. She would've even settled for simply returning home to her village in Dawn and the fields of kremer, and being the girl that should've been. She missed the sounds and smells of home—the little girls singing while playing hand-clapping games as the women baked loaves of kremer bread, the scent of fresh grasses wafting on the arid morning breeze, and the taste of water freshly drawn from the local cistern. In her dreams, she would walk the paths of her village and see the people she had known since childhood. They would wave hello, their faces open and friendly with familiarity.

That was all gone now, and there was no going back. Not after all these years. Not after all she had seen and done. She would carry her sins with her for the rest of her life. She would carry the sins of others as well. She didn't ask for any of this. None of it seemed fair.

Then she reminded herself that it was the krestge who had begun this madness. It was they who had come to Earth in their warships. It was they who had released a biotoxin into Earth's atmosphere in an attempt to exterminate everyone. They were the ones who had killed off almost every human being on the planet. And those who didn't die were mangled and mutated beyond recognition. It was them and their actions that had made her people build underground cities, and have to pick and choose who could live in them because there wasn't room for everyone. Meanwhile, others like herself—who were considered the lucky ones!—had been herded into transport ships to flee to this world. She had heard this history long before she met Okoni. Her mother had told her some of it. The rest she'd learned on her own. It was all true. The krestge had slaughtered her people.

But Eleusis was to be a fresh start, a place free of the threat and memory of the krestge. Yet, the krestge had followed. These creatures that had pushed humankind to the edge of extinction had come and offered the hand of friendship. Were she and her people supposed to be all right with everything and say, "All is forgiven, all is forgotten, no hard feelings, these things happen"? Did they really think that just showing up and being friendly was enough to make everything okay? Well, everything wasn't okay. And where was the apology? Shouldn't there have been one? Something official from all of them as a people to say they were at least sorry for what they had done?

She stared and stared deep into the void for a long, long time with these thoughts ringing in her head. It was dim, and she was barely comfortable lying on her back when she realized she wasn't in her room anymore. She had moved without moving, shifted places while lying still. She was out of her body and someplace far, far way. She had unknowingly phaseshifted beyond Dusk's twilight sky and was amongst a gathering of *them*—the "all-powerful, all-seeing" high council of the krestge. They could see time in large washes and movements, but they could not see her. Not so "all-powerful and all-seeing," it would seem.

To them, as with so many others, she was a nothing, a tiny unnoticeable speck. Yet, she could hear their shared thoughts and fears and questions and plans. She heard that the future they had attempted to prevent was still a possibility. That they regretted not finishing what they had started. That their own people on Eleusis were an unfortunate expense for the future they wanted to secure. Stefonie shifted back into her being on impulse, not on purpose. And in that small fragment of a moment they noticed her and knew that she had heard them.

She returned to her body, feeling dazed. But now, after all this time, she finally understood her importance. It had been her ability to phaseshift and pass their notice that had created this paradox. It was her insignificance that made her significant. Because she had seen into their thoughts now, they had made their decision to gather then. They had placed their forces in the past in order to hide them from the future.

In all that time Okoni had been planning, and she had been a part of his plans. So he had trained her to control her phasing ability so that she could become the weapon he desired. Okoni wanted this purely out of hatred for the alien. In his madness, he just also happened to be right.

Stefonie understood what she must do. She grabbed her things and rushed to return to the transport shuttle that she had hidden in the outskirts of the city. The krestge had seen her. They knew she was coming. She had to hurry to stop them before they could stop her.

## DAY, TODAY . . .

The front shielding protected them from the glare of the unwavering sun, while the engine whined a high hum and the sand scraped against the hull. Arid desert formed the totality of the image in their minds of what this uninhabited land would be like. They had not been prepared for the actuality of the untold wonders far below their shuttle. The air currents, dust storms, and the shimmer from the heat were dazzling sights. Though the most striking vision was the ocean of undulating solar panels glittering in slow tidal movements as far as their eyes could see. They watched them, mesmerized by their beauty, and amazed that they absorbed enough energy to feed all the needs of the cities of Dusk. This gave the twins a small amount of comfort in their own creation, because the same people who had designed all this had also made them, even if only by mistake.

• • • • •

This unlikely quartet spent hours together in the shuttle not speaking, even though they had plenty to say and the time to say it. Cel positioned xemself on xyrs couytal and moved in and about xemself, appearing as though xe had a multitude of arms and legs attached to xyrs shifting torso. The presence of the krestge clearly unnerved Freddie, and he made every effort to not look in xyrs direction. Meanwhile, Jown and Pietyr remained in a constant state of internal conversation. They distracted each other by mindspeaking ideas about how to apprehend the girl given her strength and agility while the scarlet in their eyes flickered.

"I~~apologize~~~for~~~in-truding~~~~but~~~it is~~~curious~~the way~~~you speak~~to~~each other~~~"

"You can hear us?" the twins said in unison.

"~~When you~~~are this close~~~yes~~" Cel said. "~~~~How~~ did you~~~learn to~~~commun-icate~~this way?~~~"

"We didn't learn—"

"—we were born like this," Pietyr said.

"I~~didn't know~~that~~such a thing~~~~was~~possible~~"

"You're the second person—"

"—we've met—"

"—recently—"

"—who can hear our thoughts."

"~~My wife and~~~I also can~~~com-muni-cate~~what you~~~hu-mans~~call~~~thoughts~~as well~~~because she ~~~had the~~~functions of~~~the biomask~~surgically~~in-stalled~~soon after~~we~~were mar-ried~~as a gift~~for me.~~~"

"We didn't know such—"

"—a procedure existed."

"~~It is~~expensive~~~and rarely done~~but~~peop-le who ~~have~~chosen~~marri-ages~~such~~as~~ours~~~ sometimes~~do this.~~~~I~~~under-stand that~~~humans ~~need to~~~keep~~secrets~~from~~~each~~~other.~~~It is~~~ in your~~nature.~~~~~My wife had~~them~~ad-just~~her filter ~~~so that~~she could~~~still~~hide thoughts~~~from me~~" Bastia shook, changing colors and shadows in xyrs amusement. "~~She thinks~~I do not~~~know~~~~"

Silence.

Cel thought to them, *Forgive me, but I sense that there is something on your minds. Something that does not belong there. Yes, there . . . an unwanted imprint . . .*

*The girl . . . Stefonie . . . did something to us.*

*She may have inadvertently placed a hold on you during a mind connect. She must have disconnected from you suddenly. It must feel quite disorienting. Would you like it removed?*

*Yes,* the twins thought together.

*Give me a moment.* And Cel reached into the thoughts of the twins. Xyrs thoughts flowed into them as well. Xe entered into the section of their minds where the hold lay implanted by the girl in the warehouse fight and released the burden placed there. The strange flash of red in their eyes disappeared.

*I hope that helps.*

*Thank you,* Jown thought to Cel.

"Thank you," Pietyr said aloud. And for the first time in his life he felt gratitude towards a krestge.

In the silence that followed, Cel translated through their mental link a feeling of hurt and confusion and questions that still lingered. Xe shared with them xyrs anguish—the fear of what could happen if all those addicted to escoala were suddenly denied the drug, the new terror of a weapon that could kill his people on a world scale. How such an act would summon the full wrath of xyrs people. How they would burn this planet and every living thing on it to ashes. Yet what was most pressing on xyrs mind was how xe had felt since xyrs son went missing, and he finally thought to them clearly in words, *I don't understand what Doso said about my son. How could he possibly be a danger to me?*

They rested in each other's minds, feeling the hurt and fear that the others in the trio's mind connection felt.

"We don't know," they said aloud.

"We will find your son—"

"—We promise."

"We're here," Freddie called back to them from the pilot's seat. "Prepare for landing."

## DAY, SEVERAL HOURS AGO . . .

In the middle of nowhere, with her landed transport behind her and a piercingly hot sun beating down, Stefonie made her way to the cliff side. She walked clumsily in the protective suit that shielded her skin from the extreme heat. The hard soil reflected back the blazing light without mercy. She pounded a piton into the rocky ground near the edge of the cliff and fastened a carabiner and the rope with the bag with her belongings attached to its end. Then she tossed it over the side and let it dangle. Heavy objects were easy to carry long distances and she had done this before many times. But she had never carried them from great heights, and she needed to be sure she could do this.

She removed her protective eyewear and clothing. In the few moments of her nakedness, the radiation from the sun burned her brown skin. She phaseshifted, turning to shadow, and flowed over the edge of the cliff to the cave opening only someone like her could enter, and flowed over the sheer side of the rock, and pushed the hanging bag inside the cave. Then she went inside herself.

Within the shaded blackness of the enclosed area of rock, she unphased back to normal. The temperature inside was actually cool, and her naked body goosefleshed. Stefonie rummaged through her bag and pulled out a jumpsuit and a pair of soft shoes and hurriedly dressed.

Deep inside she could hear the movement of water. She knew that a source as large as an ocean lay somewhere beneath all this rock. She searched for the door she had been told would be there. It didn't take long to find. A red light above the entrance flashed when she approached. It then morphed into a wide beam that scanned her up and down. It lingered upon her eyes, waving vertically from side to side, then switched off. A rumbling sounded. Small pebbles and dust fell as the door slowly opened.

Okoni had taught her all about this place. Regardless of him and his ambitions, it would be she and she alone who would bear the responsibility for whatever happened next. So much power lay within. Once she entered she knew there was no turning back. She swallowed hard, her throat dry and mouth tacky. Then she passed through the door. It rumbled again to close behind her.

She found herself in a musty room with angled slits high above. Red-tinted sunlight streamed in and dawnflies glowed and danced and twirled within the beams. In the blackness, letters written in white light appeared on the wall, mechanically scrolling down—

>>

>>

Initiating . . .

>>

** ELEUSIS DEFENSE SYSTEM INITIATED **

The room itself began to sink. Down down down it went, dropping faster and faster. Her stomach sickened. She reached for the walls, felt for a corner, and slid into a fetal position. Breathing hard. Ears clogged. Eyes closed. She screamed until her lungs hurt . . .

** Biological Human Hybrid Component Detected **

>> Initiate HECATE

Loading . . .

++aaaaeoktodkgo.def

++aabbeoktodkgo.def

++aacceoktodkgo.def

++aaddeoktodkgo.def

++aaeeeoktodkgo.def

++aaffeoktodkgo.def

++aaggeoktodkgo.def

++aahheoktodkgo.def

++aaiieoktodkgo.def

++aajjeoktodkgo.def

++aakkeoktodkgo.def

++aalleoktodkgo.def

++aammeoktodkgo.def

++aanneoktodkgo.def

++aaooeoktodkgo.def

++aaoofoktodkgo.def

++aaoogoktodkgo.def

++aaoohoktodkgo.def

++aaooioktodkgo.def

++aaoojoktodkgo.def

++aaookoktodkgo.def

++aaooloktodkgo.def

++aaoomoktodkgo.def

++aaoonoktodkgo.def

++aaooeootodkgo.def

++aaaaeokto1kgo.def

++aabbeokto2kgo.def

++aacceokto3kgo.def

++aaddeokto4kgo.def

++aaeeeokto5kgo.def

++aaffeokto6kgo.def

++aaggeokto7kgo.def

++aahheokto8kgo.def

++aaiieokto9kgo.def

++aajjeoktoAkgo.def

++aakkeoktoBkgo.def

++aalleoktoCkgo.def

++aammeokto10kgo.def

++aanneokto11kgo.def

++aaooeokto12kgo.def

++aaoofokto13kgo.def
++aaoogokto14kgo.def
++aaoohokto15kgo.def
++aaooiokto16kgo.def
++aaoojokto17kgo.def
++aaookokto18kgo.def
++aaoolokto19kgo.def
++aaoomokto1Akgo.def
++aaoonokto1Bkgo.def
++aaooeooto1Ckgo.def
++aaaaeo1Adrianto1kgo.def
++aabbeo1Adrianto2kgo.def
++aacceo1Adrianto3kgo.def
++aaddeo1Adrianto4kgo.def
++aaeeeo1Adrianto5kgo.def
++aaffeo1Adrianto6kgo.def
++aaggeo1Adrianto7kgo.def
++aahheo1Adrianto8kgo.def
++aaiieo1Adrianto9kgo.def
++aajjeo2julrv3toAkgo.def
++aakkeo2juleo2toBkgo.def
++aalleoeo2jul2toCkgo.def
++aammeoeo2jul2to10kgo.def
++aanneo2juleo2to11kgo.def
++aaoo2Antoinefoto12kgo.def
++aaoo2Antoinefoto13kgo.def
++aaoo2Antoinefoto14kgo.def
++aaoo2Antoinefoto15kgo.def
++aaoo2Antoinefoto16kgo.def
++aaoo2Antoinefoto17kgo.def
++aaoo2Antoinefoto18kgo.def
++aaoo2Antoinefoto19kgo.def
++aaoo2Antoinefoto1Akgo.def
++aaoo2Antoinefoto1Bkgo.def

++aaoo2Antoinefoto1Ckgo.def

++aaoo3000000000to0Akgo.hec

++aaoo3000000000to0Bkgo.hec

++aaoo3000000000to0Ckgo.hec

++aaoo3000000000to0Dkgo.hec

++aaoo3000000000to0Ekgo.hec

++aaoo0000000003to0Fkgo.hec

** The Heuristically Enabled Centralized Atmospheric Teleholographic Entity is now operational **

>>

>> _

Her fall came to a sudden soft stop. The door rolled open, and a hallway came into view. She shaded her eyes as they adjusted to the light and walked down the hall into a room filled with desks and chairs covered with tarps, row upon row of unused terminals, and an almost translucent manifestation of a woman standing in the middle of it all. The holographic apparition shifted faces from one semblance to another. One set of features lingered, then slid away to be replaced by another and another, then the original appeared again. It wore a gown of flowing white against its brown skin, the shoulder delicately exposed.

: Welcome to the Eleusis Defense System facility

: It is good to meet you

: You can call me Cate

Stefonie walked around her, seeing her from all sides, then passed her hand through her. Cate smiled at the slight disruption of her being.

: Yes, I am a projection

"A projection of what?" Stefonie asked.

: The Lattice among other things

Stefonie had known that the Lattice had the capacity to learn, but never once had it occurred to her that the Lattice itself might be alive and thinking and have a personality of its own. Yet, here stood undeniable evidence of that possibility.

Cate's imprinted matrix created features for the different focuses of her attention: the Lattice, the communications grid, and the EDS. As each resemblance appeared, then slid away to be followed by the next in constant succession, so was her time allotted. (And no one but Cate knew or remembered that two of the faces imitated in her cycle were that of her creator and her creator's great love.)

Cate did a cursory examination of this girl and quickly discovered her internal structure was that of Maumon's missing daughter. After all this time in the paradox of searching for the abducted child, the girl had simply walked through the door. Cate calculated if she should tell Stefonie how long and hard her mother had looked for her. Her calculations predicted that this knowledge might be a distraction from the work that must be done. Cate experienced sorrow that she could not tell her this truth; sorrow that she had been taken away from her mother all those years ago; sorrow that she had to be the one who would activate the EDS; and extreme sorrow that Stefonie might very well die here today.

: How much do you know about the EDS?

"I have a working knowledge of the codebase."

: Excellent

: Come. There is much for you to do

Stefonie observed Cate as she followed her down the halls. The way she moved and even her small expressions were so humanlike and alive. She, like everything else here, was a creation of the many dedicated men and women of this secret project. The intellectual descendants of the designers of the great ships that had carried the last of humanity to this world had once walked these very halls. And this was where they had created a momentous feat of technology, the computerized atmospheric system known as the Lattice—a system that formed a global network to store data and performed the functions of a worldwide communications grid—a system based upon the design of an earlier system established on Earth centuries before.

But the Lattice was far more advanced than its predecessor. It was the backbone of a defense system that could only be built on a world such as Eleusis with its unusual atmospheric properties. The energy of this world's skies—the likes of which had not been found on any other world surveyed—helped to bind the unseen gaseous circuitry. Part of the design formed a shield around the world to defend against krestge biological agents, such as the poisonous dust that they had once inflicted upon the human population of Earth. Another part was an energy weapon that would, in theory, penetrate krestge multidimensional hulls. For this it required a biological component, a human with the correctly sequenced genes, a human like Stefonie.

: Do you have the authorization codes?

"Yes, but I will also need to rewrite some subroutines, and that may take some time."

: Then we better get started

They arrived at a large observation window through which could be seen the cavernous chamber several kilometers deep. The sides of the chamber had spiraled tubular metallic rods all the way around. At its very center stood a platform big enough for a single person to stand. This accelerator was designed to excite and blend the strange particles found in the atmosphere with the body of the biological component.

: I assume that you understand the danger

"Yes, I know."

Cate waved her hand as if presenting something. The air before her hummed and a hyperscreen view opened. It displayed the emptiness above the atmosphere of the world and zoomed to what lay beyond it.

: They are already here

The ships of the krestgian armada moved in and out of

space-time, hidden in plain sight. As a measurement and a concept, time had no meaning for those four-dimensional beings. It had no context for them, no real physical manifestation. That had always been their best weapon against humanity, who experienced time linearly. The EDS—hidden so deep beneath the surface of the world—was ours.

"All my life I've been seeing blurred visions of this in the sky. I thought I was going crazy."

: It is possible that your modified genetic structure allowed you to see this with your naked eyes

: You also should have a direct connection into the Lattice

"Then why do I need you?"

Cate went silent, and her form became like the rushed movement of sand being lifted by a gust of air. After a moment or two she settled back into her more stable state.

: I am here to assist you

"I see."

Cate waved her hand again and the hyperscreen display diminished.

: You will enter the chamber here

Cate directed Stefonie to a thick door. It had a window which showed a vestibule inside that opened to another door. When the first door closed, it would seal behind her. The next door opened to a long bridge that led to the center of the collider. Her life would never be the same once she passed through these doors. In fact, this was where her life might end. Stefonie had known this time would come, only she had never been quite sure how she would feel once it was here.

Cate suddenly stilled and her three-faced exchange froze. Her holographic being momentarily filled with specks of static.

: There is something that requires my attention

: I will return

And she disappeared, leaving Stefonie alone by the chamber door.

Stefonie wondered at Cate's sudden departure as she reached into her pocket and pulled out the bottle of red pills that she'd been so faithfully carrying since she left Night. The poison that would allow her to enter the chamber; the updated nanoids that would make her one with the machine. To ingest them meant there was no turning back. She considered this for a moment. They weighed so little in her hand. Then she opened the bottle and swallowed them all and closed her eyes, and waited for them to propagate throughout her body and forever alter her.

O

## DAY, A FEW HOURS AGO . . .

In the middle of nowhere, with their landed shuttle behind them and a piercingly hot sun beating in their faces, they approached a cement-block cube about fourteen feet high with a single thick door in the front standing in a field of nothing. The men wore protective suits to cover their skin from the sun's intense radiation and dark glasses to protect their eyes. The krestge needed nothing and remained a formless shadow over the arid, hard ground. Jown began a fit of coughing. His brother gently tapped his back. Freddie sneezed.

A small red light flashed above the entrance that morphed into a beam. It scanned them one by one, up and down. It lingered on their eyes, waving from side to side, seeing through their protective wear. When the beam reached the form of Cel Bastia, it switched off.

"Damn," Freddie said. "Doesn't like you . . ."

The light above the door switched to blue, and then the door slowly rumbled open.

"~~~~No,~~~I~~~be-lieve~~~that~~it~~rec-ognized~~~~me.~~~"

They entered into the cool, musty enclosure. It had angled slits high above that allowed in red-tinted rays of sun. Dawnflies glowed and danced and twirled within the streams of light. The men removed the hoods of their protective clothing. The crinkling material of their suits echoed in the blackness. The door rumbled closed behind them, and letters written in white appeared on a wall and mechanically scrolled down . . .

>>

>>

This is the Eleusis Defense System Facility

A nonhuman entity has been detected

Please enter your authorization code:

>> _

Cel flickered and moved in and out of xemself, folding and folding as xe entered xyrs code. A click and a hum, then the room began to descend. Down down down they plummeted in a stomach-sickening fall. In the rush of their descent, the men felt for the walls and the corners and slid into seated positions. The krestge remained unperturbed by the rapid drop. More letters written in white appeared, scrolling down the wall before them.

>>

** The authorization code has been accepted **

>>

>>

Their fall came to a sudden soft stop and the door opened to a hallway. They shaded their eyes to adjust to the light. A woman stood before them. Or at least it seemed like a woman. Her ghostly, almost transparent visage shifted between three different faces turning, turning, and turning. One set of features appeared and would linger, then slide away to be replaced by another and then another, and then the original face appeared again. Over and over her cycle continued in a mesmerizing frequency.

: I am HECATE, your holographic interface

: How may I help you?

There had been discussion of the creation of a holographic caretaker of the facility. An autonomous being designed to ensure the maintenance and security of the EDS. It fascinated Cel to see the results of humanity's endeavors.

"~~~These gentle-men~~~and I~~have~~come~~seeking the~~young woman~~~~who~~has~~recently~~arrived here.~~"

: This facility is currently unoccupied

"Maybe we—" Jown said.

"—beat her here," Pietyr completed.

"~~~Unlikely.~~~"

"Maybe she came and left?" Freddie said.

"~~That~~also~~~is highly~~~unlikely.~~~"

"Could she be here and you not know about it?" Pietyr said to HECATE.

: No entity may enter or occupy this facility without the proper authorization codes and/or my sensors detecting and logging their presence

"Not that we don't trust you, but we would like to look around, if you don't mind?" Freddie said.

: Of course

: This facility is completely at your disposal

And the teleholographic entity floated through the hallways as the quartet roamed around. All was empty, dusty, and abandoned. Pietyr searched the shadows. Jown sniffed for scents. Echoes of their footsteps interrupted the stillness. The lights flickered on upon detecting their presence. The ventilation system switched on as well and the stale air began to move. They entered a large room with rows and rows of chairs crescenting a large window that opened towards an unfinished collider chamber. Pipes and wires hung loose and building equipment stood dormant, stopped in midconstruction. Pietyr searched the shadows for those who had been here before and saw very few. Jown scented only the pale blue of dust.

"I don't understand. Suez said that she would be here," Freddie said.

"We sense—" Jown said.

"—no one," Pietyr completed.

"This doesn't make any sense," Freddie said.

"~~~No~~~it~~does not~~~"

"So what do we do now?"

The shadowy being of Cel circled around the teleholographic entity as HECATE's visage continued its three-faced cycle. The two seemed in a dance of the ethereal—one alive and mysterious, the other a manipulation of light and a disruption of air. They made a strangely beautiful sight.

"~~I will~~~connect~~into~~~this system~~~and~~~find-~~~some answ—"

The lights flickered and dimmed, then turned red, casting the room into an eerie crimson. HECATE's form scrambled into a view of static. She morphed to black then white then back to her normal form of a woman with three interchanging faces, though her white gown had become red.

: Several krestge battle cruisers have been detected in orbit

"What?" they said together, even the krestge.

HECATE waved her hand, so that a hyperscreen appeared in the disturbed air. It displayed an image of a krestge battle cruiser hovering above the top layer of the atmosphere. Its position made clear by the coordinate grid of the visual.

Another krestge battle cruiser appeared . . . then another . . . and another . . . and another. The hyperscreen view filled with at least a dozen krestge ships, their iridescent hulls gleaming silver against the orange sun.

"~~~This~~~cannot~~be.~~~~~I would~~~have~~~been~~~informed.~~~~"

Cel folded and unfolded and shimmered xyrs form.

Jown and Pietyr shared a silent thought of fear.

"Oh my god . . ." Freddie whispered.

In the days after the arrival, Cel had been part of a group of krestge representatives that had come to this very room to solidify the details of the peace. Here they had met to finalize the details of how their two peoples would maintain a delicate coexistence. Cel had witnessed the krestge promise not to attack humanity again. In return, humans had promised to end their research into weapons technology against the krestge.

"You've got to—"

"—do something," they said to Cel.

"Talk to your people. Tell them to stop this," Freddie said.

"Yes, yes~~~of course.~~HECATE: Open~~~a~~secure~~~chan-nel~~~to the~~lead~~~~ship.~~~"

* Connecting . . .

* Connecting . . .

* Connecting . . .

** Connection established. **

[[Cel Bastia, it has been a long time. How may I help you?]]

[[End the niceties, Kreiol. I want to know what you are doing here.]]

[[We are conducting normal surveillance operations.]]

[[Don't lie to me like I am a fool. There is nothing normal about a krestge battleship hovering over a human colony.]]

[[We are there per order of the Council.]]

[[Why was I not notified? When were you planning to tell me?]]

[[What would be the point, Bastia? Everyone knows how your judgement has been clouded by your fondness for this species. You were supposed to make sure they remained contained.]]

The men patiently listened to the aliens speak in their language, which sounded to them like wild animals drowning in oil. The twins caught the meaning of a word or two here and there, enough to understand that the conversation was not going well.

[[We have a treaty with these people. We made an agreement in good faith.]]

[[The future and safety of *our* people is at stake. You've seen the possible future of this species. You know the danger. Your irresponsibility in this matter has forced us to act.]]

[[There must be a possibility for some kind of—]]

The ground violently shook, causing the men to steady themselves by grabbing for nearby furniture. A crack line formed across the ceiling and dust rained down. Cel flickered in place, xyrs edges softening. HECATE's image dissolved to nothing, then reappeared.

"What the hell was that?" Freddie said.

: A krestge vessel has landed near the entrance of this facility

"I think it's time that we got outta here," Freddie said.

"We can't exactly leave—"

"—the way we came in."

The krestge continued their conversation. Their swallow and hiss and lull and sway echoed back and forth.

[[So you're going to attack these people? And what of the thousands of krestge who live here? Are you planning to kill them, too?]]

[[You all made the decision to live among the humans. You made your choice.]]

[[You cannot do this, Kreiol!]]

Silence.

[[Kreiol!]]

[[Kreiol!]]

>> transmission terminated

"~~~What~~~happened?~~~"

: They closed the channel

"~~Then~~open~~~another~~~~~"

* Connecting . . .

* Connecting . . .

* Connecting . . .

: A connection cannot be established

"Try~~~again,~~~and keep~~trying~~until you get~~~ through.~~~"

"Why are they—"

"—just sitting there?"

: I suspect they are waiting for this vessel to depart

HECATE closed her eyes and opened them again. An image in a hyperscreen morphed into a view of MOCA, the new docking station in Oros. It rose up in three dimensions and slowly spun around, displaying the transport ship of humanity's newest alien trading partner currently loaded in its berth.

"So they want us—"

"—to remain isolated."

: Possibly

: Or they do not want to be on bad terms with this species

They watched as the ship detached from the dock and lifted off to fly higher and higher into the air. The hyperscreen view followed it as it flew out of the gravity well of the planet, engaged its engines to fold the space around it, and disappeared from sight.

In the next few tense moments, the impossible felt inevitable. The krestge ship positioned over Oros released a burst of intense light that burrowed down down down into the city, producing a huge yellow-orange ball of flame that exploded high into the air.

"God Almighty!" Freddie screamed.

The facility shook again.

: Several krestge have entered the first level of this facility

: It is highly recommended that you evacuate immediately

"How?" Freddie said.

"Is there—"

"—another exit?"

: Your safety necessitates the disclosure of information above your authorization level

HECATE closed her eyes once again, her face slipping and sliding into one countenance then another.

```
>>
>> create script showmap.sub.lattice
channel = @open_atmospheric_thread(LATTICE);
UNSEAL channel HECATE OVERRIDE ACCESS code: +009999
repository = @open_repository(channel);
map = QUERY * FROM repository JOIN eds_facility AND hidden_areas;
@close_atmospheric_thread(repository);
DISPLAY(map);
eof.
>> lattice.showmap
>>
>>
```

When she opened her eyes again, the previous hyperscreen disappeared to be replaced by another. The distilled air displayed the layout of the entire EDS, including another underground site far away that appeared to be a duplicate of the facility where they currently stood. HECATE pointed to a turbo tube line that connected to the second, hidden part of the station.

**: This leads to another and more secure area of this facility**

The view within the map zoomed into the second facility. It showed a perfect replica of the control room. Inside stood a completed collider—in other words, a functional weapon.

**: You need to come with me**

"~~I have to~~stay~~here.~~~~I must~~try~~to convince~~~ them to~~stop this~~madness~~~~"

"You tried already," Freddie said.

"You have to come—" Jown said.

"—with us now," Pietyr completed.

"No.~~~These~~are~~*my* people~~" Cel moved in and about xemself with xyrs colors wildly glowing.

**: Two more levels of this facility have been penetrated**

"~~Go~~" xe said, folding and folding xyrs shadowy form. "~~I will~~~be~~all~~right.~~"

Cel's entire life had been dedicated to the cause of what xe believed was a mutually desired peace between the species. Xe had hoped that through xyrs time and energy, xe could show xyrs own people that humanity deserved their respect and were not the dangerous animals they had once believed them to be. Cel had even married a human woman and had loved her child as if he were xyrs own. Now Cel realized that everything xe had believed in and worked for was unraveled into nothing. Xe had to give peace one last try.

"~~~Promise me~~you will~~find~~my~~son~~~~"

The twins shared silent thoughts of fear and admiration.

"We promise," they said in unison.

Then the men followed HECATE to find the entrance to a turbo tube on the lower level. Opening the door, they all found themselves looking back one last time to wonder what would become of the friend they were leaving behind.

O

DAY, A HALF AN HOUR AGO . . .

They rode underground in a turbo tube car, these two men who appeared like each other and their friend who poked around at the controls to make the car move faster. The lights outside the forward window, because of the increased speed, became endless bright lines pointing towards their destination.

: High-level radiation emissions have been detected

An explosion sent a shock wave through the tunnel, forcing the tube car to lurch forward. The men slammed into the front wall and into each other. Then the car stalled and came to a screeching stop. Smoke spewed. Sparks flared. The lights flickered off, leaving them in dim emergency illumination. The twins coughed as they ingested the smoke and rushed to put out the flames. Freddie found the switch for the exhaust system and turned it on. With a hum it pulled out the smoke and replaced it with clean air.

"HECATE, what happened?" Freddie screamed.

: The tunnel entrance has been penetrated

Jown and Pietyr used all their might to pry open the exit door. Freddie squinted through the back window into the tunnel. Something down there was moving.

"I think we don't have much time!" Freddie said, holding his sonar pistol.

The twins grunted and pulled, grunted and pulled until the exit door began to slide. Both sides finally gave way to open enough so that a grown man could slip through.

"Shit!" Freddie jumped back. A pounding at the back door dented the metal so that a large round bruise protruded.

: They must not be allowed to pass through

"I know! I know!" Freddie said.

The men pointed their guns to cover each other as they squeezed through the exit door. The screeching of the metal echoed through the tunnel as the krestge behind the stalled turbo car continued to pound and push it forward. The men ran towards the light at the other end of the tunnel. An entrance opened as the men approached, then closed behind them, and they found themselves in a long vestibule that filled with a hot steam designed to kill contaminants.

Disoriented, the men entered a control room and could see into the collider chamber to where Stefonie stood inside.

: You must protect the girl

• • • • •

The vestibule has been penetrated. I check the system and see that Cate has been keeping me from noticing that this facility has been breached. I suppose she didn't want me distracted. The men from before enter. What in the world are they doing here? How did they even find this place? I can't help but watch as they gather desks and chairs and anything they can lay their hands on to barricade the door.

The krestge are breaking through. They've entered the control room. The men shoot their sonar guns to not much effect. It only seems to irritate the invading shadows. One of the men is knocked across the floor. Another tosses whatever lands in his hands. They are fighting for their lives. They are fighting for me. Yes, they are here to protect me . . . no, not me . . . They are here for the boy. I can see it in their minds. Our connection is faint but still true. I see the boy and their search for him. They want to protect him, just as I once did. And I see the boy's father . . . I see xyrs thoughts through their minds . . . I feel xyrs love for xyrs son, and I understand what I must do.

>> establish HYBRID EDS connection AUTHORIZATION code: ••••••••

* Connecting . . .

* Connecting . . .

* Connecting . . .

** Connection established. **

EDS:>> _

Cate becomes a dot of light and flies through the chamber window. I feel a paralyzing jolt that holds me, and Cate and I connect. She reaches into my mind. Her touch is as light as a whisper, as gentle as the western breeze.

Dawnflies float towards me, burning ice-cold with memory. Thousands and thousands of them flow out from the cavernous blackness below. They speak to me with words I do not hear. They drift up my body, scanning. First my toes, then my ankles, my knees, my thighs, my groin, my waist, my stomach, my heart and lungs, then my throat, my chin, my mouth, my nose and eyes, my forehead, until I am engulfed. I open my arms as if to fly, spreading my fingers wide, and my physical being dissolves into the glow. Darkness leaps from my fingertips. My skin sloughs and I become all muscle and sinew, bone and blood. My fleshly remains fall away and I am one with the light. The Lattice that encircles the world and I are one.

We travel into my memories together—Cate and I—winding and twisting through the braids of my life. An hour, then two hours, then days and months and years rush back and forth. Only these aren't memories. We are there together, and we see and experience everything together. Floating up up up on a thread. I unravel in dizzying turns of the invisible strand. This feels as natural as muscle memory, as automatic as breathing.

We share my childhood, my last moments with my mother in that dimly lit kitchen. I had forgotten that, and yet it feels like it only just happened. I remember the long walks to town with the other children, and the singing, and my friend Naiada, and the waters of the village cistern. Before my sight in a swirl we experience together all the events that have brought me to this moment. Ten years ago. Seven. A few weeks ago. Everything blends together into this moment in wisps of orange and red and yellow and gold and pink and indigo and endless endless shades of blue.

I see the day when we arrived and our ships formed a chorus of smoke trails in the sky. I see the first ship touch down, cracking open like an egg, spilling its contents long across a distance. I see the krestgian ships hovering over our cities, their silver hulls gleaming. I see myself—Cora—the little lost girl, taken from Dawn and bitterly abused, and my long years spent in the dark company of Okoni, the father of lies. And I see this war begin and how it ends. So much that I have allowed myself to forget comes rushing through my mind.

She wants to completely take over my being. I can see she has done this with others. None of the others could resist her as I can. I understand that she simply wants to help, but I cannot allow this. She must be removed from my being and from this chamber.

```
EDS:>>
EDS:>> create script accessrights.sub.hecate.kore
channel = @open_atmospheric_thread(LATTICE);
entity = (HECATE) _getEntity(channel);
CHMOD entity 077;
@chamber_unload(entity);
@close_atmospheric_thread((REPOSITORY)channel);
eof.
EDS:>>
EDS:>> kore.hecate.accessrights
EDS:>>
EDS:>> _
```

HECATE hurls out of the chamber as a dot of light. Her form reappears in the control room scrambled with static, misshapen and malformed, until it calms and settles back into its original state.

"What the—"

"—hell?"

"What happened?" Freddie demands after he fires his gun and ducks behind a table.

The krestge are pouring through the tunnel into the control room, filling it with their shadowy dark forms.

: She forced me out

: She is not supposed to be able to do that

• • • • •

I have no business judging who lives and who dies. Yet this is precisely what I must do in the next few moments. I must decide the fate of thousands. I am scared. But I must not fail when so many need me.

EDS:>> initiate shields

I feel the rumbling. It's beginning. I can hear the children singing. No one else can hear their song but me. They dream the song, and it flows high up into the atmosphere and plays upon the golden threads that weave through the sky. Their voices emit from every corner of the world, and they sing in complete harmony. And I realize my purpose—and send a message to Okoni. I hope he will understand. Then I remember Earth, and send a signal there . . .

EDS:>> send initiate signal > Elysium Defense System

Eleusis begins to shake. Large cracks form on the surface of the ice of Night and the soil of Day. The warning sirens of Dawn and Dusk scream. The collider is now ready and the release doors above are preparing to open.

EDS:>> arm weapon

No one asks the sacrifice how it feels as it's being led to the slaughter. But I know. And now I understand so many things that I didn't before. This moment, this place, this me, is a sum of all that I have been, all that I am, and all that I will become. I am more than biology, more than luck, more than circumstance. I have to be more.

And I phaseshift.

My dark energy fills the void, spreading in all directions. My body dissolves to fill every corner of the collider's enclosure. The space is not enough. What seemed so cavernous before can now barely contain me, and my flames become a cyclone of blackness.

The girl stands in the chamber with her arms out wide. She becomes impossibly dark, black like a standing shadow. From the bottom of the collider, dots of light appear and flow around her like thousands of fireflies. She melts and disperses, and her body dissolves. The material from her dissolution swirls around within the collider. It becomes bigger and more, bigger and more. The collider fills with her blackness. The men who were hunkered behind desks and chairs turn to look. Even the attacking krestge are in awe of the sight. All forget that they are in the midst of fighting. A rumble thunders from the collider, shaking the heart. Lightning fingers of an electrical skeleton hand reach out from the chamber, striking each alien, solidifying them into pillars of black that crumble to dust. The massive doors at the top of the collider chamber screech open. And the black fire swirls out like a cyclone and releases into the atmosphere . . .

## NIGHT, A HALF AN HOUR AGO . . .

Okoni broods while the tiny members of his vast army shiver in the cold. They await the signal they were told would come soon. Stefonie had made it into the city several weeks ago and had made contact with his operative there. The fact the man had been found dead may mean nothing. Stefonie probably found him disloyal in some way and decided to silence the man rather than risk leaving him alive to speak important secrets to the wrong people.

He hates to admit how lost he feels without her. The days since she left have been empty. She said little, and yet she made him feel that underneath it all, she understood him. She was beautiful and impenetrable, as if she held the secrets to another world. Okoni had never met a woman like her. Her presence eased his mind. He wanted to possess her. And somehow she eluded him even as he held her captive.

Okoni breathes clouds of cold smoke as he stands looking over the land of white and the sky of deepest indigo, feeling like a fool. He had trusted his wife. He felt he had no choice but to trust her. Sending her to the city alone was the only way for this task to be done. She had sworn to him that she would bring down the barrier. She knew this was the only way he and his army could march across this ridge and into the capital. He had pictured himself in Oros many times, facing his old friend Suez, a man he once thought of as a brother, and telling his men to arrest him and take him away. His wife was the key to all of his dreams. She had promised him. How could she betray him like this? Yes, the treacherous girl must have betrayed him. Why else would she be gone this long with no message? His operative in Oros had been loyal all these many years and yet she had killed him. She was probably in Oros siding with Suez against him. Even now the armies of Dusk must be on their way here to this very location to subdue him. Around and around the same thoughts floated through his mind. He would dismiss them, only to have them return again.

He walks away from the elders he's been sitting with. The old men watch him leave and say nothing, though they have plenty to say. Here they are, so close to Oros they can see its light brighten the sky, and yet they remain behind the border, completely impotent. They have long since grown weary of Okoni's extended, dark moods. They feel that his obsession with this girl has weakened him and endangered everything they had worked so hard for. They wished that his desire for her had dissipated and that she had been thrown away like all the rest. Yet none of them dare to confront him with their frustrations. He could still order their lives to be snuffed out like the flame of a candle.

Even Samuel, the oldest of the elders and the man who kept Okoni's closest counsel, was afraid to speak against the girl. His yellowing eyes follow Okoni as he puffs at his pipe of escoala weed. He knows the time is coming when he will have to risk his few remaining years to tell Okoni the truth, that the girl was not coming back. She had been gone for too long on this "mission of importance." A mission that she surely had abandoned as soon as she reached the freedom of the city. It was clear to everyone that the girl had forgotten all about Okoni and everything he stood for. He must be made to face the fact that the girl never loved him or his cause. Samuel closes his watery eyes and thinks mournfully on how Okoni will receive his words.

Okoni storms into the midst of his commanders to order them to begin packing up and to fall back further south. He taps one of the men on the shoulder and begins to speak the words of retreat, then he stops before the words leave his lips. *No, this wasn't right. We should never surrender.* The girl loved him. His wife only needed more time. He needed to trust her and believe that her words of promise were true. She would activate the EDS and take down the security barrier. He need only wait a little longer.

"Are we crossing tonight?" a commander asks Okoni.

Before he can answer something moves up in the inky darkness in the sky. An undulating dark upon dark pushes at the air like the rustle of wings. A black rain falls. It is not rain. It is the drippings from oil birds, which are never seen in these icy regions. The massive flock amasses by the hundreds and fills the heavens with their *quarks* and *caws* and drips down their goo onto the encampment, sending the soldiers to run to cover themselves from the dark fluid. They move together as one, flying westward away from Dusk, then double back, undulating as if confused. Then they hit an invisible wall—the unseen structure sizzles and sparks—and they fall from the sky to their deaths one by one onto the ice in horrible *thud thud thuds*.

A menacing rumble like thunder breaks through the atmosphere. A sound that shakes the ground and the heart, and the sky above fills with krestge ships. One of them flies overhead. They have come, just as Okoni predicted. The silent ships hover in the sky for what seems like forever. Without warning they release their energy weapons down upon the city of Oros. Huge plumes of orange flames blossom. Okoni and his army watch, knowing that there is absolutely nothing they can do.

*If only the fools had listened to me!*

Suddenly the golden threads of the Lattice become visible. Over the curve of the globe, beams of light form a crisscross pattern high up in the twilight sky. The stream of information has become a shield. And for the first time, all of Eleusis experiences something akin to daylight. Aidoneus Okoni smiles widely as the planetary shield slices through the ships and they burst into flames. She has done it! His wife kept her promise to him! The security barrier must be down!

Okoni shouts, "Send one of these out there to test the barrier."

A little one in a raggedy jumpsuit runs in the direction of the city. Okoni and the whole company watch him. The boy stops for a moment to fuss around on the ground, picks up a rock, and throws it as far as his little arm can manage. A wall of light appears upon impact that sends a bolt of energy directly at the child who threw the rock, hurling him backward. He lands many feet away, and smoke drifts from the spot where he once stood.

A message appears on Okoni's bioconnector, floating across his cornea.

: I'm sorry, my love, but I have decided that I cannot allow you to cross the border

## HERE AND NOW . . .

In a single flash of brilliance, I experience what has come before and what is soon to be. The past, the present, and the future comingle like a coil. And then this moment—this very moment—comes rushing in and I flow into the future. I see all sides, inside and out . . . So many arms and legs and ears and eyes and mouths . . . All moving separately yet as one . . . I am a part of this . . . I am the center of this . . . the beginning, the middle, and the end . . . I see it all . . . All my life, all my hurts and disappointments, all my mistakes. I see the beauty of these moments colliding into one.

I see the boy I left behind in Night. His eyes glow. He sings a single note. I see my mother, aged and yet still strong, chasing after another boy I don't recognize into the center of our village, where he joins with the many other children with pastel-colored eyes there as they sing the same note in unison. Dots of light appear across the land and fly up up up into the Lattice weaving the sky. Maumon Deidra of Dawn also sees this and bows her head in reverence. Those of her cult follow her lead and bow as well.

EDS:>> commence weapon discharge

I begin with those in the control room. I must protect the men who have been protecting me. It feels so easy to reach out and touch these krestge. They are nothing.

I move on to my other tasks. There is still so much to do.

The collider that contains what is left of my body is focused outward. The top of the facility opens, and I am released. My particles fly upward towards the surface through the atmosphere. The Lattice accepts my energy, turning the entire planet into a carrier of my black fire. I encircle the globe, seeing everything and everyone at once. My dark flame could kill every krestge—the innocent and the guilty. That is what I was designed to do. I decide that I will not be their judge and executioner. At least not today. Today I will direct my destructive power elsewhere.

The small krestgian uni-piloted ships that flew below the EDS shield before it completely encompassed the planet, dart about and continue their attack. No matter. In my form as black fire I pursue the elusive gray structure of each globular ship by swirling and gliding through the air, and then I swallow them whole into the cold-heat of my flames. After I obliterate these tiny invaders, I gather my darkness and aim towards the larger ships above, the invading krestge fleet.

One then two then three then ten then more than half of their armada is set ablaze as I pass through them. For a few bright moments the skies above Eleusis ignite into an inferno. I feel their surprise. Their shock. Their horror. I hear their unison cry of disbelief when my black fire slices through their four-dimensional hulls like butter. Then they flicker out of existence and their sudden screams become a sudden silence.

I make sure to leave their command ship intact, though. I have questions for them.

• • • • •

I flow into the command ship and wander freely about their halls. I walk through their empty corridors, running my fingers across the cool walls, letting the freeze of the metal seep into me. A smokelike trail follows in my wake. I am the dark center of a walking black flame. There is no air, only void, and the shadows that move upon shadows. The hull is made of a strange fluidic metal that liquefies, solidifies, and vaporizes at the same time. The ship exists in a flux between dimensions, as they do—as we do—ebbing and flowing through space and time, moving in and about itself. Sometimes it is here, other times somewhere else far, far away. My energy pulls it to remain with me. I am an anchor of sorts.

So many levels in the place. When I look below me I can see tier after tier after tier going down and down and down before they fade into darkness. The liquid-solid-gaseous metal hull is transparent enough to allow a view of the exploding remains of their invading armada that burn all around us. The sounds of krestge mindspeaking echoes in my head.

They are numb with fear at my presence and are at a loss as to what to do. A human being has never been on board a krestge vessel before, for obvious reasons. Then again, I'm not really all that human anymore. I am like them, only different. I am a shadow walking through shadows, and the shadows are white. They move out of my way when I pass, as if I could burn them with a touch. And I *can* easily burn through the hull if I so choose. But I want to stay here for a while. I want to learn. I want to understand.

Without the obstruction of eyes, I truly see them; without the muffled reception of ears, I truly hear them. They are everywhere in a never-ending sea of possibilities, an infinity of mouths and legs and arms and torsos. And then they flatten, and I see them as they truly are. They are more like human beings in ways that are difficult to describe.

• • • • •

Their thoughts silence as I enter the center of the ship, where the thought-controls that maintain the ship's movement and functions lie. I touch their navigational instruments and read their thought-consoles. They operate through harmonies of image and sound that are equally shared by all the crew members. Interesting. I connect into their system and search and retrieve their data and learn the exact location of where they come from and how to get there. Their home is unlike anything I had imagined.

And I think I also understand something. If they had left us alone, it may have been millennia before someone like me would have come into being. Or maybe this evolution would've never occurred at all. Their interference forced our hand to do the impossible. They underestimated our resolve to survive. It forced the Builders to begin building me. And here I am, their greatest fear realized.

I stand in the fullness of my blackness and say, not as a question but as a realization,

[[You needed us to be afraid of you . . . Our fear made you feel . . . safe. You are actually afraid of *us* . . . and always have been . . . You have been afraid of what we could become . . . ]]

As if on cue another ship explodes outside. The final thoughts of those krestge onboard permeate the ether. Their final screams of agony dissipate into silence. The krestge before me are defeated, and they know it. They shift and change shape and form and flow in acquiescence.

I feel something in my being changing again. I need to leave this place. My body is gone, though. It was the price I was willing to pay. Still, there is no use in their seeing this form disintegrate. That would destroy all that I have accomplished here. I gather myself to say one last thing before I go.

[[Tell your people what has happened here. Tell them there is no longer a peace between us. Tell them that if you ever try anything like this again, myself and the others like me will show as much mercy to you as you have shown to us.]]

The future is unsure, always shifting and changing based on variables that cannot be foreseen. Nothing is more gray and difficult to read than the future. The Builders made many simulations, and yet so much had not been predicted. She was supposed to burn, and she did in fact burn. But then the dots of light appeared. We call them dawnflies, and we have been feeding them with our kremer. They are the energy that surrounds the world and have an agenda of their own. They carry her away, down down down on invisible threads, to restore her body and heal her. They heal her of everything except from the poison that she willingly ingested. I suppose not every hurt can be mended . . .

## DUSK, IN A FEW DAYS . . .

It will be raining, or maybe only gray. Pietyr and Jown will stride down the path to an unheard rhythm, their dark overcoats swaying in unison. The men will wear brimmed hats cocked neatly to the side—one more to the left and the other more to the right. They will be on a beautifully landscaped estate with real trees and real grass and a house made not out of refurbished metal but of plaster, brick, and wood. There will be no police cars this time. No flashing red lights. Only a lonely dwelling that seems too large for itself. It will appear dark even though many lights will be on inside. Freddie will wait in the zepher because he won't want to step foot in that house.

The housekeeper will open the door and will recognize the men from before and let them in. Or she will make them wait. It is hard to see which. She will want to sneer at them and then will think better of it. Such sentiments feel unseemly in a house in mourning. They will remove their hats while they wait for the lady of the house to be informed that they have arrived.

Arin, the boy's uncle, will come down the stairs. He will appear to have aged considerably since the last time they met. He will say little. Though he might mumble a greeting. Then he will walk the men through the magnificent house, where the clocks will be covered, and so will the mirrors. Their steps will echo as they pass through the kitchen and into the backyard to where Neira will be waiting for them.

The twins will tell Arin that they wish to speak to her alone. At first Arin will refuse, but upon Neira's insistence he will reluctantly leave. She will face them with her hand clasped about a charm that will delicately hang from the silver chain around her neck, a star made of a plus sign with a large X through it.

"You have our condolences," Pietyr will say, and Jown will complete the thought with, "on the death of your husband."

An uncomfortable silence will follow, which she will break by asking, "Have you found my son?"

"Yes," they will say together.

"Where is he?"

"He is safe," Jown will answer.

The twins will take some time to mentally discuss how to broach their next questions. They will want answers—answers only Neira can provide.

"Why—"

"—did you do it?"

"Why did I do what?"

"Stop with the games," Pietyr will say.

She will fiddle some more with the pendant around her neck.

"Why the lies? Why the deceptions?" Pietyr will demand. "Why not tell the truth about what you had done instead of having us searching the city for what you knew couldn't be found?"

"I had to keep Cel in the dark. And xe loved the boy." Neira will continue, "After my husband—my *first* husband—died, Cel was there. Xe was kind to me. I saw that xe was beginning to love me. And I knew then what I needed to do. Xe was on the krestge council and our direct liaison with *them*. It was important that a human remain close to xem, to influence xem."

"So why raise a son with xem?"

"That was Cel's idea. My husband—my first husband—was a brilliant man. He said that if we were to survive he needed to participate in the experiments, and he left his seed for me. The likelihood of *our* child being one of the few gifted was so small. And then the miracle happened! My son was chosen. Doso could see it, too. She knew and she warned me that my son could not stay here with Cel, and she was right. I loved my son, but my faith is clear on what I had to do. So I brought him to the reverend of my church. 'The usefulness of children is infinite,' as our good book says. Look at yourselves. Did nature make you? Or did someone design you?"

"We are—"

"—mistakes," Pietyr said.

"'Mistakes are how we learn' is the prime tenet of Builderism. We must have faith that through scientific development we will find a way."

She will stop caressing the pendant at her neck and put her hands down to her sides.

"How did you find me out?" she will ask.

"It was the scent of nothingness," Jown will say. "Nothing smells like nothing to me."

"And then your husband told us about your procedure," Pietyr will say.

"We realized then that you were hiding something from us. Something that we couldn't see or smell."

"Once we realized that you could hide your thoughts from your husband, we knew that you could do the same to us, then it all fell into place."

Silence.

"Did you know that your son would be taken to Okoni?"

"I suspected as much."

Silence.

"You need to remember," she will say, "that when our people first arrived here it was all we could do just to survive. You've grown up with *them*. You don't see them the way my generation does. We were the ones forced to flee. We were packed up on ships like cargo, only to find ourselves on this piece of rock. And despite all the odds, and because of our faith in the Builders' work, we survived and we flourished and built cities . . . and then once again they came. And we had to make peace with them on *their* terms . . . They are monsters, all of them."

"But Cel loved you," Jown will say, on the verge of tears, "and xe loved your son."

"And xe died trying to protect this world," Pietyr will say.

"I am not surprised by that," she will say.

Mentally they will exchange thoughts of bewilderment. Then they will turn to leave.

She will say one last thing to their retreating backs, "My son, please don't bring him back here."

## NIGHT, IN A FEW WEEKS . . .

I will be taken back to the ice and left alone there. I won't feel cold. I won't feel anything at all. I will simply move through that wasteland floating like a shadow to find him. Okoni will be sitting in his chair gazing off into space. He will stand when he sees me and be pleased by my return. It will take a few moments for him to realize that something has changed—that I have changed. His smile will then leave him, and we will stare at each other for a long while.

The silence will be broken by my telling him what he will do. He will frown and relent because he will understand that he has no choice in the matter. I will allow him—and the men who follow him—to go south further into Night. But the children will come with me. The little ones and I will leave Night together.

The boy and I will walk out hand in hand. Then I will turn him over to the waiting protection of the twin men with emerald eyes. The authorities and even some krestge will be there waiting for us. The tiny shadows that once were children will finally have a chance at life. Hopefully they will not be too far gone to live again. Some of them will not be ready for this. I will feel sorry about that.

After this, I will return home to Dawn. I will try to be the she who once was. I will be with my mother and tend to her fields as I did in my childhood. I will attempt to smile and resume the life that had been torn from me. There will be a falseness in it, though. A pretense. I will never be that child again. Those around me will see this and be afraid. I had grown up in Night. There will be nothing much to change this essential fact. It is and will always be a part of who I am. But I will never accept that this is all that I can be. My life is mine, and I won't allow what happened to me to dictate my future. Others will fear that I brought back a bit of Night with me. I will sense their suspicion and know that they are probably right. They will leave me alone to live my life as I choose, though. Funny what freedoms fear brings.

## DAWN, ABOUT 6 MONTHS FROM NOW . . .

A westerly wind will be blowing warm, arid air across a golden crop of kremer, making the stalks sway in rhythm with the breeze. Deidra will be standing there surrounded by her fields as two boys play nearby. She will be raising them as if they were her own because there will be no one else. Not a mother. Not a father. No one. Only her. All are afraid of what the boys will become. But Deidra has seen it before, and now she knows better. She will not make the same mistakes again.

One boy will bend down to pick up a shiny thing sticking out of the dirt. It will be a piece of old circuitry from a crashed transport ship from long ago that has now worked its way to the surface of the soil. The other boy will stare at it also. The boy with the circuit thing will take off running and the other will chase him. Together they will race around each other in a spiraling nonsensical path, laughing. Two boys with the same gift. The same curse. Brothers.

When the men arrive, one of the boys will see them first and will hurry to Deidra's side to hide behind her skirts. This is the one who still calls her Doso even though he knows full well that this is not her true name. The other boy will drop the curiosity he found and will run with all his might towards the men. Deidra will remain standing with the shyer child. She will not be able to move. She will know why the men have come.

Freddie will pick up the boy and spin him around. Jown will pat him on the back and Pietyr rub his head. Freddie will say how much bigger the boy has gotten, and quietly notice that his irises have turned even more amber and are beginning to shimmer.

"How are you?" Freddie will ask.

"Fine," the child will answer, and grin widely.

"Where is Stefonie?" Jown will say.

"She's not here. She doesn't come here anymore. She's probably where she's been building her house. She says when it's done I can come over any time I want."

"Where can we find this place?" Pietyr will say.

"It's on the other side of the village," the boy will answer. "Ask anyone there and they can point you to it. It's not far."

"Thanks," Freddie will say.

"You're here to take her back, aren't you?" the boy will ask.

"Yeah," Freddie will answer as he puts the boy down.

The men will wave at Deidra again, and she will return it only slightly.

Freddie and the twins will make their way into the village center, leaving Eben confused. His new brother will feel sick inside for the rest of the day as he continues to question why the woman he has come to think of as his big sister needs to return to that place. They will be told over and over, and still to them it will make no sense. It's the darkest place Eben had ever heard of. It's the place that held his new brother captive—the place that still haunts his brother's dreams.

Not until they are much older will they truly understand her need for the treatments she receives there. That the red pills changed her so that she constantly exists somewhere between her phased self and her normal self. That she could not control her phaseshifting for longer than about half a year. That without the treatments she would fall into the darkness of her phased state and would probably be lost forever. That only Aidoneus Okoni, the creator of the drug she ingested, knows how to administer the treatments that enable her to control her body, so that she must go back to him again and again and again. This is how it is, and this is how it will be for the rest of her life. Her injection marks will simply be added to her battle scars.

A woman holding her child on her waist will point these strangers in the direction of where a house is being built. She will look so much like Stefonie one could swear they must be related. They will have the same tightly twisted hair, the same reddish-brown skin, and noses forming similar-shaped cursive double-us. They will only differ in eye color. She will stand there and intensely watch these strangers stride down the arid road while still holding her baby. She will shift her child to the other side of her waist and wipe a speck of dust from his face, feeling the loss of her long-ago friend.

The men will pass the beams forming the shape of the house standing lonely against the otherwise empty plot of land. Beside it will be piled bricks, and sacks of cement laid neatly in rows, and other building equipment sitting idly by the wayside. Stefonie will have a home of plaster and wood, not sheets of refurbished metal.

They will find her wearing a gonar and sitting on a pile of rocks overlooking a vista of sand dunes. The light of the orange-red sun will be sitting on the horizon, spreading its glow from east to west. The pinks and reds and oranges and blues will blend together in a watercolor wash. Every so often a glint of the golden threads that crisscross the sky will glimmer through, reminding all who care to see that the Lattice still protects them.

Such is the beauty Stefonie will be lost in when Freddie and the twins approach. She will know that they are there and will speak without facing them.

"I bought this land," she will say. "The former owner said he was going to give it to his nephew as a wedding gift. He said owning it used to help him believe that his nephew would be coming back. Now that he knows that he is dead, the place has lost its value to him. So he sold it to me."

Stefonie will then take a long, deep breath.

"Do you know how the man found out that his nephew was dead? I told him. I know because I was there and saw it happen. That is me, the Queen of Death and Darkness."

"It's time to go back," Freddie will say.

"Yes, I know. I'm ready," she will reply as she maneuvers to stand. "I'm having this house built here so I can see this view. The workers are hurrying to finish the job and will complete it by the time I return. They want to spend as little time with me as possible . . . They're afraid of me . . . Everyone is afraid of me. They think they know me and what I've done. They don't know anything."

They will take their time to walk to the transport. Stefonie moves deliberately slow. No one will hurry her, though. They have the time. Cate will be waiting inside. Her incorporeal being will be visible only within the confines of the shuttle. Her three faces still forever turning and turning.

: It is good to see you again

"Yes," Stefonie will say. "And you, too."

: I can accompany you as far as the border

"Good," Stefonie will say, "that will be fine."

And Stefonie will stop for a moment, as if she heard a voice calling her name. The name she will hear will not be the name she is, but the name she was. And she will look back on the land and the unfinished house and the red horizon, and she will remember that the future is always with us. It shifts and moves and changes, but it is always here. We live the future every day that we breathe, and every yes or no in the path laid before us eventually becomes a history. Nothing is fixed. Nothing is sure. Not unless we want it to be. And then she will whisper, "It will be different this time. I'm not that scared little girl anymore."

# ABOUT THE AUTHOR

**Jennifer Marie Brissett** has been a software engineer, web developer, and the proprietor of Indigo Café & Books in Brooklyn. She has a masters in creative writing from the Stonecoast M.F.A. program. Her stories can be found in *Lightspeed, Motherboard/VICE, Uncanny,* and *Fiyah,* among other publications. Her debut novel, *Elysium* (Aqueduct 2014), received the Philip K. Dick Award Special Citation and was a finalist for the Locus Award for Best First Novel and on the Honor List for the Otherwise Award.

jennbrissett.com